AMONGST THE DEAD

Amongst the Dead is is the third in the series of crime-caper novels set in 1940s Australia that feature William Power; it is preceded by *Good Murder* and *A Thing of Blood.* Robert Gott is also the author of *The Holiday Murders* and its sequel, *The Port Fairy Murders.*

To my parents, Maurene and Kevin,
for whom no number of dedications
would be sufficient.

AMONGST THE DEAD

ROBERT GOTT

SCRIBE
Melbourne • London

Scribe Publications
18–20 Edward St, Brunswick, Victoria 3056, Australia
2 John St, Clerkenwell, London, WC1N 2ES, United Kingdom

First published by Scribe 2007
This edition published 2015

Edited by Margot Rosenbloom
Typeset in 10.5/15 pt Janson by the publisher

Printed and bound in Australia by Griffin Press

The paper this book is printed on is certified against
the Forest Stewardship Council® Standards.
Griffin Press holds FSC chain of custody certification
SGS-COC-005088. FSC promotes environmentally
responsible, socially beneficial and economically viable
management of the world's forests.

National Library of Australia Cataloguing-in-Publication data

Gott, Robert. / Amongst the Dead: a William Power mystery.

9781925321074 (paperback)
9781922072092 (e-book)

1. Murder–Fiction. 2. Crime–Fiction. 3. World War, 1939-1945–
Australia–Fiction. I. Title.

A823.4

scribepublications.com.au
scribepublications.co.uk

This is entirely a work of fiction. All of the main characters are products of the author's imagination, and they bear no relation to anyone, living or dead. Only the streets they walk down and the bush they struggle through are real.

CAST OF CHARACTERS

William Power
Brian Power
Mrs Agnes Power
Peter Gilbert
James Fowler
Nigella Fowler
Corporal Glen Pyers
Major Archibald Warmington
Captain Manton
Pete, the driver
Luther Martin
Sister Lucille
Charlie Humphries
Corporal Andrew Battell
Private Nicholas Ashe
Private Rufus Farrell
Private Fulton Power
Isaiah
Ngulmiri
Captain Dench
John Smith
Baxter
Major Purefoy
Captain Collins
Major Hunt
Sergeant Clarence Preston

CONTENTS

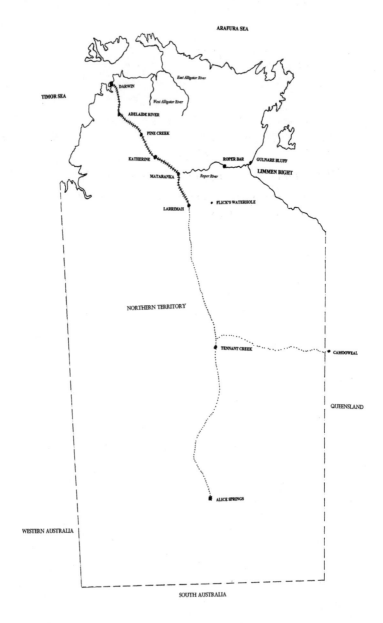

ARAFURA SEA

East Alligator River

TIMOR SEA

DARWIN

West Alligator River

ADELAIDE RIVER

PINE CREEK

KATHERINE

ROPER BAR

GULNARE BLUFF

LIMMEN BIGHT

MATARANKA

Roper River

FLICK'S WATERHOLE

LARRIMAH

NORTHERN TERRITORY

TENNANT CREEK

CAMOOWEAL

QUEENSLAND

ALICE SPRINGS

WESTERN AUSTRALIA

SOUTH AUSTRALIA

'… Alcibiades
Thou art a soldier, therefore seldom rich
It comes a charity to thee, for all thy living
Is 'mongst the dead, and all the land thou hast
Lies in a pitched field.'

Timon of Athens, Act 1

PART ONE

Chapter One

SIGNING ON

WHAT I REMEMBER MOST about the first time the Japanese dropped bombs on me — and, yes, I did take it personally — was not the shrapnel but the mosquitoes. I was lying face down in what was called a trench but which was, in truth, a drain. In my view, a trench is a piece of real estate distinguished from a drain by the absence of putrid, foetid, and greasy water. When the warning siren went off just after 2.00 a.m., my brother Brian and I were amongst those who hurried from the Sergeants' Mess at Larrakeyah Barracks and tumbled into this so-called trench.

I crouched, initially, rather than lay, reluctant to saturate my uniform in the evil-smelling water. The shocking explosion of the first bomb encouraged me to forget fastidiousness in favour of safety, or the illusion of it. By the time the second and third bombs had fallen, I was ready to start burrowing. I feel no shame whatsoever in declaring that the early morning of Wednesday, 28 October 1942, in the northern capital of Darwin, marks the precise time and place where I experienced, for the first time, a fear so intense that I thought I might die of it. Up to that point in my life, 'died of fright' was an expression I assumed belonged to melodramatic fiction.

I put my hands over my ears and tried very hard to believe that a drain offered an impregnable defence against a bomb dropped from above. We'd been told on our arrival in Darwin, just an hour earlier, that we could expect to be inconvenienced by raids at all hours. Since the initial, devastating attacks in February, the Japanese had punished the mostly evacuated town dozens of times.

'You get used to it,' we were told by a sergeant. 'They're nuisance raids, mostly — small, anti-personnel bombs rather than big bastards. They spray shrapnel close to the ground, so if you keep your head down you should be OK.'

'But what,' I asked reasonably, 'if one of them lands in a trench?'

'If that happens, you'll probably die, or wish you had.'

'And does it happen?'

'All the time,' he said. 'That's the thing about bombs. It's hit and miss. They hit, or they miss.' He'd implied in his tone that he thought I was a bit of a dill.

Every muscle in my body was tensed to aching point, and I sensed that Brian, lying close to me in the dark, was similarly rigid. There was a whining, vibrating hum that I took to be the air rushing around the cylindrical bombs as they plummeted to earth. However, the constancy and weird proximity of the sound turned out to be a cloud of mosquitoes; and they so harried me that, even through my life-threatening terror, they caused me unimaginable distress. I loathe mosquitoes, with their nasty, probing syringes and their ghastly, bloated abdomens, swollen with the blood of others. If I'd been capable of being objective, I suppose I should have been grateful to them. They were so vicious, and in such biblical numbers, that they offered a distraction from the whomp and crack of bombs, and drowned out the deadly zip and ping of shrapnel. I endured them, and thought how strange it was that just a few weeks previously Brian and I had been sitting in the offices of Army Intelligence in Melbourne, eagerly agreeing to an assignment that would put both our lives at risk.

It was Monday, 5 October 1942, and Australia's most important Catholic leader, Archbishop Daniel Mannix, was comfortably ensconced at Raheen, his mansion in the Melbourne suburb of Kew, instead of lying sprawled and very dead on the altar steps at St Patrick's Cathedral—only because, I modestly assert, of my intervention. While my achievement had been worthy of accolades, I couldn't expect any—certainly not the kind of accolades I'd been used to receiving as an actor. I'd fallen, temporarily, out of acting, and into Army Intelligence; and in Army Intelligence, mum is definitely the word.

In a small room in Victoria Barracks, the man who'd recruited me, James Fowler, and his sister Nigella, floated the extraordinary idea that I and my younger brother Brian (still a little shell-shocked by the behaviour of his now estranged and catatonic wife, Darlene) should attempt to discover the truth about three suspicious deaths which had occurred somewhere near Darwin. Why, in a time of war and extravagant killing, these deaths should matter so much, was one of the questions I eventually asked. I say 'eventually' because my initial response was unalloyed excitement at the prospect of returning to the profession for which I was best suited—acting. We were, you see, to be sent north as entertainers, and not as dreary foot soldiers, trapped in the hideous daily round of soldiery, a role for which both Brian and I were manifestly unsuited, having been identified as flat-footed—not in any disfiguring or disabling way, I hasten to add. My feet felt quite at home treading the boards, but would have rebelled at the prospect of a forced march.

Nigella Fowler, a young woman of unexceptionable appearance for whom I had nevertheless formed a strong attachment—an attachment which had acquired the urgency of what I supposed was love, after she had saved my life and saved the day simultaneously in St Patrick's Cathedral—looked at me and repeated what James had already stressed.

'This is dangerous work, Will. Once you're up there, there's no way out.'

I thought I detected a small tremor in her voice that may have betrayed her feelings for me. Coolly professional, I understood that she couldn't express them at this critical time for fear that I might swerve from my patriotic duty in favour of pursuing her. Catching that momentary glimpse of attraction only made me more determined to solve whatever problem Army Intelligence needed solving in Darwin. A successful resolution would surely do more in the way of securing Nigella's affections than a month of mawkish wooing.

'We understand the dangers,' I said, 'and I'm sure I speak for

Brian as well when I say that we're ready to face them.'

'I can speak for myself,' said Brian, with a characteristic little note of churlishness in his voice, 'and it so happens that Will is right. I'm ready for this. More than ready.'

James Fowler nodded his neatly groomed head and tapped his desk with the end of a fountain pen.

'Actually, neither of you is ready, although your willingness is admirable, and all we need to be going on with. There simply isn't time to train you properly, but we'll do the best we can in a short time.'

'Training?' I raised an eyebrow in imitation of my doppelganger, Tyrone Power. 'I'm a professional actor, James. I don't need training. Rehearsal time, yes, but not training. Brian, of course, will need …'

James held up his hand to silence me, and Nigella interjected.

'Only yesterday, Will, you admitted that you knew nothing.'

Here I saw a startled look on Brian's face. James took over.

'I think you should start from that excellent premise, Will.'

Not wishing to jeopardise my return to performing, I held my tongue, and I felt my love for Nigella curdle just a little.

'Your real training will begin tomorrow,' James said. 'The details are being worked out even as we speak. For now, it's enough that you get some background on the unit we want you to infiltrate.' He paused, gauging our preparedness to listen.

'Go ahead,' Brian said.

'Earlier this year there was a bloke stationed here at Victoria Barracks—an anthropologist named Bill Stanner. He'd done a lot of work before the war with the natives up north, and he managed to convince the Minister for the Army that what we needed was a special unit that would provide surveillance in the north, in the most rugged and inaccessible parts of the country.

We all knew that there were any number of places where the Japs could come ashore, and Stanner argued that the existing coast-watching set-up was woefully inadequate. We knew that, too, of course. Stanner's idea was to raise a unit of men with bush experience, and to provide them with horses rather than vehicles, because where these blokes would be going, vehicles would be next to useless. Stanner's plan got up, incredibly, and the North Australia Observer Unit started recruiting back in August. Your brother Fulton was one of those who signed up.'

'He wouldn't know one end of a horse from the other,' I said.

'Yes, well,' said Nigella, 'it was optimistic of Bill to think that he'd get exactly the men he wanted. In the end it was decided that the most critical skill was signalling. If you were adept at Morse, you were in, and you could learn to ride a horse later. The whole point of these Nackeroos, as they call themselves, is that they're mobile in difficult terrain, and in constant radio contact over great distances. If the Japs land, the Nackeroos' job is to follow them and report their movements—not engage with them in combat.'

'This is all new stuff for us,' said James. 'The unit's only just sorting itself out in the field.'

'How many men are we talking about?' Brian asked.

'All up, maybe four hundred and fifty all ranks, maybe seventy-or-so Aboriginal guides, and a few others.'

'Are you saying that the entire north coast of Australia is being watched by four hundred and fifty men?' I asked

James Fowler smiled.

'That's four hundred and fifty more than before the NAOU was formed. I can't even begin to imagine the conditions under which these blokes are operating, Will. They work mostly in groups of five or six, sometimes fewer, and go out on patrol for weeks at a time. I'm sure most of them thought this would be an adventure. The reports we're getting, even at this early stage, suggest that life up there is a mixture of privation, terror, and boredom. The thing is this, though: very few people know that the NAOU even exists, and it's important that it stays this way. We don't want Jap intelligence knowing that there's a guerrilla waiting to track their every move once they land. These deaths we want you to investigate — they happened in A Company, which is the company your brother is attached to.'

A quizzical expression must have crossed my face.

'The unit is divided into three companies, A, B and C, and each company has responsibility for a different territory. A Company patrols terrain around the Roper River and up towards Darwin. We're talking tens of thousands of square miles of mostly unexplored and unmapped territory. The distances are mind-boggling. All the companies are coordinated from Unit HQ in Katherine. I know all this sounds terribly complicated. It'll become clearer when you get up there.'

'So you think these deaths are suspicious?'

'Ah, we know they're suspicious. What we want to know is whether our suspicions should lean towards fifth-column sabotage or simple psychopathy. That's what you and Brian will need to find out.'

'In between singing and dancing,' Brian said.

James Fowler laughed.

'It sounds absurd, doesn't it? But, believe me, there are little troubadour groups out and about all over the place. When you get out there you'll be appreciated, don't worry about that. But that's the endgame. You've both got a lot to get through before Darwin.'

'Which brings us, neatly,' said Nigella, 'to Corporal Pyers.'

James Fowler picked up the telephone on his desk, waited a

moment, and asked for Corporal Pyers to be sent in. The man who entered didn't immediately inspire confidence. He was unhealthily thin; his uniform was clearly designed to dress a more robust example of the adult male. He looked, frankly, ill. I couldn't imagine, from the look of him, that he had anything useful to impart. His face glistened with feverish sweat, and his dark eyes were dull with fatigue. I placed him closer to the end of his tether than to its beginning.

'Corporal Pyers,' said James Fowler, 'has recently returned from New Guinea, and is something of a specialist in remote troubadouring. His job is to teach you as much as he can in as short a time as possible.'

It seemed to me that it took all of Corporal Pyers' skills to ensure continuous inhalation and exhalation, but I refrained from showing even the mildest dubiousness as to his abilities.

'These are the blokes, are they?' he asked, and his voice was thin and bland, entirely lacking the depth and sonorousness one would expect from an experienced actor. He shook my hand weakly, one might almost say limply, and then shook Brian's.

'I think we should get started immediately,' Corporal Pyers said, and it didn't escape my notice that his tone implied that he thought not a moment was to be lost if we were to be brought up to scratch. The sooner I demonstrated the power of one or two speeches from *Timon of Athens* the better.

Both James and Nigella stood up to indicate that the Victoria Barracks part of the proceedings was now at an end, and we were informed that we were to accompany Corporal Pyers into town, to the workshops behind the Tivoli Theatre in Bourke Street.

'We'll talk as we walk,' the good corporal said, although I didn't see how his health could accommodate both simultaneously.

I shook James' hand and turned to speak with Nigella; but perhaps fearing that emotion might get the better of her, she'd already reached the door and offered no more than a nod, and a quiet 'Good luck,' directed at the room generally rather than at me specifically.

'You're to report here at eight o'clock tomorrow morning. Sharp. Bring nothing. Your kit will be here, including uniforms, and you'll have left Melbourne by midday. I hope this isn't happening too quickly for you.'

Brian said that he couldn't leave Melbourne quickly enough at the moment, and added that whatever lay ahead had to be an improvement on what lay strewn behind.

Corporal Pyers, or Glen, as he volunteered as soon as we were outside Victoria Barracks and heading into town, observed that it was a measure of how desperate things were that the army was dragooning civilians into the entertainment corps, and that he knew something was wrong when he'd been recalled so quickly from what was supposed to have been a lengthy convalescence.

'Dengue fever,' he said. 'Picked it up in Milne Bay. Christ, what a shithole that is. Believe me, the only thing exotic about New Guinea is the range of diseases you can catch. Copped a fucking terminal dose of khaki dermatitis, too.'

Not wishing to appear completely ignorant of army life, I didn't inquire as to what exactly khaki dermatitis was. Its name seemed sufficiently self-explanatory to prompt the comment, 'I suppose it's a bugger to get rid of,' from Brian.

'It is up there, mate. It gets so your balls go mouldy.'

With the unpleasant image of what was lurking behind Glen Pyers' flies now lodged in my mind, we crossed Princes Bridge, and at his insistence paused for a drink in the bar of Young and Jackson's Hotel.

'You two look fit enough,' he said—a compliment perhaps provoked by Brian's paying for the beer. 'I was bloody fit as a Mallee bull before Milne Bay. That was back in August. We hardly got to perform at all up there. I've never worked so bloody hard in my life, or been so bloody scared. They had us stretcher bearing, digging, driving, shooting at the fucking Japs—you name it. Got to do a bit of magic here and there, and then this fever hit. Thought I was going to die. Hoped I was, at one stage.'

Before what began to look like a rapid descent into maudlin reflection could gather speed, I distracted Glen by asking him what he meant by 'magic.'

'I was a magician on the Tivoli circuit before the war. So that's what I do in the shows. Bit of mind reading, sleight-of-hand, that sort of thing. What's your act?'

'Shakespeare,' I said.

Glen Pyers laughed.

'Christ Almighty. You'll be shot by your own audience if you trot that stuff out.'

'I think you'd be surprised at how receptive audiences can be.'

'Well, yes. Yes, I would. And you, Brian? What does the army need you for?'

Brian has always had an alarming tendency to blurt out the truth. Given that we were now, strictly speaking, in the employ of Army Intelligence, and given that we'd been instructed to trust no one—and no one would surely include Corporal Glen Pyers—I experienced a moment of trepidation when I thought Brian was about to reveal that his acquaintance with the great craft of acting came no closer than having been a teacher—a profession notorious, it's true, for attracting those with the desire to act but without the talent to back it up. Brian looked over his beer at Corporal Pyers, furrowed his brow and, with intense seriousness—as if he were delivering very bad news indeed—said, 'I'm a comic.'

It took Corporal Pyers' fevered brain a moment to make sense of the dichotomy between what was said and how it was said, but when he got it he bestowed the acknowledgement of a broad smile.

'All right,' he said, 'let's see what we can scrounge in the way of dress-ups.'

He led us to the Tivoli Theatre in Bourke Street, an establishment I'd visited only twice before—both times against my will, and both times at the behest of my late father who, when I look back on it, seemed determined to expose me, in the guise of birthday treats, to experiences more calculated to appal and alarm than to reward or entertain.

I think I must have been fourteen when he first took me to the Tivoli, and I distinctly recall letting him know that I thought it common, vulgar, and dull—a formless concatenation of grotesquery. Quite apart from the dreary warbling and mirthless comedians, I have a strong memory of being repulsed by an acrobat of such horrifying spinal elasticity that, with very little effort, he could assume a position where the slightest nudge would result in his head disappearing up his own arse. After the show, I mentioned to my father that vaudeville seemed to be a place where unattractive people with unappealing skills played to undiscerning audiences.

He took me again on my birthday the following year—having forgotten, I suppose, my distaste. I recall, though, that I reiterated it firmly. The year after that, the only thing that prevented, yet again, another visit to the Tivoli was my father's death. In most respects he was taken too early; in this one, he was taken not a moment too soon.

Brian's face lit up when he saw the Tivoli bill. He had a taste for the vulgar — witness his now-distracted wife, Darlene. Brian and the Tiv were old friends. He actually insisted that this was what real theatre was all about, not the frightful drawing-room comedies that infested the grander theatres in town. (Not that there was anything on at the moment, grand or otherwise.)

When we reached the theatre it was close to four o'clock, and the two o'clock show had recently released its hostages into Bourke Street. A few of them, including one or two American soldiers, were loitering around the garish billboards which ludicrously declared that the price of a ticket would deliver the extravagance that is the Folies Bergères. What the patron would actually see was a bevy of local girls in skin-coloured body tights, forbidden by law to make a move, with befeathered dancers moving amongst them to the moaning of a popular ballad.

'This,' said Brian, 'is a humdinger of a show.'

I remained silent.

Corporal Pyers led us down the side of the theatre and into a warehouse behind it. This was clearly the storage space and workshop for the theatre. Props leaned against walls, scrims and backdrops were in various stages of being painted or retouched, and racks of costumes were lined up, awaiting repairs.

'Wait here,' he said, and disappeared through a door beyond which, I presumed, lay offices. He returned a moment later with a severe-looking woman dressed with the self-conscious eccentricity of a person who believed that employment in any capacity in the theatre demanded quirkiness of appearance. She wore pince-nez that forced her head down to enable her to look over them, and her neck was strangled by a loop of over-sized amber beads — raw, shapeless, and ugly. She might as well have strung links through rubble, and worn that. She was holding a slip of paper, and looked Brian and me up and down.

'I'm not happy about this, Glen,' she said, and the familiar way in which she spoke his name indicated prior acquaintance. 'The army can't just go on requisitioning our costumes like this. We're as hard-pressed as everybody else getting decent materials.'

'This,' said Corporal Pyers, 'is Joycey Dover.'

'I'm William Power,' I said and held out my hand. She took it, exposing to my notice a ring that looked more like an attachment with a medical purpose than a piece of jewellery.

'I'm Brian,' said Brian, and merely nodded.

'All right,' said Joycey Dover. 'What do you need, Glen?'

Glen manoeuvred Brian and me so that we stood back-to-back.

'Same height, more or less; same weight, more or less; same frame, more or less. This makes things easier. So, one set of tails in my size — black. White's hopeless. One set in their size. Toppers, of course. Collapsible. That's all really, Joycey. We haven't come to strip the cupboard bare.'

He then turned to us.

'Which of you is the femme?'

'I beg your pardon,' I said. 'Why is it necessary for either of us to be the femme?'

'What's a femme?' Brian asked.

'A femme, Brian,' I said, 'is a man who dresses as a woman, and not in sensible tweed and flat shoes.'

'No,' Corporal Pyers said, and walked to a rack of costumes. 'More in this line.'

He pulled forth a satin sheath which would have looked fabulous clinging to Jean Harlow's body, and not quite so fabulous clinging to mine or Brian's.

'What about you, Glen?' I said. 'You look thin enough to carry off a dress like that.'

He smiled.

'I'm the magician, I'm afraid, unless one of you gentlemen is The Great Levante. The men up north expect the magician to have a pretty sidekick.'

He raised an eyebrow. Brian was out of his depth, I could tell. I didn't want him getting cold feet this early in the piece, so I agreed to be fitted for the dress.

'I'm not saying I'll do it,' I said quietly to Pyers, 'but if it's altered to fit me, it'll also fit Brian. We'll work out who's doing what later.'

Joycey Dover manhandled me into a corner and told me to undress. Despite being conscious that both Glen Pyers and Brian were watching me with smirks on their faces, I did so without hesitation. A professional actor doesn't baulk at a simple fitting. Wardrobe mistresses are like sculptors. To them, a body is little more than an armature on which they hang cloth instead of clay. I stood in my underwear as she measured me and jotted down figures.

'You'll have to take everything off,' she said. 'The dress can't be adjusted properly if it's competing with singlet and underpants.'

Without batting an eyelid, I did as requested, and Joycey Dover slid the satin sheath over my head. I closed my eyes and thought of England as she tucked and pinned.

'Very nice,' she said. 'It fits well, but you'll have to tape your bits down at the front. You can't go on stage with a bulge sticking out the front of the dress.'

Brian had the gall to guffaw like a schoolboy.

'That's something that won't be such a problem for you, Brian,' I said.

It took only a few more minutes to be fitted with a wig and to find a pair of shoes that almost fitted. When I took stock of myself in the mirror, my reflection wasn't the grotesque, pantomime dame I was expecting. With a bit of make-up and a close shave I felt I could give some of the Tivoli scrubbers a run for their money. Not that it would come to that. I'd decided that Brian was to be the femme in this outfit. I had more to offer than a lithe silhouette.

Afterwards, when Corporal Pyers had headed off with his bundle of costumes, Brian didn't take the opportunity to pass any remarks about my appearance as a woman. I knew he wanted to, but I suppose he thought that if he remained silent he'd escape the grim possibility of his winding up as the femme. In the tram on the way up to our mother's house in Princes Hill, I told him frankly that, as he had no other skills to offer, slipping into a satin sheath would have to substitute for talent.

'Well,' he said. 'We'll see,' and he managed to inject a surly, defiant note into this otherwise bland riposte.

Our mother's anxiety about our imminent departure was mollified by the assurance that we'd be seeing our youngest brother, Fulton, to whom she wrote every day, and from whom she heard little. This was hardly surprising, given that he'd been posted to Darwin, and Darwin wasn't ideally placed at this time for normal postal deliveries. I now knew, as well, that Fulton wasn't even in Darwin, but that he was somewhere 'out bush' with the North Australia Observer Unit. Our first loyalty was to Army Intelligence, and neither Brian nor I revealed to our mother the truth about Fulton's position. She was sufficiently pleased that we were able to confirm that Fulton was alive and well, and that in only a few short weeks, when we returned, we would be in a position to bring her more detailed news about her youngest son.

I was perfectly, and unconcernedly, aware that our mother had a hierarchy of affection where her three children were concerned. I came a distant third behind Fulton and Brian, perhaps because as the oldest I reminded her most strongly of our late father. It hadn't escaped my attention that whenever she pointed out the similarities they were attached to traits she considered unpleasant. I was only sixteen when my father died, so I can't confirm the truth or otherwise of Mother's observations. Given that she'd been having an affair with the family solicitor, Peter Gilbert, even before her husband's death, I'd respectfully submit that her views on my character must, at the very least, be open to question. I have no objection to being least favoured, but I confess a resentment towards being ill-favoured; and if it weren't unseemly, at the age of thirty-two, to express such a resentment, I would do so. My strong sense of personal dignity forbade raising such matters with Mother. Her indignation would have been epic, and I've never been fond of the epic form.

Over dinner that night, we told Mother as much as we could about our new roles in defeating the Japanese menace.

'I'm not at all sure,' she said, 'that I understand any of this. Are you, or are you not, soldiers?'

'Not soldiers exactly,' said Brian. 'We'll be in uniform, but that's sort of part of the act.'

'Our job, Mother,' I explained, 'is to raise morale, and no one's going to shoot at us.'

'Your morale-boosting efforts haven't really been all that successful in the past, do admit, darling,' said Mother, with chatty indifference to my feelings.

'Fortunately we won't have to battle the collective simple-mindedness of the general public,' I replied. 'Soldiers are hungry for entertainment, and if I were out in the middle of nowhere I'd certainly appreciate hearing a bit of Shakespeare for a change, instead of the drone of the moron I'm obliged to bunk with.'

Mother looked at me over the rim of her raised teacup.

'Don't despise your audience, Will. They'll know it, and they might throw grenades instead of flowers.'

I was rescued from the necessity of defending myself by the arrival of Mother's lover, Peter Gilbert. I hadn't yet reconciled myself to the fact of their relationship, let alone to its duration. I had no wish to cast moral aspersions against my mother—although her affair with Gilbert did begin adulterously—but I couldn't quite bring myself to greet him with anything but cool disdain. He was, anyway, impervious and insensitive to my feelings about him. Brian shook his hand warmly, and their cosy display of mateship was so cloying that I couldn't prevent my lip from curling with disgust. Mother saw it, and shook her head slightly. I'm sure if we'd been alone this would have been one of those occasions when she claimed I reminded her of my father. I excused myself and retired.

I didn't sleep well, and not because of my agitation about Peter Gilbert and Mother, but because of my excitement at the prospect of returning to the stage—my natural home, and the only place where, in the guise of various characters, I could truly be myself.

The following morning, Peter Gilbert, still in his pyjamas, intruded upon me in the bathroom while I was shaving.

'It's customary to knock,' I said.

'A custom more honourecd in the breach than the observance?' he said, and inflected it upwards to indicate that he considered the quote so apt as to be witty.

'As you see,' I said while drawing the razor carefully across my chin, 'the bathroom is occupied.'

'And by the very person to whom I wish to speak.' He sat on the side of the bath and crossed one leg over the other. 'It isn't actually any of your business, so I'm telling you this more as a courtesy than a duty. Your mother and I intend to formalise our relationship. You'll no doubt be appalled by the resulting change in our connection; but the fact is, when we're married, you'll become my stepson.'

'Should I congratulate you?'

'It wouldn't kill you.'

I caught his eye in the mirror.

'We should learn to tolerate each other, Will.'

I turned to face him.

'My father has been dead for sixteen years. For all of that time, and longer, you've been having an affair with my mother, and neither of you thought it worthwhile to mention the fact to Brian, to Fulton. or to me.'

Peter Gilbert actually smiled.

'That's true up to a point, but both Brian and Fulton were aware of how things stood between your mother and me, and we assumed you must have known, too, but that you chose never to discuss it — a strange obstinacy, if you don't mind my saying so, very like your father's. To be fair, we never really talked about it with your brothers, either. It was all terribly discreet.'

Here he paused and coughed.

'I had my own family, you see.'

'So this was adultery on a biblical scale.'

'Fortunately, Will, we don't get stoned to death in this country for loving the right person and marrying the wrong one.'

I turned back to the mirror and finished shaving.

'So, now you're divorced and free to marry.'

'No,' he said. 'I'm widowed.'

I couldn't hide the disbelief in my voice.

'You were waiting for your wife to die?'

'That's what you do when you marry a Catholic.'

He stood up.

'Now you know.'

He crossed to the bathroom door but, before leaving he said, 'I have two children, Will. Both of them are grown up, of course. Cloris is twenty-eight and John is twenty-six. You'll meet them when you come back from up north.'

I was so distracted by this avalanche of unwanted information that all I could think of to say was, 'Your last name is Gilbert and you called your son John? Isn't that a little vulgar?'

'My father's name was John. Not everything is connected to the movies.'

He left. I splashed water on my face, and a little bay rum, and returned to my bedroom to get dressed.

Chapter Two

SETTING OUT

OUR FAREWELLS HAD BEEN AWKWARD; or, at any rate, mine had been. Mother and I had had no time to discuss her impending nuptials, and we were both aware, as she kissed me lightly on the cheek, that this rather large and important issue had not been broached. She'd no doubt read my silence on the matter as disapproval—and she wasn't a million miles from being right about that—but her response was a familiar demonstration that my feelings weren't, after all, of much interest or importance to her. She sent me off with that small, reluctant kiss, and a chilly smile — a smile that had begun warmly when it was turned on Brian, but which had lost all its heat by the time it was directed at me.

Brian and I arrived at Victoria Barracks as instructed, at eight o'clock on the dot. James Fowler and Corporal Pyers were there already, and on the floor in the office were three kit bags. Folded on a chair were two uniforms, and beside the chair were two pairs of shoes.

'As soon as you change into these,' James said, 'you belong to us.'

With the recent news of Mother's arrangements still running around in my head, I couldn't wait to shed my civilian skin and turn myself over to Army Intelligence. The uniform was scratchy and immediately uncomfortable, and after only a few paces around James Fowler's office I knew that the shoes would be torture. Nevertheless, as I moved inside the heavy, ill-fitting material, I felt something close to elation. As far as I was concerned, this wasn't a uniform. It was a costume.

James Fowler looked at his watch.

'I've got two hours to give you some idea of what's in store for you. Obviously we don't have time to turn you into real soldiers, but I'm afraid you can't go where you're going without a crash course in a few basic skills.'

Over the next hour or so I began to wonder whether I'd made a ghastly mistake in signing up for this run, if I might use a theatrical term for what now appeared to be rather more military in nature than I'd bargained for. We were to be put on a troop train immediately and sent to somewhere called Ingleburn in New South Wales where, God help us, we were to learn how to fire a gun and, worse, how to ride a horse.

'The Observer Unit is basically a cavalry unit, so being able to ride, even inexpertly, is essential. Did I mention that yesterday?'

'No,' I said calmly. 'No, you didn't.'

'I'm sure I did.'

'You didn't actually say that we'd have to learn how to ride,' Brian said.

'Ah, well, there you are,' he said.

Corporal Pyers was to accompany us to Ingleburn, where he, too, would be taught to ride, and where he'd rehearse us in preparation for our performances.

'Today is the sixth of October,' James said. 'The NAOU training course is generally eight weeks. You have eight days. In ten days, on the sixteenth, you'll be onstage for the first time with the Third Division Concert Party, in Maryborough.'

'That's Maryborough, Queensland?' Brian asked.

'Correct.'

'You're kidding.'

His interjection was timely because I was speechless.

'I understand,' James said, 'that Will had a few difficulties up there recently, but I'm afraid they're immaterial to this operation. The Third Divvy CP happened to get going in Maryborough, back in August, and they're just about ready now to put on their first show. From our point of view, the timing is perfect. You, Will and Glen, are replacing two blokes who've dropped out. After Maryborough the concert party heads across to Mt Isa, and then up to Darwin. On the way, in Katherine, you'll make contact with the Unit HQ there and get your instructions. Any questions?'

I had too many to settle on one, so I remained silent. Brian asked, 'Any more surprises?'

'Just one,' James Fowler said. 'His name is Archie Warmington, and you'll meet him in Ingleburn.'

The closest I'd come to troop trains was seeing them in newsreels at the cinema pulling into, or out of, stations, their windows writhing with the vermicelli of excited soldiers waving and smiling, and their carriages graffitied with names and clumsy sketches. The train we found ourselves on, bound for Sydney, was a sad disappointment. It was crowded, noisy, and noisome. We were crammed into a carriage with a group of soldiers, none of whom could have been older than twenty, and their demeanour and conversation was unappealing to say the least. After a few hours of their pointless, witless larrikinism, I wasn't entirely certain that they and I belonged to the same species.

Corporal Pyers, however, saw this as an opportunity to relieve these raw recruits of what little money they had about their persons by demonstrating, and taking bets on, sleights of hand that were remarkable. He was able to make coins and notes appear and vanish with unpredictable and astonishing dexterity. The fingers that closed over a coin in the left hand opened a moment later on an empty palm, and the foolish soldier who'd laid a whole pound on its whereabouts found himself a poorer man. Pyers was able to undo a watch without the wearer knowing, and spirit it into the pocket of a baffled companion. He produced cigarettes out of nowhere, one after the other, until every man in the crowded compartment had one. I was sitting beside him, and I didn't detect the mechanism of any of his tricks. Corporal Glen Pyers went up in my estimation.

Apart from Glen's entertainments, the journey to Sydney was tedious and uncomfortable. When we arrived we were directed, like so much livestock, onto trucks, and driven west towards Ingleburn and an army camp that had been set up there in 1939. If the facilities were primitive, I thought, they would at least have the advantage of being relatively new.

We arrived late at night and, to my surprise, Corporal

Pyers, Brian, and I were separated from the mob and taken to a wooden hut some distance from the long barracks that housed most of Ingleburn's recruits. There were three cots set up, and I fell soundly asleep moments after stretching out on the one I'd claimed as mine.

I woke next morning to the sweet and cloying smell of clove tobacco, an odour new to me at the time, and which I came to associate indelibly with the man who was sitting with his back to us in the open doorway of our hut. He sucked deeply on his exotic kretek, flicked the butt end away from him, and entered the hut. By this time I was up on my elbows, and thought from the man's confident stance that he was about to bellow an order like some ghastly caricature of a pissed-off sergeant major. Instead he said, in a rather beautiful, mellifluous voice — every vowel round and every consonant acknowledged — 'Good morning. I hope it wasn't the pong of my kretek that woke you.'

'No,' I lied, reacting with an instinctive reluctance to offend him.

He leaned towards me and extended his hand.

'Major Archibald Warmington. But I think Archie will just about cover it.'

'William Power. Will, please.'

'One of these recumbent fellows must be your brother Brian, and the other, Glen, who is, I believe, a prestidigitator of some renown. As you see, I'm quite well informed.'

'I'm Brian.'

'I see a family resemblance.'

Corporal Pyers had by now stood up and, in the harsh light of the morning, exposed as he was in his underwear, looked emaciated and more in need of medical attention than whatever Archie Warmington had in store for him.

'We'll have to look after your hands,' Archie said, 'and I'll get some fruit into your diet.'

He swept his eyes over each of us.

'My instructions, gentlemen, are to do no more than teach you three things — how to shoot, how to ride, and the rudiments of signalling. There'll be no square-bashing, no six-mile hikes or runs, no gruesome exertions of any kind. The four of us are temporarily in a little bubble of privilege, and I've never been one to moan about privilege.'

It was then that I noticed that Archie Warmington's uniform was discreetly tailored, and that there was an air about him that wasn't quite fey, but which wasn't at all the air of a commando, either. He must have been in his late thirties, perhaps even early forties. His dark hair was cut close to his skull, and his face was lean and so strongly boned that it spoke of a body beneath it that must have been all muscle and sinew. He carried it loosely, though, and his movements suggested that its explosive potential was calibrated to dance rather than violence.

I'd been dreading Ingleburn — dreading being a part of the vast and impersonal machinery of the military. As it happened, the eight days we spent there count amongst the happiest of my life. Archie Warmington made it his business to protect us from the rigorous banality of army training. Indeed, we were so thoroughly protected that we were barely aware that the business of preparing recruits for battle was going on around us. Distant shouts, the sound of gunfire on the range, the tramp of feet — this was as close as we came to the day-to-day routine of these inchoate diggers. We weren't obliged to engage in the faux camaraderie of mess-hut conversation with people whose only commonality was their possible violent death. We took our meals in our hut; they were delivered by motorcycle, and they weren't the slop that everyone else was eating.

I'm not suggesting that the food available to us was luxurious, but its preparation was more akin to restaurant dining than to the trough-feeding one associates with army food. The menu included plenty of fruit—rather more pineapple than I would have liked—and the innovation (under the direction of Archie Warmington) of rice for breakfast, as a consequence of his long association with Bali. In only a matter of days, Corporal Glen Pyers began to look almost healthy. I didn't make any inquiries regarding his khaki dermatitis, for fear that he'd show me either its improvement or its steady deterioration. Either way, peering at some dark corner of the Pyers body wasn't something I'd volunteered for.

After breakfast on our first day, we were shown the guns that we'd be required to master.

'You won't actually be issued with any weapons,' Archie said, 'but you may have to use one nonetheless—if not against the Japs, then possibly against wildlife.'

'I'm sorry,' Brian said, 'did you say "wildlife"?'

'You may have to shoot something for food,' Archie said casually. 'And then, of course, crocodiles can be a problem.'

I laughed, assuming that Archie was lightening the mood with humour. His eyebrows moved slightly upwards, a minimal gesture that was surprisingly eloquent and horrifying. I pushed the notion of crocodiles to the back of my mind and turned my attention to the weapons lying on the table in front of me. These were, I learned, a .303 rifle, a .22 rifle, a 12 gauge shotgun, a German Luger, and a Thompson submachine-gun. When I picked this up it proved heavy and difficult to wield. I was familiar with it from American gangster movies, where it sat more easily in the hands of George Raft and Edward G. Robertson. The Luger was Archie's own. Lugers were, apparently, regularly captured from German soldiers and issued to Allied officers. This was fine in principle, and Archie declared that his Luger was a marvellous weapon, but maintaining a steady supply of ammunition for it was problematic at best.

I surprised myself by discovering that I had rather a facility for shooting, and in a very short space of time became not only comfortable with guns, but adept at firing them accurately. I was certainly a better marksman than either Brian or Glen. I don't know why I assumed that an accomplished magician would be able to shoot straight, but Glen fired a rifle with the skill and accuracy one might expect from Teiresias. Brian wasn't much better. He was, however, much better than I was at understanding the arcane workings of the FS6 transceiver, a device the mysteries of which defeated me, despite Archie's patient explication.

Glen proved to have a previously unknown affinity with horses. He'd grown up in Hobart and had had very little contact with them. Certainly, he'd never ridden one, but as soon as he climbed aboard the wiry creatures at Ingleburn—horses Archie called 'walers', and which he assured us were the favoured mounts of the Lighthorse—Glen looked, and felt, at home. My own relationship with the horses was more fraught. When I sat astride one of the quivering, snorting animals, I was uncomfortably conscious of how far I was from the ground, and that the security of my seat depended entirely upon the whim of the horse. I had no confidence in my ability to control its savage urges.

Given the brevity of our training schedule, Archie sensibly decided to play to our strengths, and was happy enough to allow us to acquire minimal competence in our weakest areas and to more carefully hone where we were strongest.

The acquisition of these skills took place during the day. After dinner, Glen rehearsed us for our roles in the Third Division Concert Party production of something called *Camp Happy*.

This was a grab bag of sketches, songs and comedy acts, with no coherent through-line — a necessity, given that performers would come and go.

At our first rehearsal, Glen blithely announced that he'd audition us for the roles that had fallen vacant. With epic self-control, I kept my indignation in check. The idea that my acting talent should be judged by a mere magician, however accomplished, was abhorrent and absurd. The expression on my face must have betrayed something of my discomfort, because Glen, in a clumsy attempt at conciliation, said that all he really needed to know was which of us was better able to project his voice without amplification.

'This isn't about who's a good actor, Will. It's just about who can make himself heard.'

I needn't have been concerned. I knew how to use my diaphragm to push my voice out across the footlights and up into the gods. Brian, when he attempted to project his voice across even our relatively small room, failed, because it was all coming from the throat. There was no resonance, no thrust; but, to his credit, he accepted with measured good grace that he'd be spending a good deal of time sashaying about in a slinky, satin sheath.

'Archie will teach you how to walk in heels,' Glen said.

'My God,' I said to Archie, 'is there anything you can't do?'

'I don't yodel,' he said. 'But, of course, that's not as useful a skill as walking in heels, so I never bothered to learn.'

'You ride, you shoot, you know Morse, you walk in heels. This is a surprising range of skills.'

'I think my life has been very different from yours.'

Archie spoke in a way that aroused in me an inexplicable little vibration of envy.

The parts I was required to learn were unbelievably awful.

Being the utility actor in any variety show is a thankless job. Whoever I'd be playing against had the best lines. I was there to set up the punch line, and there was no place for improvisation, and certainly no room for any excerpts from the Bard. It was clear, after looking through the whole program, that soldiers were prepared to sit still, and maybe even shed a discreet tear, for some indifferent tenor's rendition of 'Ave Maria,' but there was no room for poetry. I consoled myself with the thought that once we were released from the constraints of the concert party, and we were troubadouring, *Timon of Athens* would ring out above whatever parallel it was that we were near.

Despite the unsatisfactory nature of the material I committed to memory, the eight days at Ingleburn sped by. I rehearsed my parts with Brian, who read the other parts for me so that I could get the timing right. Surprisingly, as the days went by, he became less and less resentful of having been allocated the femme role. He rehearsed separately with Archie, and then with Glen, and he became so at ease with his role that, on the evening before our departure for Maryborough, he happily set about the time-consuming task of shaving his arms, legs, and chest. He refused, however, to show me what he'd learned. I'd have to wait to see it in performance. There wasn't a skerrick of embarrassment or shame in this refusal. It was almost as if he knew that my reaction to his appearance on stage would be astonishment.

Neither Brian nor I had pleasant memories of Maryborough. Only a few short months before, I'd been embroiled there in a hideous and violent series of events which had resulted in my unjust alienation from my eponymous acting troupe, who were still in Maryborough, working under the direction of my leading lady, Annie Hudson. Brian's recent memories of Maryborough could hardly have been more pleasant than my own. Having come up from Melbourne, ostensibly to help me, he'd embarked upon a ludicrous and dangerous affair with a madwoman.

We'd been told that Maryborough was the place where we were to connect with the Third Division Concert Party, but I'd put it out of my mind for the most part during these training days, and consoled myself with the thought that the estranged members of my troupe wouldn't be in any audience to which we played. They were civilians, and the concert party was dedicated to entertaining the troops. Perhaps I could get in and out of Maryborough without making contact with any of my former colleagues. The person I most wanted to avoid was Sergeant Peter Topaz, a copper whose low opinion of me was out of all proportion to the one or two small errors of judgement I'd made.

Archie Warmington wasn't coming with us to Maryborough, and I was genuinely disappointed that I might now never get the opportunity to find out where he came from, and who he was. He'd obviously made an impression on Brian as well because, on the morning of our departure, while he merely shook my hand, he put his arm around Brian's shoulder in a gesture of mateship. I suppose the bond that forms when you teach someone how to walk in heels is stronger than the bond that forms when you teach someone how to fire a Thompson submachine-gun.

Chapter Three
IN CONCERT

WE ARRIVED IN MARYBOROUGH in the back of an army truck, and as we drove down Ferry Street I became absurdly and irrationally anxious about being seen by members of my former troupe. I was particularly anxious about meeting Arthur Rank, the person to whom I'd been closest and who had more reason than the others to despise me—given that I'd almost killed him with a blow to the head. I imagined that he'd be fully recovered by now (the blow had fallen a month ago, after all), but in the intervening time I'd been troubled by the collapse of our friendship.

Initially, I admit, I thought Arthur's attitude towards me had been peevish. I'd assaulted him in good faith, if such a thing is possible. Now, though, I was prepared to acknowledge that perhaps my actions had been ill-conceived; and so, although I'd have welcomed an opportunity to offer a sincere apology, I was also crippled by the inevitable mortification that this would entail. Brian, who'd got on famously with the troupe, was untroubled by the prospect of seeing them. Indeed, he said he'd seek them out at the first opportunity, and he helpfully provided Glen with a thumbnail sketch of each of them.

The truck passed the town hall, and a sign out the front proclaimed that the Hudson Players, so recently the Power Players, were currently performing *Pygmalion*. Annie Hudson transformed from guttersnipe to princess? Sadly, she didn't have the range to accomplish this alchemy, and her performance would provide irrefutable proof that a guttersnipe in a ball gown is just that—a guttersnipe in a ball gown. And who amongst the others could play Professor Higgins? Arthur had only one arm, and while Shaw doesn't actually specify that Higgins have two arms, audiences would expect him to pull on two gloves when he takes Eliza Doolittle to the ball. Adrian Baden, who'd be more interested in seducing Freddy Eynsford Hill than Eliza, would make an adequate Higgins, so I hoped the company had the sense to appoint him over Bill Henty, who'd want to do the role bare-chested, or Kevin Skakel, whose club foot was less of an impediment than his inability to act.

I was pondering the casting of *Pygmalion* when we drove through the gates of the showgrounds, which was where the Third Division had set up camp. We were deposited inside the front gate, and I thought I detected a slight sneer on the face of the corporal who checked our papers when he discovered that we were members of the concert party. We were given a tent number and vague directions as to its whereabouts. Finding it was easier said than done. The showgrounds had been converted into a small city of tents, but an inquiry to a passing private led us to a section dominated by a fair-sized stage, with its sides and roof made of large tarpaulins. There was a great deal of activity around the stage, which seemed to be quite well set up, with an effectively painted backdrop and a row of lights — powered, I supposed, by a generator kept at sufficient distance to minimise the noise.

My excitement grew, despite the banality of the part I was expected to play. There were actors on stage, one of whom was practising an impressive pratfall. I was glad that I wasn't obliged to engage in knockabout comedy. I didn't think it was funny, and it hurt. There were musicians as well, including one who was off by himself coaxing a racket out of an accordion — an instrument whose portability is its only redeeming feature. The overall impression was one of busy rehearsal, and it seemed to involve a large number of people.

The sight of the stage caused Brian's face to lose its colour. The reality of being expected to perform in front of a large crowd must have just hit him.

'Quite a set-up,' I said to Glen.

'According to the schedule, there's one performance tomorrow night and then the whole thing comes down, and we head for Mt Isa.'

'I'll need to find the people in my sketches,' I said. 'I don't think slipping into their routines will be too difficult. It's not like I'm a last-minute replacement for King Lear, is it?'

Glen narrowed his eyes.

'This is a professional outfit, Will. Don't underestimate how sharp you're going to have to be. You'll be up there with people who do this for a living — people who've performed in London — and they'll expect you to be up to speed and up to scratch.'

I took his little homily with good grace.

We found our tent, stepped onto the wooden flooring at its entrance, and went in. There were four cots inside, and on one of them sat a thin young man who was sewing a sequin onto a garment that fell across his knees with the unmilitary and sinuous drape of a vamp's gown. He looked up when we entered and said 'Gedday' in an accent more suggestive of slip-rails than slips. 'Sergeant Rothfield'll be pleased to see you blokes. I'm Lon—as in Chaney.'

He didn't get up, but his demeanour was perfectly pleasant and I immediately warmed to him. We'd barely made our introductions when we were joined by Sergeant Rothfield himself, who must have been alerted to our arrival. There was no room in the tent for five men to stand, so we sat awkwardly, with the sergeant choosing to sit beside me. He was, it transpired, the producer of *Camp Happy*. Without much ado, and giving the strong impression that he was pressed for time, Sergeant Rothfield handed us the latest running sheets for the production.

'It's two-and-a-half hours,' he said. 'Non-stop. Twenty-five separate items, no breaks. One comes on as the other goes off. You can see where your cues are, and you'll get a bit of a run-through this evening and tomorrow. I presume you know your lines, Will; but as the sketches are old Tivoli standbys, you probably knew them before you came on board anyway.'

I refrained from correcting him on this point, even though I was stung by his assumption that I was the kind of performer who'd be well acquainted with tired Tivoli standby acts.

'Tomorrow's performance starts at six, and it goes on no matter what—rain, hail, earthquake, volcanic eruption. I'll leave you to it. Lon here will look after you.'

'He's a good bloke,' Lon said. 'Writes plays, apparently. I've never read any of them but.'

The running sheet confirmed that *Camp Happy* lurched from low comedy to tear-jerking renditions of 'Danny Boy' and the inevitable 'Ave Maria'. There was a baritone, a tenor, a swing band, a ventriloquist, sight acts, Glen's magic spot, a ukulele player (ugh), a classical pianist, and several utility actors. Lon was to appear in the first half as a hillbilly, a type whose comic appeal escaped me, and in the second as a burlesque femme called Lola. 'Something,' he said, 'in the Carmen Miranda line. I get plenty of whistles.'

'Brian here will give you a run for your money,' Glen said. 'He's my beautiful assistant.'

Lon laughed.

'Mate,' he said, 'you'll be beating them off with a stick.'

That night's rehearsal was so energising that I stopped minding the inanity of my lines. I was just happy to be on a stage and in the company of real actors. The men I was playing against were far from amateurs. They were assured and slick, and appreciative of the fact that I was obviously a dependable and skilled replacement for whoever it was who'd fallen ill. It all happened so quickly and in such a blaze of lights and noise that I didn't take in anyone's name, but stood on the sidelines when I wasn't required and watched in a kind of mesmerised ecstasy, moved foolishly to tears by a maudlin tune—not because it touched me, but because I felt, suddenly, for the first time in a very long time, that I was home.

It has always been my experience that joy is an emotion that is peculiarly susceptible to rot. It therefore wasn't very surprising that my pleasure at being back on stage was short lived. The morning's rehearsal didn't go well, with my acting partners being openly hostile to the small improvements I'd made overnight in my part. My defence of the changes was met with an uncompromising, 'Just play the fucking part as it's written.' Not wishing to behave with the prima donna selfishness my partners were exhibiting, I acquiesced; but actors are fragile, volatile creatures, and my gall at wishing to give myself just a couple of memorable lines damaged my standing in the company. Where Brian was welcomed and chatted to, I was sent to Coventry and treated with cool, dismissive indifference. There were no complaints about my performance; but after each run-through I found myself in the wings alone.

I didn't mind. *Camp Happy* was just a conduit through which Brian and I were obliged to pass before undertaking the real purpose of our trip. Indeed, any deep attachment to the concert party would have been inadvisable, given that we'd be leaving it in a matter of days.

After lunch, Brian suggested that we hitch a lift into town and visit the George Hotel where my old troupe would, no doubt, still be staying.

'No,' I said firmly. 'I don't want to see any of them.'

'Not even Arthur?'

'Especially not Arthur.'

As is often the case with my brother, he mistook my tone and assumed that I was defiantly clinging to the notion that I bore no responsibility for my poor relations with Arthur. Before I could ask him to pass on my sincere and profound regrets, he'd left, and I could only hope that he wouldn't take the liberty of speaking on my behalf. I would have followed him, but I decided then and there that all that had happened prior to this day, Friday, 16 October 1942, was to lie undisturbed. Encroachments from both the recent and more distant past were unwelcome and I'd resist them, and beat them back, whether they came as single spies or whole battalions. I'd defend the bridge from the past to the present with the determination and courage of Horatio.

I spent the afternoon running through my unchanged lines, and as the time approached for costume and make-up I began to feel the adrenalin-flutter of nervous expectation. The dressing-room was the back of a three-ton truck, parked out of sight of the audience, behind the stage. It wasn't ideal, and most changes took place on the ground outside, with costumes being handed down from racks. My make-up was basic — something to accentuate the eyes, the eyebrows, and the mouth — and in my top hat and tails I couldn't wait to step out into the warm embrace of the audience. When I looked at myself in the mirror, and adjusted my bowtie, I knew that acting wasn't just a profession; it was a vocation. The moment was spoiled somewhat when the mirror was shared with a fellow actor who said, unnecessarily, 'Remember, Will, just speak the fucking lines as written. Your lips are too red, by the way. You look like a fucking nancy boy catamite.'

I spoke my lines as written, and the audience couldn't have known how aggrieved I was at being reduced to a cipher. I fed the other actors their lines, to which they responded and got the laughs, despite the antiquity of the jokes. The soldiers in the audience were so generous as to be almost undiscerning. Perhaps a sense of imminent death helps breathe life into old gags.

I came off stage confident that I'd done my job well, although no one patted me on the back. Things were hectic, of course.

I'm almost certain there was no deliberate slight.

It was Brian who stopped the show. The moment he walked on stage next to Glen—who looked like a poor man's Mandrake—was the first time I'd seen him in full costume. His hand rested on Glen's arm as he crossed to the centre of the stage, and he moved with the fluid grace of a woman who, if she knew anything at all, knew that she was sufficiently beautiful to snag the glances of watching men. Glen manipulated ropes, cards, coins and silks, and brought a member of the audience to the stage where, with Brian's help, he divested the hapless private of his watch, his wallet, a filthy handkerchief and a gold chain. The audience howled when Brian wove himself around the victim and, in one quick, deft movement, seemed to reach into the soldier's trousers and withdraw a fully extended, army-issue condom, creating the bizarre impression that the soldier had come to the concert wearing it. His protestations only made the crowd laugh louder. Brian didn't speak a single line, which preserved the spectacular illusion of femininity he'd created. Unlike Lon, who appeared later as Lola, Brian hadn't chosen to play his role as burlesque, but had attempted the infinitely more difficult task of causing an observer to ask, 'Is he, or isn't he?'

Afterwards in our tent I was unstinting in my praise, and I think Brian was pleased to hear it.

'I saw everyone today,' he said. 'At the hotel.'

He waited for a moment, hoping to elicit a response from me. Having already bolstered his ego, I decided against giving him this small satisfaction. When it became clear that I had no intention of asking after their welfare, he volunteered, 'They're all fine. I thought they might want to know how you were going, but nobody asked.'

'I see,' I said, 'and you thought it was important to tell me that.'

He must have realised suddenly that he'd been guilty of an undeserving meanness—and whatever flaws might be found in his vast catalogue of them, meanness wasn't one of them—because he tried to save the situation by saying, 'I just meant that they didn't say anything nasty, so that's a good sign.'

'No, Brian. There's nothing nastier than silence.'

I slept well, despite being vaguely troubled by my acting troupe's snub.

The next morning, the Third Division Concert Party was loaded into three trucks and a parlour coach. The stage had been dismantled during the night, mostly by a working party whose brawn we wouldn't have access to in Mt Isa. We'd all be expected to help put together this cumbersome structure and then to pull it down, almost immediately.

I've never been particularly good at small talk, so the two-day journey to Mt Isa, crammed into a bus with perhaps twenty others, some of whom had taken a set against me, promised to be something of an ordeal. The promise was soon realised; but well before we'd arrived in Mt Isa, conditions on the bus had become truly awful and the lack of goodwill had become general.

All conversation in the bus died when we entered Mt Isa. I say 'entered,' but it isn't the kind of place you enter. More correctly, we passed through a cloud of roiling dust into a world that struck me as so 'other' as to generate an uncertain, but definite, fear in all of us. The presence of the American military was immediately apparent. Trucks ground their gears and blew their horns with abandon. The most astonishing thing of all was the unexpected realisation that the US army was populated by black men. We'd seen only a few of these fellows in Melbourne, but here in Mt Isa they seemed to outnumber white soldiers ten to one. It was explained to me later that the Australian government had reluctantly suspended the White Australia Policy on the understanding that black Americans would be relegated mostly to the back blocks; and if the streets of Mt Isa were any guide, the American administration was keeping its end of the bargain.

I don't think I will ever again experience the strange contrast of noise and crowds to the utter desolation of the surrounding landscape.

The dust that blew into the bus like smoke was so thick that I couldn't understand how, whenever we breathed it in, it didn't simply turn to mud in our lungs and drown us. The bus crawled through the vehicle-clogged streets towards the racecourse where we were to spend the night, and where we were to raise our theatre for one performance of *Camp Happy* to an audience of, obviously, mostly Americans. Conditions at the racecourse were appalling, but the necessity of putting up the theatre denied us time to assimilate this fact until the prospect of sleeping in the open, in the dust, could no longer be ignored. It wasn't the sleeping arrangements that stunned me initially. It was the flies. No plague in Egypt could compete with them.

Having been raised with fastidiousness about germs, I considered each individual fly to be an explosive threat to good health. To be covered in them from head to foot as they sought out moisture around my nose, lips, eyes, and ears, on any exposed skin, and anywhere on my clothes where there was the promise of sweat—and I was sweating profusely, the heat being intense—was horrifying to me. It was a sudden leap to go from hunting down a single fly in a room to be swarming with them like a piece of carrion. I was afraid to open my mouth lest dozens of them crawl inside, and I knew that many of them would have come from the pit toilets that must have been dug to accommodate this influx of soldiers.

Nevertheless, it is amazing how quickly one becomes inured to something as disgusting as insistent flies. It was impossible to keep them at bay, so eventually they crawled with impunity, depositing microbial horrors where they willed.

The theatre was more or less raised by nightfall; so, after a stomach-bogglingly awful meal, it was decided that, as this was to be our only free night in Mt Isa, we'd wander into what passed for the centre of town. This turned out to be more complicated than anticipated, though. Mt Isa wasn't a sleepy little town. Its position as a railhead meant that thousands upon thousands of tons of equipment were routinely unloaded here for transport north by road into the Territory. With tons of war materials came thousands of personnel, and the Americans didn't travel light. Mt Isa had become a de facto military base, but a posting here was no picnic. The black soldiers were acutely aware that many of their white colleagues were idling comfortably in towns on the east coast, an option that was largely closed to them because of their inconvenient colour. Consequently, the mood in Mt Isa was unpredictable, and we were told that it was inadvisable to venture off the racecourse without carrying a sidearm at the very least.

Whether or not it was true that we could expect every G.I. we met to be armed with a knife or a razor, it was bound to have a discouraging effect on easy social intercourse to imagine that a wrong word might lead to an open jugular. Brian blithely volunteered that I was handy with a gun, and someone produced a Luger—borrowed with permission, I was assured, from a captain who was confined to his patch of bare earth by a ferocious bout of diarrhoea. I strapped it on reluctantly, but I could sense that it improved my standing amongst my fellow actors immediately. I thought perhaps I might contrive to be armed during any further discussions about scripts.

Everything about Mt Isa was gruelling. Walking to the main street was gruelling; finding a place to buy a beer was gruelling; buying the beer was gruelling; even drinking it was gruelling. There was too much of everything—too many flies, too many people, too much heat, too much dust, too much noise, too much aggression, and too much boredom. No wonder that the main streets were jammed with M.Ps. in jeeps, usually travelling in groups of four, and almost all of them black.

I didn't start the fight, but in retrospect I probably shouldn't have fired the Luger. It was really Glen's fault. Somehow our small group ended up outside the American PX, which had been set up in a large tent on a vacant piece of baked earth in the main street. (There can't be too many towns that boast vacant, blasted blocks in their main street). The crush here was awful, and Glen saw an opportunity to fleece some doughboys of their dollars. He did spectacularly well, aided by the inebriated state of his victims, but the entertainment to be derived from watching cards vanish and your sure bets fail is short-lived when money changes hands. The G.I.s weren't as gracious about losing as the diggers on the train had been, and they were losing more, and to an undeclared enemy.

Before I really understood what was happening, American soldiers began to coalesce on one side of Glen, and Australians on the other. It could only end badly. Glen was sitting down behind an upturned crate on which he was laying out his cards and conning his audience into laying their bets. Perhaps from his position he couldn't see that sides had formed because, instead of packing up his deck and retreating, he asked smugly, 'Anyone else?'

A soldier pushed his way to the front of the group and stood before Glen. He was tall and lean, and so dark that it took a moment to register that he wore a neat moustache. Everything about him was neat. He seemed to repel the dust and grime that clung to the rest of us. I was lost in admiration.

'I would like to place a bet with you, sir,' he said, in a voice that bore no relation to the black-American caricatures familiar to me from the movies.

'I'll be happy to take your money,' Glen said, and all the invisible ties that bound us were pulled a little tighter. You could see it as people tensed, or became suddenly more attentive. Glen was oblivious, concentrating no doubt on setting up his trick.

'Here's the deal,' he said. 'You choose a card from this deck, and show your buddies, but don't show me. Put it back in the deck, I'll shuffle, and you think of a number between one and fifty-two. Can you manage that?'

The ties tautened.

'Tell us the number you thought of, I'll hand you the deck, and you start turning the cards over one by one until you get to that number. That'll be your card. You turn them. I won't touch them. Do you reckon you can do that?'

Before the soldier had a chance to reply, Glen produced fifty American dollars, dollars he'd won earlier, and slammed them on the crate.

'Tell you what. That's fifty bucks, fifty-until-recently-Yankee bucks. If this doesn't work, the fifty is yours. All you have to do is put up ten. You could win fifty, but you can only lose ten. That too complicated for you?'

With frightening civility, the soldier said, 'I'll risk five dollars. That's all.'

'No worries, mate. I'm glad to see that you understand it is a risk.'

'Yes,' he said ominously, 'it is a risk.'

Glen was a good magician, but his instinct for danger was poor. He held the deck towards the soldier, who took a card from it and made a show of displaying it to a few men nearby. He returned the card to the deck, and Glen began to cut and shuffle.

'OK,' he said, still shuffling. 'Think of a number and tell us.'

'Twenty-eight.'

Glen furrowed his brow in a bad approximation of concern, as if this was the one number he'd hoped not to be chosen, and continued shuffling. He handed the deck to the soldier and said, 'Start turning them over, Private. When you get to the twenty-eighth card, that'll be the one you picked.'

Slowly the count began. What should have been a simple entertainment was mutating before our eyes into a bitter contest. When the twenty-sixth card was turned, the air was electric, and I prayed that Glen had been sufficiently canny to get the trick wrong and lose the fifty dollars.

The soldier turned over the twenty-seventh card, and Glen said, 'Before you flip it, tell us all what card you picked.'

'The two of hearts,' he said, and his carefully modulated voice did nothing to calm my nerves. On the contrary, his self-discipline was terrifying, and he turned the card with agonising deliberation.

It was the two of hearts.

There was a moment when all those assembled might have laughed and applauded. It ended when Glen folded his arms in the smug certainty that he'd made a fool of not just this soldier, but all of them. My mouth became dry and I began to breathe with shallow, rapid inhalations.

It was the flash of what I took to be a knife, or a vicious razor, that caused me to draw the Luger from its holster. The effect was as if I'd taken a cattle prod and poked each and every G.I. in the groin with it. They recoiled, and a cry went up from somewhere amongst them that the 'Ossies' (with the 's' over-emphasised in that frightful American way) were about to fire on them. The inevitability of a riot breaking out struck me so forcibly that raising the gun and firing two quick shots in the air to quell it seemed to me to be entirely reasonable. However, the crack of the Luger had the perverse effect of galvanising Glen's audience into violent unanimity, and they surged towards us with fists flailing.

I was one of the first of our group to be knocked to the ground and trampled mercilessly beneath heavy, U.S. army-issue boots. I curled into a ball, protecting my face and head, and so didn't see the rapid arrival of numerous M.P.s, who brought the situation under control with ruthless efficiency. I heard gunshots, but was distracted from any proper assessment of the state of play by several sharp and painful kicks to my back, buttocks, ribs, and legs. I knew from experience that bruising would be extensive. I hoped that Brian had protected himself against a similar battering. A heavily bruised femme would create the unfortunate impression of an unhappy domestic situation.

I don't think I fell unconscious at any time, but at some point I was lying amid a forest of trousered legs, and at another I was sprawled in the dirt with no one around me, and with flies reclaiming their temporarily abandoned demesne. There was a great deal of shouting, with the M.P.s bringing their soldiers under control largely through screaming abuse at them. The other Australians had sensibly melted away as soon as it was safe to do so. They were actors, after all, and were unaccustomed to fisticuffs, unless they were carefully choreographed. The

Americans would have pummelled them into the dust. I understood this but, nevertheless, it would have been nice if someone, Brian or Glen perhaps, had remained long enough to help me to my feet.

As it was, I stood groggily, and endured derisive laughter and a couple of pointless shoves from a sweating private. I think he said 'Faggot', but I can't be certain because his accent was absurd. I smiled at him graciously, and he responded by spitting at my feet. When I looked down to check that the gobbet of saliva had missed my shoe, I suddenly realised that I was no longer holding the Luger.

I scanned the ground, hoping to see it lying half-concealed by dirt, but it was nowhere to be found. There were still many soldiers milling about, so it wasn't possible to get down on my hands and knees and scrabble about for it. The Luger was gone, and I knew that I'd be held responsible for this, even though the real responsibility was squarely Corporal Glen Pyers'. With any luck, the captain whose weapon it was would be too incapacitated by loose bowels to make enquiries about his Luger until we'd moved on. If my own bowels were tortured by flux, I didn't think I'd be worrying about a purloined German handgun.

I found my way back to the racecourse and, despite the blanketing darkness there, even managed to locate the paltry rectangle of bare earth that would serve as my bed. None of the men with whom I'd gone into town had yet returned, and I could only suppose that they'd found somewhere to drink themselves into a stupor. That suited me well. The drunker they were, the less likely they were to ask questions about the wretched Luger.

I wasn't yet ready to retrieve my duffel bag from the bus and attempt to make a rudimentary bed from spare clothes. I headed to the area where the stage had been raised, and found that there were people making adjustments to the rigging, and there were even a few musicians practising their parts. There didn't seem to be anything I could do to help, and I felt a sudden reluctance to offer assistance. Any promise of camaraderie that might have resulted from attachment to the concert party had failed to eventuate. This wasn't really my fault, although I knew I lacked Brian's common touch. I've never been comfortable disappearing into the herd, and this is the principle upon which camaraderie turns. Pulling together, and running with the pack, are distinctions without difference. I withdrew and returned to my quarters, as it were.

Sleep was impossible. The ground was hard, despite layers of dust so thick that they ought to have provided a cushion. My body was tender in key areas after the riot, and passing soldiers stumbled into me, and over me, and kicked up dust that stifled me and made breathing a torture. I must have fallen into a light doze, though, because I was wakened from it by Brian's and Glen's drunken arrival. They'd had, it transpired, a wild and rollicking evening with the very soldiers who'd knocked me to the ground and booted me from pillar to post. Apparently, they were tremendously good fellows who were quite reasonably agitated by the discharging of my Luger. There was no point arguing with them. Their systems were too flooded with alcohol to allow them to see sense. I held fire, even when Glen said, 'That was a dickhead thing to do, Will. Someone could've been killed.'

I couldn't put this level of stupidity entirely down to booze, so I had to suppose that his extraordinary sleight-of-hand skills were nature's way of compensating him for low intelligence.

'Go to bed,' I said. 'I probably saved your life so, yes, I suppose that does make me a dickhead.'

Glen laughed derisively and dangled the missing Luger close

to my face. When he spoke, his voice assumed a sharp, rather nasty, edge.

'You dropped this. Just add me to the list of people who've spent their lives picking up after you.'

He let the Luger slip from his fingers, and the barrel caught me painfully just above the right eye. I immediately felt the warm ooze of blood, but I didn't make a fuss. Brian and Glen, who'd fetched their duffel bags before they found me, set about clumsily laying out the groundsheets. This proved quite difficult, given their lack of coordination and the darkness. I felt disinclined to help them, and took some satisfaction in the sure knowledge that their next day's brutal hangovers, allied with the heat, dust, and flies, would be unspeakably unpleasant.

I stayed out of everyone's way throughout almost all of the following day. I wandered about swatting flies and then regretted eating lunch, which was filthy, after finding the cookhouse and looking inside. The English language lacks a descriptor that would do it justice. 'Squalid' is altogether too grand.

By late afternoon my nerves had been stripped raw after hours of attempting to keep Beelzebub's minions away from the small wound Glen had opened. The thought of one of those creatures settling above my eye after traipsing over someone's stool in the cesspit was almost too much to bear. I'm not by nature squeamish, but I had no desire to repeat Emily Dickinson's transcendent banality of hearing a fly buzz when I died. I found solace in preparing for that night's performance. As soon as I fell into the rhythm of dressing and making up, and going over my lines, my dejection eased. I couldn't, of course, lose myself in a character, but I had a responsibility to deliver the best performance possible — in spite of, not because of, the material.

That night's audience, a mix of Australian and American soldiers, greeted *Camp Happy* with a response that verged on the ecstatic. They whistled, howled, laughed, and applauded in a kind of frenzy of gratitude. When Brian crossed the stage I thought the roar would tear a hole in heaven.

There was, though, an ugly incident after the show involving Brian and a completely sober G.I. I witnessed it, and was amongst those who intervened to prevent what threatened to be something akin to rape. A tall, pallid, red-headed private, with an accent that an American Professor Higgins might have been able to pinpoint to a grim cabin in a remote corner of Mississippi, waylaid Brian as he came off stage. Unless Brian excited in him an uncontrollable need to express a transvestite passion, he genuinely believed that he'd found the girl of his tortured dreams amid the choking grit of Mt Isa. Brian attempted to repel his advances in his masculine, light baritone, and one can only surmise that the boy's mother had an unnaturally deep voice, because he was unfazed by the sonorous dichotomy between form and sound, and pressed his case rather too insistently.

It was at this point that Brian's ability to balance in high heels was revealed as being confined to the predictability of floorboards. The uneven dirt that lay between the stage and the costume truck caused him to totter inelegantly when he shoved his admirer forcefully in the chest. Brian fell, and instead of bringing out the gentleman in this southerner, the spectacle of the now prone and flailing Brian caused him to pounce with the blind determination of an animal on heat. It all happened more quickly than the time it takes to describe it — a fact that Brian later chose to ignore when he accused me of allowing the assault to progress beyond the point where it was either humorous or safe. As I wasn't the only witness, I, in my turn, pointed out that events unfolded too rapidly to allow anyone to grasp the gravity of the situation. As soon as Brian hit the dirt there were several pairs of hands, including mine, dragging his over-enthusiastic beau off him.

'Pairs of hands,' I said, 'that I could have done with last night. Where were you when I was being stomped on?'

'I didn't see that. After you fired that shot it was chaotic.'

'Sure. We're supposed to watch out for each other, Brian. Maybe you should try to remember that.'

If he'd still been in wig and make-up, I'd have described his response as unmistakably a pout. It wasn't, as I told him, an attractive addition to his repertoire of emotions, and we both went to bed—a ludicrous expression for what was in essence lying down in the dirt—in a state of simmering mutual discontent.

Chapter Four

DARWIN

THE EVENTS OF THE FOLLOWING DAY dispelled the ill-feeling between my brother and me. I awoke, peeled the flies from around my mouth—God knows how long they'd been ensconced there, vomiting and reingesting their foul efflux—and attempted, like everyone else, to shave and get clean. It struck me as absurd that the army expected its soldiers to be clean-shaven, and then placed them in situations where this simple daily routine became torturous, time-consuming, and disfiguring.

We learned, after a breakfast of something that may have been porridge, but which may equally have been warmed gravel, that our bus wasn't sufficiently robust to survive the journey from Mt Isa to Camooweal, and thence to Katherine. Instead we were to be crowded into the back of American transport trucks. I was alarmed to find our black driver, and the other drivers in the convoy, all of them black, donning respirators before climbing into the cabin. We'd barely pulled away from the racecourse when the need for the respirator became apparent. The convoy moved in great, boiling clouds of red dust.

There was no protection for us in the open tray of the truck; yet, when I settled on the uncomfortable bench that provided the only seating, I thought the trip might be just tolerable. I changed my mind when the convoy moved away from Mt Isa and gathered speed. Conversation became impossible and, distressingly, so did sitting down. The road declined into an endless run of bone-jarring, teeth-shattering corrugations which the drivers attempted to cheat by pushing their trucks to terrifying speeds. To sit was to bounce; to stand was also to bounce. But bouncing on the balls of one's feet is considerably less painful than bouncing on one's buttocks. This was a nugget of knowledge I could have done without.

An hour into our journey—and given that it was to be a journey of more than a thousand miles, an hour represented a trivial portion of it—I began to think I didn't have the stamina to endure it. I was exhausted and parched, and every jolt aggravated with exquisite and agonising repetition the bruising I'd suffered at the feet of our so-called Allies.

In the first of many paradoxes I would come to associate with life north of Capricorn, my bladder was urging me to expel precious fluid while my throat was screaming for water. The latter I could accommodate, with difficulty, and at great risk to my teeth, by taking juddery swigs from my water bottle. The former was more complicated. The trucks stopped for no one and for nothing, and that included the dysentery-afflicted captain whose Luger I'd borrowed. In an awkward and dangerous manoeuvre he squatted with his arse out over the tailboard of the truck. All bodily evacuations for all of us were managed over the rear edge. It was only desperation that made it physically possible. It was essentially passing water and jumping up and down at the same time—a combination of movements not generally practised, but which might have some application in an obscure branch of vaudeville. The driver of the truck behind was spared the worst of the spectacle by the impenetrable clouds of dust thrown up by the vehicle in front.

The convoy stopped briefly for lunch, which was a tin of peaches, and to refuel. All the tension between Brian and me had been juddered out of us, and we speculated, along with Glen, about what awaited us in Katherine. None of us had travelled overland this far north or west before; to our eyes, the landscape was brutal.

'It's not all going to be like this,' Brian said, assuming his irritating, teacher's voice. 'It's the wet tropics where we're going to end up, not this arid stuff.'

I was reassured, and began to entertain visions of cool gullies and dark rainforests, where dust never blew and where crystalline streams flowed over picturesque moss and lichen. The four days it took to reach Larrimah, from where we caught a troop train to Katherine, remain a blurred progression through desert, spinifex, termite mounds, sudden expanses of grassland interrupted by the startlingly white trunks of lone ghost gums, great stretches of thin scrub, and always, always the obliterating miasma of dust, dust, dust. Camooweal, Banka Banka, Elliott, Daly Waters—these are places we passed through, but the character of which I can't attest to. The overriding impression was one of persistent grimness, although this may be symptomatic of my usual optimism having been shaken loose and jostled into the disarray of despair. I do recall that the shared hideousness of the journey created an unexpected intimacy amongst my fellow travellers, and particularly between Brian, Glen, and me.

The makeshift camps at the end of each appalling day enabled us to talk; and, despite being harried and horrified by rats, scorpions, centipedes, ants, and an entomological encyclopaedia's worth of flying insects, our talk was easy and warm. By the time we'd reached the railhead at Larrimah on Saturday, 24 October 1942 I was confident that, whatever befell us, I'd be glad of Brian's and Glen's company. In a completely unexpected rush of fraternal emotion, I even began to look forward to meeting my youngest brother, Fulton, who was still, as a result of the years that separated us, a child to me. Given that he was now an admired member of a secret army unit, I had to concede that perhaps he'd left his childhood behind. I began to wonder whether I'd even recognise him. His face was indelibly etched in my mind as the face of a boyish eighteen-year-old, which was probably the last time I'd looked at him closely. I don't think he'd even used a razor then. It seemed extraordinary that, at twenty-one, he was now unequivocally a man.

The lorries were brutal, but the train from Larrimah to Katherine put paid to any notion that soldiering generally, and entertaining specifically, were glamorous. We were herded into cattle trucks still redolent of their former occupants, and the symbolism wasn't lost on me, I can assure you. I was too discreet to mention slaughter and abattoirs to the men around me, although I did make the observation, sotto voce, to Brian, who nodded and disconcertingly pointed out that the irony extended to us as much as to anyone else. He was right, of course, and it is a testament to the understanding between us that I wasn't in the least irritated by this, and confined my response to pointing out that 'irony' wasn't really the word he was looking for.

When we arrived in Katherine it was just before lunchtime, and we were in the process of locating the members of the concert party when Sergeant Rothfield, the show's producer, whom I had barely seen since our arrival in Maryborough, found us.

'Slight change of plan,' he said, and he made no attempt to disguise his annoyance.

'You three have been redeployed. No idea why. It's not my business, but it leaves us short for tonight's performance, which is my problem, but a pain in the arse.'

I tried to look both sympathetic and surprised, an unexpectedly difficult combination. He indicated a vehicle parked beneath a spindly tree, making it clear that this was to take us somewhere. It was what the Americans might call a 'jalopy,' and was in such a parlous state of disrepair and so rusted that it didn't look so much as though it had been parked near salt water for an age, but that it had been parked *in* salt water. If this was representative of the North Australia Observers' Unit's clout when it came to requisitioning necessary materials, we really were on our own. The driver was a man who was on the wrong side of fifty—one of those men who'd lied about his age in order to serve (lowering it, rather than raising it)—and he was dressed in a strange amalgam of the familiar and the antiquated. It transpired that this was the unit's non-combative dress, and it consisted of Australian Light Horse surplus from the First World War.

We drove in silence some small distance out of what I supposed was the town, and stopped in a sparsely wooded place which was busy with men and vehicles. There were a few substantial buildings, but most of the accommodation was in tents, and many of these had their canvasses propped up with rough bush-timbers. This was the beating heart of the NAOU. Aesthetics were not as important, it transpired, as the fact that the camp was difficult to see from the air because it nestled amongst the comparatively riparian fertility of this section of the Katherine River. When it was pointed out to me that Katherine had been bombed several times, the drab tents suddenly assumed a more pleasing aspect.

The three of us were shown into a large tent, one whole side of which was open: it held a motorbike, several drums of what was possibly fuel, crates, small boxes and, at one end, a desk, unattended at the time. We were soon joined by a soldier who took up his position behind the desk without uttering a word, as if he were too distracted to notice that three people were standing before him. He wasn't wearing a shirt. His only clothing was a pair of shorts, boots, socks, and a well-worn hat which he placed on the edge of the desk. Clearly the more formal attire of our driver was reserved for excursions outside Unit HQ. He must have been forty, although he looked somewhat haggard, despite a torso that was fit and hard. His hair was cut very short, and looked like it had been hacked haphazardly by himself without the aid of a mirror.

'Captain Manton,' he said, and didn't offer us the opportunity to introduce ourselves. 'I'll be perfectly frank with you blokes. I have no fucking idea what you're doing here or why I'm expected to hold your hands.'

Glen unexpectedly raised his hands and said firmly, 'See these hands? No one's asking you to hold them. Sir.'

Captain Manton shook his head.

'You don't look like Nackeroos, but you've got their fucking attitude to discipline.'

His tone softened slightly, but he still didn't encourage introductions. Doubtless he already knew who we were, but I didn't see why courtesy had to be added to this war's crowded casualty list.

'All right,' he said. 'We all know better than to ask too many questions in this unit. My instructions are to provide you with some specialist kit, which doesn't amount to much more than a long-sleeved shirt and a hat with insect netting. You're leaving in an hour, in a truck driven by one of our blokes. He's experienced, and you should get to Darwin in one piece late tonight, unless he does an axle.'

My heart sank at the prospect of more hours spent rumbling over corrugations. My face must have given me away because Captain Manton added, 'The road between here and Darwin's been upgraded and it's not too bad. If rain holds off you shouldn't be delayed. Get yourselves some lunch and be back here in an hour.'

He stood, and seemed to be expecting a salute. When nothing eventuated he sighed, and muttered an inaudible imprecation before leaving us.

The mess hut was inside a large, corrugated-iron shed, and the food provided, despite the constant attention of flies, was quite satisfactory, although its adequacy might have been the result of its comparison to tinned peaches.

The truck that was to take us to Darwin was driven by a teenager who said he was twenty. I would've been unsurprised to learn that he was twelve. His name was Pete, and he displayed all the pointless enthusiasm of youth. The truck, requisitioned in Darwin — its windshield bore half-a-dozen bullet holes, the consequence of its having been strafed during a bombing raid — was the first vehicle he'd ever driven, and he felt for it as one might for a living, breathing creature. Since being assigned as its driver he'd crawled over and under it and he spoke of it with the intimate familiarity of a gynaecologist.

'She's got expensive taste in oil,' Pete said. 'Four gallons every hundred miles.'

There was pride in his voice as he described the truck's inefficient, oil-guzzling capacity, as if it were a personal extravagance that was an expression of class.

I volunteered to sit in the back with the oil drums as companions, generously leaving the front seat to Brian and Glen, who would earn their relative comfort by conversing with Pete.

The allegedly upgraded road remained an allegation as far as I could tell, and it was busy with traffic, all of it military. It wasn't possible to sleep, though I had to close my eyes against the glare and dust. I thought of my parents, who'd spent what my mother called her 'year of heat' in Darwin and Broome more than thirty years previously. My acquaintance with 'north of somewhere' had so far been brief, and I supposed that its attraction had yet to reveal itself, but I couldn't imagine Mother moving through this humidity, heat, and dirt, to say nothing of the insect life, with anything approaching equanimity.

In mid-afternoon rain fell, or rather it flowed from the sky as if a vast reservoir somewhere above had been breached. This was my first experience of the Wet—and it was a Wet that would prove to be the most unpleasant on record. If my mother's year had been one of heat, mine would turn out to be one of mould.

Miraculously, despite the road becoming a river of churned mud, Pete's truck remained mobile. Where the way was impassable, small detours had been cut into the scrub, and a corduroy track laid. There was no danger of losing our way, having joined a sort of unofficial convoy. The going was slow, although the traffic thinned as trucks pulled out at Mataranka, Adelaide River, and Batchelor. We passed roadblocks into

Darwin just after 1.00 a.m. In the darkness I had no sense that there was a town there at all—I could only make out the shadowy forms of low trees and what looked like the shattered silhouettes of one or two bombed houses. The air was tainted with the unmistakeable odour of something rotting.

Pete, who said he was following orders, dropped us at the Sergeants' Mess at Larrakeyah Barracks. The tropical night was faintly luminous, and I was surprised when I looked about me to see the dark outlines of substantial, undamaged buildings. Not even the thinnest thread of light escaped from any of them. We farewelled Pete, who disappeared into the night and, not knowing what else to do, knocked. There was no reply, so we entered and groped our way to a further door. A faint nimbus around it indicated life within. We went in, without knocking this time, and came upon two men, both smoking and wearing what I was to learn was the uniform of the north, mosquitoes permitting—a pair of shorts and boots, and nothing else, apart from a tin hat when danger threatened.

'What are you blokes doing here?' one of them asked, and managed to sound pompous despite wearing no shirt. 'This is the Sergeants' Mess.'

'It's all right, Bill. They're expected.'

The voice came from behind us. He must have followed us in. He was more formally dressed than his fellow sergeants, if the addition of a sweat-stained shirt can be called formal. He couldn't have been more than twenty-five-years old, but there was something about him that was grave and impressive, and it didn't come from his rank. It occurred to me, as I saw the other men defer subtly and without rancour to him, that if he survived the war he'd amount to something.

'Luther Martin,' he said, extending his hand. 'My parents thought it was amusing.'

'I imagine the joke's worn a bit thin over the years,' I said.

He smiled, and revealed a startling gold cap over one of his front teeth.

'By the age of twelve I was choosing my friends on the basis of whether or not they resisted the temptation to say anything.'

He didn't sound like a soldier, but I suppose in a time of war the army is full of people who aren't by inclination military men.

'Sit down, please,' he said. It was then that I noticed that the room was furnished with an eclectic mix of domestic chairs and sofas.

'Bloody hell,' Glen said. 'I feel like I'm in somebody's lounge room.'

'In a way you are,' Luther said. 'It's all looted from houses around here.'

He shot the other two sergeants a glance.

'Hey,' the one he'd called Bill said, 'I wasn't even here when all that was going on.'

'Neither was I,' said his mate. 'We all sit in them, though, don't we?'

Luther acknowledged the justice of the remark with a cock of the head, and explained.

'Back in February, after the first raids, blokes went a bit crazy. The civilians had been mostly evacuated, so their houses were unprotected, and lots of blokes—army blokes, mind you—had a field day. You hear stories of bloody grand pianos being loaded onto trucks. What the hell would you do with a grand piano?'

'Maybe it's in the officers' mess,' Brian said.

They laughed.

'Well, anyway, it was a bloody disgrace,' Luther said.

'Better to be sitting on it than just letting it get blown to pieces,' said Bill.

'So it'll be returned, will it, if the house survives and the owners come back?' asked Luther.

'The spoils of war, mate.'

'As a general rule,' Luther said calmly, 'that's meant to refer to stuff you win from the enemy, not old Mrs Whatever-her-name-is who lives in Cavenagh Street.'

'Fair enough,' was the response, and it was clear that no one was interested in pursuing the ethical ambiguities of looting. Luther told us then that we could expect an air raid, but that the barracks probably wouldn't be heavily attacked.

'Unlike the RAAF base,' he said, 'we've never been carpet-bombed. The odd high explosive job, daisy cutters, strafing, but they've chosen not to reduce us to rubble. Some bloke reckons he heard from someone in Intelligence that the Japs want to use the barracks after they invade. Makes sense, I suppose. It's not like we're hard to see.'

'Those bastards bombed the crap out of the hospital,' said the man who wasn't Bill, 'and it's only a hundred yards away.'

A few minutes later, the wail of an air-raid siren sounded, and we were bundled outside into the uncertain safety of a slit trench.

I don't know how many bombs fell, or even how long the raid took. The crump and thump of bombs and ack ack fire, the squall of shrapnel and mosquitoes, and a terrifying sense that I was about to die, all conspired to make time stand still. As the noise faded and I realised that all I could hear was the mosquitoes droning, someone gave me a small shove to indicate that it was safe to stand up. Spears of bright search-light flew upwards, and the air was thick with the awful smell of explosives.

An incendiary had hit a building a small distance away, and men were already scrabbling to put out the flames. I was glad of the darkness because I was afraid the people around me might see my trembling as unmanly.

'Not a bad show,' someone said.

'Oh yes,' I thought. 'Let's bring on the fucking dancing girls.'

We returned to the Sergeants' Mess with Luther. The others went off to help put out fires and assess the damage.

'I don't think people down south know that Darwin is still being bombed like this,' Brian said. Luther crossed to a desk and withdrew from a drawer a sheet of paper with the words 'Army News' in a banner across the top.

'This came out two days after the first raid. The twenty-first of February. Printed here. Not a bad effort, considering.'

I ran my eye over it, expecting to read something significant about the bombing. It turned out that it wasn't considered sufficiently important to warrant more than a few bland paragraphs. Or, rather, it was considered so important that it had to be censored into nothingness. There was an assurance from the Honourable A.S. Drakeford, Minister for Air, that service casualties numbered only eight. Bizarrely, no mention was made of the fact that the harbour had been attacked or that bombs had fallen in the centre of town.

'Not quite the truth?' I asked.

'The truth is that that first raid was devastating. God knows how many hundreds of people were killed in the town and in the harbour—especially the harbour. The RAAF base was more or less destroyed. I've heard stories that there were so many casualties that bodies had to buried wherever a convenient place could be found for them, and that crocodiles kept digging them up and taking chunks out of them.'

'That certainly didn't make it into *The Age* or *The Argus*,' I said.

'You'll see tomorrow that Darwin doesn't really exist anymore. It's just a whole lot of soldiers wandering around in rubble.'

'Civilians?'

'A handful. The blacks and the whites were evacuated. There are some nurses. A few others. Something else you won't read about in the papers? After the RAAF base was carpet-bombed, the airmen there were spooked, and just up and left. Headed south to Adelaide River, that's what I'm told. The Adelaide River Stakes, they called it. They couldn't get out of there fast enough. Officers, too. Some blokes I've spoken to reckon they were told to go bush. I don't know if they were scared, or just confused and poorly led. Most of them came back eventually. Thank God for the Yanks. I'll tell you something: you won't hear a bad word said about the Yanks up here. They're bloody marvellous.'

Glen, who'd said very little, suddenly spoke up. 'The bloody Japs are going to do it, aren't they? They're really going to land here. They're actually going to invade.'

There wasn't the slightest trace of fear in his voice. I imagine his experiences in Milne Bay had steeled him against panic — but neither was there any excitement. He was simply expressing a reasonable assumption. Luther nodded.

'That seems to be the general view. If Port Moresby falls to the Japs, we're next. Like I said, thank God for the Yanks.'

Brian, whose nerves were doubtless as shaken as mine by the air raid, cut across the conversation and asked rather sharply, 'So what are we doing here? I mean here, in the Sergeants' Mess? Why the privilege?'

I couldn't see that sitting in an ugly room full of stolen furnishings was a privilege, but I took his point. We ought to have been banished to barracks that housed soldiers without rank; unless, of course, James Fowler had been wrong, and Army Intelligence had alerted a few people up here to who we were and what our mission was. When I thought about this mission I realised that I hadn't allowed myself to ponder its magnitude, except in the beginning when it had seemed as safe and uncomplicated as a parlour game, where simple deduction would solve the puzzle. Who is killing the Nackeroos? No worries. William Power will find out for you. I think it was the shrapnel that made me wonder if I hadn't over-reached myself on this occasion.

'The army,' said Luther, 'despite all appearances to the contrary, is an efficient bureaucracy. I asked the Amenities people to do me a favour and lend me some entertainers from one of the concert parties, just for one day for a specialised job. You were volunteered.'

'By whom?' Glen asked.

'I just do the paperwork. I put in the request, and it came back in the affirmative.'

'All this sounds a bit irregular,' Brian said, although he couldn't possibly know what was or wasn't regular in the army.

'Well, it's the nature of the exercise,' Luther said. 'I take it you haven't been briefed at all about this?'

We shook our heads in unison, like fairground clowns waiting for someone to push ping-pong balls down our throats.

'It's straightforward, really. We just want you to pop across for a few hours to a place called Channel Island. It's close by, out in the harbour a bit. A quick boat trip. The people there have had a rough trot and could do with a bit of light entertainment.'

'I suppose they were badly hit by the bombings,' I said, now knowing how much havoc had been wrought in the harbour.

'No,' Luther said, 'they weren't hit at all. It's like the Japs deliberately avoided hitting Channel Island.'

Brian drew his eyebrows together, a facial expression he'd used since childhood to signal dubiousness about what he was hearing.

'What,' he asked, 'is the missing piece of information here?'

Luther coughed.

'Channel Island is a leprosarium.'

He looked at each of us in turn.

'I'm sorry,' I said. 'My ears are still ringing from the bombs, but just for a moment I thought you said "leprosarium".'

'You'll be relieved to know that there's nothing wrong with your hearing. Channel Island is indeed a leprosarium.'

'What,' asked Glen, 'is a leprothingo?'

In the calm voice of a patient teacher explaining something to a dull child, Brian said, 'A leprosarium, Glen, is a place where lepers are sent for treatment.'

'Lepers? You want us to entertain lepers?' Glen asked, and the disgust in his voice was unmistakeable.

I said nothing for a moment, and was busy taking internal umbrage at the thought that someone, somewhere, had assessed my talents as being suited to a leper colony.

'There are seventy of the poor bastards out there on Channel Island. Men, women, and children.'

'No way am I going to catch leprosy,' Glen said. 'Khaki dermatitis was bad enough. I'm a magician. I need all my fingers for my work.'

'You can't catch leprosy from a single visit,' Luther said. 'You have to be exposed to it for a very long time, and even then you have to be unlucky. Besides, you're being asked to sing and dance *for* them, not sing and dance *with* them.'

'It's all very Father Damian of Molokai,' I said. 'Do we have a choice?'

'Of course, but I didn't think …'

'Good,' Glen said. 'I'm not going. I don't mind being shot at, but this is germ warfare, and that's against the Geneva Convention.'

There was something so fierce and ugly in Glen's tone that I felt a compulsion to distance myself from him.

'These people aren't our enemies, Glen.'

'You don't even know who they are, you stupid bastard, and I don't care who they are. They're lepers, and I'm sticking with tradition and having nothing to do with them.'

'All right,' Brian said. 'Will and I will go.'

If he was expecting Glen to change his mind, he was disappointed. He stuck to his guns with a sullen stubbornness that made me see in him the revolting child he must have been.

After little more than two hours' sleep we woke to a slate-grey morning. The colour of such a morning in Melbourne would suggest a chilly day ahead. Here in Darwin the air didn't seem to need the sun to heat it. The sky was crowded with dense and ominous clouds, and by the time we walked out of Larrakeyah Barracks, with Luther as our guide, and without Glen, I was sweating profusely. Brian and I were both wearing shorts, our pale legs betraying us as new arrivals. We were to catch a small boat and make the short crossing to Channel Island; but first, Luther wanted to give us a brief tour of Darwin's shattered streets.

It wasn't a long walk from the barracks to what had once been the commercial centre of town. Houses along the way stood or had fallen according to a random pattern of destruction. Here, a lush and flowering garden sat unscathed, its house empty but intact; there, a garden had great gaps blown in it, the yard pocked by bomb craters, and its house a tangle of blasted, scorched timbers. At the gate of one property, Luther drew our attention to a now-faded notice dated April 1942 and bearing the mayor's signature, exhorting troops to forego looting abandoned properties and reminding them, as if they needed it, that the abandonment had not been voluntary but the result of enemy action.

It was difficult to determine what the streets might have looked like, so extensive was the damage. The Bank of New South Wales, which must have been a rather grand building, was now a crumbling shell, and its neighbours sat roofless, or boarded up, or with great, jagged holes in their walls. There were plenty of men about clearing the roads of rubble, or doing the best they could to repair what was repairable, or tear down and make safe what wasn't. Almost to a man they were dressed only in shorts, and most of them were hatless.

'A lot of these blokes are Civil Construction Corps volunteers,' Luther said. 'Not army. Without them, practically nothing in this place would work.'

'Where are they from?'

'All over. Some of them have been directed into the corps by Manpower. How'd you be? One day you're in Melbourne doing some job Manpower thinks is useless, and the next you're on your way here. You'd be pissed off.'

I couldn't disagree with him and, after looking around, refrained from suggesting that perhaps the nation hadn't lost too many significant buildings. By this stage we were approaching the enclave at the end of what had been Cavenagh Street. This, Luther said, was where the notorious, open-sewered

Chinatown had been. It had been looted bare, and more or less dismantled.

'No great loss,' he said. 'It was a squalid and immoral place, apparently.'

The way he said this reinforced for me the suspicion I'd been harbouring that Luther Martin's attitude was rooted in a thoughtless Christian revulsion for anything that might offend his God. I immediately distrusted him, and told him that Brian and I needed some time before catching the boat to work out what we were going to do to entertain the lepers.

Luther left us at the harbour, where the skeletons of many ships protruded from the water, and where men were busy repairing the wharf. We had half an hour to sort out what we'd do. We'd already decided the night before, after finding a recording of a Glenn Miller swing tune in the Mess (and having been assured that there was a gramophone on Channel Island), that we'd attempt a demonstration of the jitterbug. We agreed that it would be pointless of Brian to slip into his Jean Harlow sheath.

'We need to run through this dance,' I said.

'What, here?'

'We rehearse where we can, Brian. Our stage is wherever we happen to be.'

Where we happened to be was on the partly repaired timbers of the long wharf, surrounded by Civil Construction Corps workmen and others, all hammering and carrying and swearing. I have no doubt that, for those who looked up from their work and saw us, the sight of two men moving woodenly through the steps of the jitterbug was very strange. Woodenly at first, that is. Having established the general shape of the dance, and who was to do what, I counted us in and began to hum 'In the Mood'. Brian is an excellent dancer, and he moved easily and fluidly to the syncopation he was hearing in his head. We began apart, both gyrating independently, and then came together in a graceful and energetic rendition of the dance. I threw Brian over my hip and between my legs, and we span and twirled and stomped—and didn't believe Fred and Ginger could have done better under the circumstances. When we'd finished we were suddenly aware that work on the wharf had stopped, and men were staring at us, some with hammers poised in mid-air. If this had been a movie they would have applauded; we were rewarded instead with a few disbelieving sniggers, and the workers returned to their labours.

We were both breathing heavily; I, for one, had underestimated how much energy the jitterbug required.

'Good,' I said. 'That's good, but it's only a few minutes. I'm sure they're expecting a bit more.'

'Maybe we could teach them a few of the steps.'

'They've got leprosy, Brian. If they start throwing each other around, bits will fall off.'

The teacher in Brian, always lurking just beneath the surface, couldn't resist correcting my apparently poor understanding of the condition.

'All right. All right. I was only joking, Brian. For heaven's sake.'

'I'm glad you can see the funny side of leprosy, Will, because frankly it doesn't strike me as one of nature's wittiest diseases.'

'Well, I guess we all have our favourites. Now if I could just drag you down from your pulpit for a moment, do you have any ideas of a non-earnest variety for our programme?'

Brian sighed with familiar, exaggerated resignation and said, 'I thought I might recite "The Geebung Polo Club"—I know it off by heart—and maybe "Bellbirds", and "The Rime of the Ancient Mariner".'

I wasn't sure how the lepers would react to Brian's English curriculum, but I had to acknowledge that recitation was the go. My only difficulty was in deciding which speeches from which plays would be best calculated to make a leper forget his hideous condition for a few, precious minutes. Something from *Cymbeline* perhaps, and definitely a piece from *Titus Andronicus*, my performance of which had been thwarted a few months earlier by events beyond my control. In one of those flashes of inspiration that come whenever my attention is focussed on Shakespeare, I decided that I would sing a couple of the songs from *Twelfth Night*. I'd have to forgo the lute, of course, and do it unaccompanied, but I thought that the ostentatious plucking of a stringed instrument with healthy fingers might anyway be seen as rubbing their noses in it rather.

The boat, which was little more than a canoe, arrived, and in a few minutes we stepped ashore on Channel Island. It was a desolate place—almost without trees of any kind, as if the landscape itself had contracted leprosy. We were met by a nurse in a uniform that had once been white, but which had been poorly dyed a khaki colour. (She told us later that the white uniforms stood out dangerously in the shadows of slit trenches.) There were people moving about near a group of buildings which I supposed constituted the lazaret.

Sister Lucille greeted us effusively, and led us to a small, barren courtyard where the beginnings of an audience had started to assemble. They chatted amongst themselves, and the evidence of the awful infection that afflicted them was immediately apparent in the faces of only one or two of them. There were Europeans, Malays, Chinese, and Aboriginal people amongst the small crowd, and they sat together in the democratic intimacy of the ostracised and the diseased.

Sister Lucille found a gramophone and set it up in the dirt

at our feet. Thus far, neither Brian nor I had said a word to any member of the audience, despite their sitting or standing in close proximity to us, and I assiduously avoided catching anyone's eye. A dark-haired, fair-skinned man in his early fifties, supported by crutches, broke from the group and swung towards us.

'Welcome,' was all he said before retreating. I don't know whether it was our sensibilities or his that he was protecting, but he proffered no hand for us to shake.

'Thank you,' Brian said, and then, addressing the audience, he repeated loudly, 'Thank you.'

I moved the gramophone a safe distance from us and wound its handle. I suddenly felt sick with nerves, and wished Glen was with us to dazzle these people with the impossibility of his magic. I placed the record on the turntable and lowered the needle to its spinning surface. The opening bars of 'In the Mood' crackled forth, and Brian and I assumed our positions. It wasn't a perfectly executed jitterbug, but it was all right. The dust rose around us, and the sweat poured off us, and our audience called out for more; so we rewound the gramophone and did it again. This time we improvised new steps, and I tossed Brian over my hip as if he weighed nothing. We stood panting, vaguely astonished that two men doing a competent demonstration of an American dance could provoke such applause and laughter. Brian raised his hands, and they fell silent. He walked around the edge of the half-circle they'd formed, catching people's eyes, drawing their attention to him, and creating the impression that something significant was about to happen. At the far corner of the arc he began to speak the opening lines of 'The Geebung Polo Club.'

'It was somewhere up the country in a land of rock and scrub,' he said, and he looked about him as if this were the very land in question. He gestured to great effect, and spoke the verse with startling and hilarious clarity, assuming the poshest of voices to describe the Cuff and Collar polo team, and reverting to an exaggerated drawl to bring the Geebung Polo Club to life. Until I heard Brian perform it, I wouldn't have picked Paterson's poem as anything more than faintly amusing doggerel. But, whether they understood it or not, his listeners laughed themselves silly.

Brian bowed and handed over to me. I decided to change the pace, and sang for them, in my light tenor, one of Feste's songs from *Twelfth Night*. I think perhaps I ought to have sung, 'What is love? 'Tis not hereafter.' It was only after I'd launched into, 'Come away, come away, death, and in sad cypress let me be laid,' that I thought it wasn't absolutely on the money. I noticed conversations breaking out before I'd quite finished. The applause was merely polite, which I resented. It's never pleasant to be patronised, but to be patronised by lepers is really beyond the pale.

'I think we've lost them,' I said.

'We?'

'They've been sitting in the sun for a long time.'

We were rescued from the need for further discussion by a part-Aboriginal girl who approached us, one arm held from sight behind her back, and said, 'Show us. Show us that one. That dance.'

'All right,' Brian said before I could stop him, and he began organising the audience into laughing pairs. Over the next two hours, we painfully taught those who were willing the rudiments of the jitterbug, and both Brian and I became so engrossed in the task that all squeamishness fell away, and I forgot myself to such an extent that I placed my hand in the leprous hand of an elderly Malay woman, and danced closely with a European woman whose face bore no resemblance to what it once must have been. She didn't speak, and I had to overcome her reticence by almost forcing my attentions upon her. It must have been a long time since anyone had touched her, and I don't know whether her streaming eyes were a symptom of her condition or a response to physical contact.

At the end of the lesson, in the heat of the courtyard, in the mean shadow of the lazaret, we all lined up, and Sister Lucille wound the gramophone. As the music began, our large group began to move, not quite as one, and although we couldn't boast the precision of Busby Berkeley, when the needle slid off the record we were all aware that something remarkable had happened. I stood, grinning helplessly, absurdly prouder than if I'd delivered a perfect soliloquy from the London stage.

A man standing beside me passed me his water bottle, and I automatically and gratefully took a full swig. I passed it back to him and he took it in a hand that was misshapen, scaly, and missing two fingers. All my joy vanished in a rush of bile and panic as I realised that, for all intents and purposes, I'd swallowed leprosy. My horrified reaction wasn't something I could disguise, but if I hurt the man's feelings I was suddenly past caring.

I said nothing to Brian, believing childishly that silence might somehow quarantine me against the pestilence I'd imbibed. He was beaming, although his face soured when he saw mine.

'Jesus, Will,' he said. 'You're a mean bastard. We just did something good. Nothing's good *enough* for you, though, is it?'

I wanted to explain when I saw how badly he'd misread my response, but I was so stricken that I could do nothing more than stare at him, thereby confirming his ugly, misguided beliefs about my flawed character. He shook his head in disgust and accepted the congratulations offered by Sister Lucille.

We returned to Darwin in the same small boat that had taken us to Channel Island, and Sister Lucille returned with us.

She never stayed on the island overnight. There was a nun who lived with the lepers, but she was away and not expected back for several more weeks.

'Does she have leprosy?' I asked, and marvelled at the awful sound of the question. Sister Lucille knitted her brows as if she disapproved of the inquiry.

'No. Why?'

'I was just wondering. I don't know very much about it, that's all.'

Brian chimed in with, 'Will probably thinks he's caught it.'

'If it's any consolation, Will, even if you have caught it, it can incubate for thirty years before it appears, but you won't have caught it. It's not like you had any contact with body fluids.' There was a steely little quality in her voice that came, no doubt, from countless ignorant inquiries and assumptions about the people she nursed.

'I shared a water bottle!' I blurted.

Sister Lucille and Brian exchanged a glance, the meaning of which I couldn't read, but I had the impression that Brian's face arranged itself into a smirk before he turned it towards the approaching wharf.

'I've caught it then, haven't I?' There was an involuntary catch in my voice.

Sister Lucille reached behind her and produced a water bottle.

'Is this the one?'

'It looks like it.'

'This was provided for your use and for Brian's. It might have been passed to you by a patient, but he wouldn't have drunk out of it.'

My relief was so overwhelming that I felt my eyes water, and I looked down to disguise the fact.

'Of course,' she said, 'he might have taken a swig. We'll know in thirty years' time. Did you drink from it, Brian?'

'No, no, I didn't. So, if it wasn't full …'

'You'll be disappointed to hear that it was full,' I said, but I couldn't remember whether it was or wasn't, and I was aware that my voice expressed this slight doubt. Brian reached out and took the water bottle from Sister Lucille. I thought he was going to take a swig, which would have been a reassuring gesture, but instead he removed the top and emptied its contents over the side.

'Just to be sure,' he said.

This was a small, unnecessary cruelty whose roots must have lain coiled somewhere in childhood. He watched me as the water trickled out, and he must have been satisfied with the effect because, as he replaced the cap, he smiled at me in a way that suggested the evening of some score. In Brian's head there was a tally board, and only he was privy to where each of us stood on it. I decided then that, at some point, I would demand to know.

When we disembarked at the wharf it was late in the afternoon, and we were surprised to find Corporal Glen Pyers waiting for us. We were even more surprised to discover that he was surrounded by our kit.

'Will's got leprosy,' Brian said, 'so resist the urge to kiss him.'

'We have to hurry,' Glen said. 'The boat has to leave now.' He indicated a ketch that hadn't been at the wharf in the morning. It had seen better days. It had a single mast at the bow end, and railings that were bent out of shape and which came no higher than the thigh—clearly not a safety feature, unless the boat's owner was a dwarf. There was something approximating a cabin, and in front of it I could see the bent back of a man arranging something in the hold. There were many boxes and drums on the deck, and when he straightened to pull one towards him, he saw Glen and called out to him.

'Righto! Let's go.'

I'd been looking forward to going to the pictures that night. There was a movie house in Nightcliff that hadn't been bombed, and it was showing *A Yank in the RAF*—an appalling bit of rubbish, no doubt, but starring Tyrone Power, an actor I was always interested to see. Glen bustled us onto the boat, which smelled unpleasantly of fish and rot, and our feet had barely touched its deck when its ancient motor turned over and caught with an unhealthy splutter. The master of this tub was busy behind its wheel, so introductions were delayed until we were out of the harbour and chugging across Port Darwin towards Larrakeyah Barracks. We rounded Emery Point, headed up Fannie Bay, passed East Point, and sailed out into the Timor Sea. With the boat set on a secure course, our captain called to Glen and told him we'd be there by morning.

'And where,' I asked patiently, 'is there?'

'While you two were healing the sick,' Glen said, 'I was helping load this thing with supplies.'

We were sitting on the deck near what in a grander boat might have been called its prow. Glen indicated the fellow behind the wheel at the stern.

'That's Charlie Humphries. He's a Nackeroo who sails this thing around the coast, as far as the Roper River.'

We waved to Charlie Humphries, who touched his hat in reply.

'So we're on our way then,' said Brian, 'to where Fulton is.'

Glen nodded.

'They've set up camp somewhere near the mouth of the West Alligator River. There are half-a-dozen blokes there, and when they're not scared shitless about the Japs, they're bored shitless waiting for them. We're going to cheer them up.' He paused and looked directly at me. 'Apparently.'

I didn't bite, and in fact bestowed a smile upon him before standing up and making my way perilously to Charlie Humphries, from whom I hoped to gain some useful information about what lay ahead.

I introduced myself and he pushed his hat back on his head, nodded, and said, 'You fellas are actors, is that right?'

I was immediately defensive and said, rather more snappishly than I'd intended, that we all fought our own war in the best way we knew how. He suggested that I might like to keep my hair on, and that he hadn't used the word 'actor' in any pejorative way. I was so startled to hear the word 'pejorative' in the middle of the Timor Sea that I immediately apologised for my tone. I'm always taken aback when people around me express a familiarity with their mother tongue that goes beyond a vocabulary sufficient to secure them a feed or a fuck.

I looked more closely at Charlie Humphries. I think he was well short of thirty, although the creases around his eyes were deep. His colouring, fair and more suited to the limpid light of Ireland, had become adjusted to the fierce tropical sun, not by freckling or tanning, but by roasting to a sort of permanent sunburn. His reddish, blond hair grew high on his forehead, and was dark with sweat where it emerged from the band of his hat.

'So where are we headed?'

'West Alligator, mate.'

'Sounds rather confronting.'

'They're not after tourists, mate. The only things that live there are mosquitoes, sandflies, crocodiles, and Nackeroos. I'm happy to drop these supplies off, and I'm even happier to get out of there.'

He paused.

'So you see, I have a high level of job satisfaction.'

'And you do this on your own?'

'Not usually. I've got a blackfella who helps out, but he's off doing some ceremony business, as he calls it. Someone died, I think.'

To my ear, Charlie Humphries' speech sounded as if he'd made a conscious effort to rough up properly acquired vowels. I suspected Jesuits in his background.

'Why did we have to leave so urgently?'

'It's a tidal river, mate. To get up it far enough, you have to catch the floodtide. You ever seen any of those tides, mate?'

I indicated that I hadn't.

'They can be bloody scary things. I'm hoping this one doesn't knock us around too much.'

He squinted at me.

'Whatever you do, mate, don't fall overboard. If the water doesn't kill you there are plenty of things in it that will.'

'Thank you, Charlie. My immediate plan is to hold on tight.'

Over the next two hours, until the light faded, I talked amiably with Charlie Humphries while Glen and Brian reposed at the opposite end of the ketch. He wasn't dismissive of acting as a profession; quite the contrary. He was interested, and volunteered that the priests who'd taught him in Perth—I'd been right about that—had attempted to direct his expressed desire to perform into a vocation. Not the priesthood, or the Jesuit priesthood at any rate. They told him frankly that he wasn't quite bright enough to wrestle with Thomas Aquinas, but that perhaps he was more suited to the Christian Brothers—an order where, apparently, high intelligence was a disadvantage. Charlie's parents were enthusiastic; an enthusiasm fuelled by the financial relief promised by the seminary's obligation to feed and clothe its novices. Charlie was less enthusiastic and, as pressure mounted for him to discover that he'd been called by God, he took off. He was sixteen, and he'd spent the next six years, until the war began, 'knocking around' Western Australia, mostly in the north around Broome.

'Have you lost contact with your family?'

'The people up here are mostly splinters,' he said, and didn't elaborate. I nodded as if I knew exactly what he meant.

The sea was mercifully smooth, and I was able to eat and keep down a can of bully beef, followed by the ubiquitous tin of peaches. The storm and the savage seas that Charlie had warned might spring up failed to eventuate, and he woke us at dawn—the piccaninny daylight—to announce that we were about to turn into the West Alligator River.

My eyes were unused to scanning coastlines from the deck of a boat, and the mangroves seemed to me to form an unbroken line. Before I was really aware of it, however, we'd left open water and had entered the wide, brown mouth of the West Alligator River. Charlie assured us that its sluggishness was entirely illusory; and I could see, at its edge, that it was moving with considerable speed.

'Are we expected?' Brian asked.

'Yup, but I'll fly the flag just in case. I don't want some jumpy bastard shooting at us.'

He unfurled what looked like a hand-stitched, home-made square of cloth with the colours of the patch that had been assigned to the NAOU—a double diamond, yellow on one side, green on the other.

We travelled upriver a good distance — too far, I believed, for Fulton's unit to be doing any useful coast watching.

'They watch the river,' Charlie said. 'The Japs'll have to come up it to land. It's unlikely they'd choose to do that here; but you never know, they might send out a reccy party.'

'To be met with a hail of bullets from half-a-dozen men?' I said.

'No, mate. The NAOU is not supposed to engage with the enemy. They observe, follow, and report. Ideally, the Japs should never see them.'

The river began to narrow and split into a confusion of channels until it became impossible for me to discern which was the river and which was a flooded tributary. Mangroves grew so thickly that if there was any scrub or dry land beyond them, I for one couldn't see it. Egrets and pied herons rose as we passed, and the air smelled strongly of salt and mud.

Charlie cut the engine, and the ketch drifted forcefully towards a wall of dense, green vegetation. He swung the wheel, and we were suddenly in what looked like a small, scooped-out cove, a half-circle of mangroves with a thinned-out area at the top of the arc. There, standing knee-deep in mud, and waving his arms above his head, was a man whose only clothing was a hat.

'That,' said Charlie, 'looks like Rufus Farrell.'

'Why,' I asked, 'is he naked?'

'The only blokes who wear anything up here during the day are the blackfellas. Big skin shame. Aren't missionaries marvellous?'

As if on cue, an Aboriginal man appeared behind Rufus Farrell. He was wearing trousers but no shirt, and his chest was rippled with thick cicatrices. The boat came to rest and both men clambered aboard. Rufus Farrell wore a thin beard and, incongruously, a pair of boots, and was probably little older than nineteen. His companion, who was introduced as Isaiah, was, I estimated, in his thirties, although he might have been younger.

'We're glad to see you blokes,' Rufus said. 'We're sick of the sight of each other.'

He waved his hand over the boxes on the deck.

'What have you got for us?'

'No beer.' Charlie withdrew a list from his pocket.

'Oats, bran, tinned milk, lime juice, salt, flour, yeast, egg powder, baking powder, bully beef, onions, tinned cabbage, peaches, petrol, oil, peas, battery charger, medicines, comforts, three actors.'

'Let's get it unloaded,' Rufus said, and so began two of the most exhausting and uncomfortable hours of my life. The heat, which I hadn't really noticed until the boat stopped, was killing, and the boxes of supplies were awkward and heavy and, worse, they had to be carried first through water and then through sucking, malodorous mud—a substance I'd soon learn to despise. We were advised to keep our boots on to avoid the soles of our feet being cut to ribbons by sharp shells imbedded in the mud.

We unloaded the boxes and drums a few yards from where the mud became sand and then hardened into earth. The mangroves gave way here to ti-tree, pandanus, and thin, scraggly eucalypts. There was no deep shade.

'We'll get the other blokes to help us cart most of this lot to camp when they come in this arvo. Give us a hand with the charger, though.'

I made the mistake of volunteering to do this. The others picked up a ration box each. The battery charger was for the FS6 transceiver, and it was more than cumbersome; it was vicious, weighing more than ninety pounds. The transceivers were, though, the single most important piece of NAOU equipment. They were all that stood between these men and isolation so complete that they might as well have been camped on the surface of Mars. They also helped create an illusion, directed at the Japanese now massing on Timor, that Australia's northern coast was alive with defence forces babbling constantly on their radios. If only they knew that the West Alligator River was currently protected by a naked man, an Aborigine, three entertainers, and a chap running away from the Jesuits.

Chapter Five

FULTON

THE LANDSCAPE WE TRAVERSED bore not the slightest resemblance to the lush tropics of my imagination. There was no great canopy of towering trees, or coils of vines, or rich, outrageous flowers. Here the sun fell with almost unimpeded brutality through a sparsely spaced forest of tough, wiry stringybarks onto yellow-green tussocks, bare earth, and sharp-leafed little shrubs. I slaked my thirst from my neck bottle several times over the short distance from the boat to the camp; my body seemed intent on surrendering its moisture to the sun with an abandon that I'd never before experienced. Rufus said that they weren't short of fresh water, that there was a creek not far away that didn't suffer the brackish influx of the West Alligator's tides, and that anyway it now rained almost every day, and they were in the habit of collecting rainwater in drums.

I thought it would be unlikely that Japanese aircraft flying over this camp would identify it as such. It consisted solely of a piece of ragged tarpaulin tied to four trees, a few ammunition crates, some drums, and two peculiar mounds of what looked like dried grass but which were, in fact, the makeshift sleeping arrangements of the two Aboriginal men who'd been assigned to this outpost.

The radio sat in the shade under the tarpaulin. Having helped Rufus carry the charger to it, I sat exhausted on an ammunition box, suddenly feeling dizzy.

'You all right?' Rufus asked.

'I feel quite ill, actually.'

'It takes a while to get used to this heat. You're probably just dehydrated. That happens.'

He took my neck bag and filled it from a drum, and I drank deeply. Perhaps it was just dehydration, but the lingering possibility of leprosy wasn't far from my mind. I think both Glen and Brian were almost as distressed as I was by the exertion of carrying some of the rations, but they were determined not to show it—not just to avoid looking weak in front of Rufus, Charlie, and Isaiah, but to make me look bad. I only thought this afterwards; at the time, my mind was so disoriented that for a brief period I was incapable of independent thought or action. I may, in fact, have fallen asleep sitting up, insensible to the flies and to my surroundings. I couldn't have lost consciousness for more than a few minutes, but when I opened my eyes the only person in the camp was Rufus, and he was bent over a camp oven, manoeuvring it in the coals of a fire. I stood up groggily, and was relieved to discover that I felt better.

'Where is everybody?'

'Gone to get some more of the rations. There are comfort packages in one of the boxes.'

'Should I go back and help?'

Rufus laughed, and scratched his balls.

'You'd get lost, mate.' He told me, generously, that I shouldn't feel bad about feeling ill. 'Those other blokes'll cop a dose, don't worry.'

I noticed that Rufus's body was a mess of bites and scratches in varying stages of suppuration. He saw that I'd noted this, and shrugged.

'The Japs will shoot you. The mozzies and flies will eat you alive. Sometimes I'd like to get the jump on them all and blow my own brains out.'

He turned back to the camp oven and lifted the lid with a stick. The smell of bread reached my nostrils, and the activity of the flies intensified around my face as if the repellent creatures could feed on the odour alone, being unable to settle closer to the fire.

'Could you see if there's any jam in those boxes?'

I found a tin of jam, and Rufus's face lit up.

'There are cans of butter, too,' I said.

'It's shit. Rancid fat. This is good damper, worthy of jam. The boys are gunna love it.'

'Where are the boys?'

'They've been out for a couple of days now. Reccy.'

'And you and Isaiah are left here on your own?'

'Someone's gotta do the radio. It was my turn to stay behind. Not that I mind. Fulton's the best at it. He can do it in the pitch-dark in a howling gale.'

'Fulton's my brother.'

'Is he? Jeez, I'd never have picked it. We were told that two of his brothers were coming. Brian's the other one, is he? He looks a bit like you.'

A sudden clamping in my guts made further small talk out of the question.

'Where do I go to the dunny?' I asked.

'Just off in the bush. We haven't bothered with a trench or anything. The flies'll crawl up your arse. And watch out for snakes. The browns around here work for the Japs.'

I walked some distance away from the camp, lowered my shorts, and crouched over a scrape I'd made. For a moment, for just a moment, I could see how strangely beautiful this landscape was. The initial sense of its monotony gave way to the realisation that the scraggly eucalypts had trunks of brilliant white, and around me there were subtle varieties of green, tinged in the turpentine bushes with gentle purple. In the distance, through the trees, tall grass moved in response to the wind. My reverie ended with the extrusion of the first stool. Flies—huge, thunderous blowflies—appeared in a swarm, and my disgust was so intense that I didn't linger a moment longer than was necessary. So greedy were these monsters for my waste that when I pushed dirt over the mess, many of them chose burial rather than flight.

I had a small moment of panic when the walk back to the camp began to seem longer than the walk away from it had been. My sense of direction is not the most finely honed of my skills, and I've never had to utilise it for much more than knowing the difference between stage left and stage right. Here, north, south, east, and west looked the same to me. I stopped and listened, and caught the faint sound of conversation. I'd been going in the right direction after all, and when I came into the clearing, Brian, Glen, and Charlie were setting up their beds, pegging the cheesecloth anti-mosquito coverings to convenient saplings or to sticks driven into the ground. Isaiah was nowhere to be seen, and Rufus was examining the contents of several newly arrived boxes.

'Anything interesting?' I asked.

'The usual tinned shit, army biscuits, but at least they've sent us some medical stuff—iodine, metho, antiseptic powder, razor blades, lucerne tablets, Salvital. No soap, no shaving cream.'

He pulled another box towards him.

'Aha, comforts. Let's see what the Comfort Fund thinks will make us happy.'

He began to unpack the items.

'Socks. Great. Toothpaste. Well, that's good. It's better than cold ash. Shaving cream! Boot polish? Are they serious? No cake, no beer. That's it. What a fucking comfort.'

'It does seem a bit meagre.'

'Nothing worthwhile gets past the bloody wharfies in Darwin. We're supposed to get two bottles of beer per man, per week. As if. We don't even get beer at Platoon HQ.'

Brian came over to where we were sitting, and offered to set up my bed—a gesture, I suppose, designed to affirm that he hadn't forgotten we were to look out for each other.

'I'll help you,' I said, and took the opportunity to talk to him about Fulton.

'I know it's strange, Brian, but I don't know very much about Fulton at all. I have no idea what he believes, how he thinks, what he likes, what he loathes. He was so much younger than I was.'

I thought he was about to make a remark to the effect that my ignorance was due more to indifference than age difference, but he checked himself and said something that stunned me.

'Fulton is very like his father.'

'Mother always accused *me* of that.'

'No, Will. Not *your* father. Fulton's father.'

I stared at him, trying to reconstruct his perfectly simple sentence into something that made sense. Before I could press him to clarify this astonishing assertion, the jingling of bridles and the sound of voices announced the arrival of the reconnaissance party.

Three white men and an Aboriginal man emerged into the informal clearing of the campsite. Behind them, amongst the trees, at least twenty horses snorted or put their heads down to graze on whatever meagre tussocks they could find. Half a dozen of them were loaded with packs; the rest were unencumbered. All were wet with sweat. The Aboriginal man and two of the white men began unpacking the animals. The third made his way towards Brian and me. Unlike Rufus, who wore no clothes at all, each of these men wore long trousers and long-sleeved shirts—I presumed it was inadvisable to walk through the country beyond the camp without some protection against sharp grasses and bushes. The man approaching had his head down, his features obscured by his slouch hat. A few feet from us, he removed his hat and smiled. He sported quite a healthy brown beard, and at first I failed to recognise my own brother. His face was tanned, and filthy with dust and sweat.

'Gedday, Brian,' he said, and held out his hand.

'You remember Will?' Brian said rather humorously, or so he thought. Fulton obviously found it amusing as well, because he replied, 'Will? Yes, I have a vague recollection of someone called Will.' He then held out his hand to me and said, 'Gedday, Will. Welcome.'

Under other circumstances I might have been won over immediately by his charm, but Brian's puzzling revelation caused me to search Fulton's face for evidence of a family resemblance.

My stare must have been so intense as to be almost rude.

'It is me, Will,' he said, and laughed. 'It's the beard, right?'

I agreed that it was indeed the beard, and shook his hand firmly. 'I'm sorry. It's just that the last time I saw you, you were a boy—and here you are, not a boy.'

'It's good to see the two of you. How's Mother?'

'She writes to you every day,' Brian said. 'Every day, and posts them off.'

'I've sent a couple, but I'm hopeless at writing, and I suppose she's waiting for replies. I hardly get her letters, though, and when they do come, they come in a rush. Don't tell her, but they're a bit boring.'

'There'll be some coming soon that might cheer you up. Very newsy, they'll be,' Brian said. 'We'll fill you in later.'

'You've met Rufus and Isaiah, obviously. Come and meet the other blokes.'

Glen and Charlie had already made their way over to where the horses were being unpacked, and Glen was walking amongst them with the kind of confidence around animals that I lacked completely. They looked boney and flighty to me, and I hoped I'd never be called upon to ride one of them.

The two remaining Nackeroos were absurdly young, both of them in their early twenties. The taller and darker of the two was ostensibly the officer in charge. His name was Corporal Andrew Battell, and when he shook my hand he looked at me with slightly feverish eyes—the consequence of a bout of dengue fever, I soon learned, to which he was resolutely refusing to surrender.

The Aboriginal man didn't come forward to meet us, but he was introduced at a distance by Nicholas Ashe, the remaining member of this section, with the words, 'The nigger over there, he's Ngulmiri. Me? I'm Nick Ashe. How are ya?'

He had very short brown hair, which would have been tightly curled if he'd let it grow, and he was in robust health. He was one of those nuggety, sinewy types who'd grown up rough, was handy with his fists, and was a good man to have on your side. I found him immediately repellent. I saw right through his larrikin grin and knew how quickly it could slide into a vicious snarl. Nicholas Ashe struck me as a young man for whom violence was the preferred form of self-expression.

'We're looking forward to the show,' he said. 'I like a good song.'

I said nothing. It wasn't quite the time to disappoint him with the news that singing wasn't a strong point in the repertoire.

'Let's get these horses watered,' Andrew Battell said, but without enthusiasm, his fever having drained him of the energy required to fuel that emotion. Isaiah appeared and took the reins of four horses; Ngulmiri did the same, although they didn't speak to each other or even acknowledge each other in any way that I could see. Nicholas, Fulton, and Glen took the reins of the remaining horses, and we began to walk away from the camp. At a very short distance we broke through the trees onto a trampled path bordered by grass that was as tall as I was. It was a narrow vein that gave way to scrub, beyond which I could see a sluggishly moving stream. When Rufus had said there was a creek nearby, I'd pictured something in the order of a bubbling brook. This was as wide as a river.

When we reached it, Charlie confirmed that it was indeed no more than a creek, swollen by recent rain and likely to become broader and faster as the Wet progressed. Isaiah, Ngulmiri, and Rufus manoeuvred the horses downstream and allowed them to enter the water to the depth of their withers, all the while moving amongst them. On the shore, Andrew Battell stood by with a Thompson submachine-gun at the ready. It was a disconcerting sight, and not one that encouraged me to dive in, despite the heat and the promise of cooling down.

Upstream from the horses, Fulton and Nicholas began what was clearly a routine by which each of them might immerse himself, albeit quickly. Fulton went in first while Charlie stood with a rifle cocked and pointed vaguely at the creek. Nicholas Ashe began throwing bits of branches and stones out beyond Fulton, presumably with the intention of dissuading crocodiles from approaching. This was so far from being a relaxing swim at the end of a long, hard day as to be ludicrous. When Fulton emerged, his legs were studded with leeches, some of them as fat as garden slugs. He brushed them off without concern, and Nicholas performed a perfunctory check on those parts he couldn't see. He pulled three leeches from Fulton's buttocks before slipping into the water himself while Fulton created the necessary disturbance. He, too, was festooned with leeches when he returned to the bank. Both Charlie and Glen swam, and were de-leeched afterwards. Brian and I demurred.

Back at the camp, the time-consuming business of hobbling each of the horses was undertaken. We all pitched in, but the exercise made me extremely nervous, and I was more hindrance than help. Bending down amongst the stamping feet of irritated horses is not for the inexperienced, and I was grateful to Ngulmiri, who saw that I was hopeless and came to my aid discreetly. He seemed to instinctively understand that my clumsiness would be seen as contemptible weakness by Nicholas Ashe and the others.

'All right now, boss,' he said. He was older than Isaiah. His cheeks were smooth, but he grew a thick goatee, unruly and streaked with grey.

'All right now,' I said.

I noticed that the leeches which had attached themselves to the legs of the horses were allowed to gorge themselves and fall off of their own accord. Pulling them off was an extra duty nobody had the energy to undertake. It was tiring enough checking each hoof and digging out small stones or clearing away mud.

By mid-afternoon the heat was almost unbearable, although the sun had been blocked out by gathering clouds. We returned to the camp without Isaiah and Ngulmiri, who remained with the horses.

'Horse tailing is nigger work,' Nicholas Ashe said dismissively, indifferent to the fact that both men could hear him.

The information gathered during the two-day reconnaissance needed to be collated, and additions to existing maps needed to be entered so that Charlie Humphries could take them back with him to Darwin. This was the section's main responsibility—providing topographical details about river courses, water holes, and access routes and, very importantly, determining where emergency aircraft landings might be made, or where airfields might be built. The information needed to be sorted out quickly, because Charlie Humphries's departure depended on the turning of the tide.

Sitting under the tarpaulin, Andrew Battell drew details on a map while the others retrieved the remaining rations boxes from the ketch. Glen, Brian, and I stayed behind, having decided that we should put on a bit of a show when the men returned. This was, after all, ostensibly the point of our presence. Brian and Glen were to do their magic act, with Brian fully costumed as Glen's beautiful assistant. I couldn't do any of the stuff I'd been lumbered with in the concert party shows because I'd been part of a cast, and here there was no cast. Thus I was presented with the perfect opportunity to offer the Nackeroos a preview of my ambitions regarding *Timon of Athens*. Having carried the tails and topper this far, it would have been ridiculous not to wear them.

We told Corporal Battell that we were withdrawing to the bush to prepare for the performance, and that when Fulton, Rufus, Charlie, and Nicholas returned, he should sit them down, along with Ngulmiri and Isaiah, and call out. Glen and Brian would then appear and do their act with a minimum of props, but with a maximum of glamour. I'd stay back until they'd finished, and then come forward and transport them to Shakespeare's Athens.

Brian didn't like being watched as he changed into his satin sheath and convincing wig. It wasn't possible to hide amongst the sparse vegetation, but he took himself some distance away and, with the help of only a small hand-mirror and a few sticks of make-up, transformed himself into the beauty who'd fooled and beguiled audiences in Maryborough and Mt Isa. Glen and I changed into our formal wear and stood in the scrub, acutely aware of how spectacularly out of place it all was.

'I'd be willing to bet,' Glen said, 'that, in the whole history of the world, we're the first people to wear tails here, in this spot.'

Brian joined us—the illusion of his womanliness slightly compromised by his failure to shave since the previous day. We were something to behold.

'I'm nervous,' Brian said. 'More nervous than I was in Mt Isa.'

I explained that it was frequently the case that smaller audiences were tougher on the nerves than larger ones. The awareness of the individual responding gets lost or muted if the audience is large. If it's small, one is much more alert to particular eyes and bodies. The judgement of the individual is more daunting than the judgement of the crowd.

Without large props to create large illusions, Glen was obliged to confine his act to sleight-of-hand. This, he said, suited him fine, and he and Brian insisted that I turn my back while they rigged their clothes with various cards, notes, coins, and other magic accoutrements. Brian had been shown the workings of many tricks in order to facilitate their successful prosecution, but I was not afforded this courtesy—an omission which I found galling. I'm not one of those people who wish to preserve the secret of a trick. My immediate desire, having enjoyed an illusion, is to know how it was done.

Andrew Battell coo-eeed, and we approached the camp. I stayed out of sight, and watched as Brian rested his hand on Glen's arm and walked with him into the clearing. He moved in his heels over the uneven ground and through the thin stringybarks and spreading pandanus with impeccable grace and control. The whistles and whoops that rose through the trees announced that they'd won the approval of their audience before a single trick had been demonstrated.

I paced and, in a low voice, readjusted the emphases in some of the verse I intended to speak. Landing hard on a word instead of gliding over it, or vice versa, might be the difference between making sense or nonsense of a character.

Laughter and applause coming from the camp meant that Brian and Glen were doing well. When I launched into some of *Timon of Athens*' meatier speeches, the change of pace would take them by surprise, but I knew I could hold them. They were hungry for entertainment, but this didn't mean they had to be fed only pap.

A sustained round of applause indicated that I was about to go on. Brian and Glen returned, laughing, and with that look that actors get when they believe they've made a success. We didn't exchange any words. I strode into the camp as if I were entering from the wings of a majestic theatre. Fulton, Andrew, Nicholas, Rufus, and Charlie were sitting on ammunition boxes in a semi-circle — each of them naked, apart from the boots. In top hat and tails, I felt perhaps a tad overdressed. They applauded politely as I assumed my stance. From the grins on their faces, I think that they were expecting me to launch into 'Puttin' on the Ritz' and to entertain them with a bit of soft shoe. Instead, I pointed my finger sharply at Nicholas Ashe and said:

> I scorn thy meat; 'twould choke me, for I should ne'er flatter thee.

He pulled back as though I'd poked him physically, startled more by the sound of the words than their meaning, which I have no doubt escaped him. The grins left the faces of the others, too. I launched into the speech, gathering momentum as I went:

> I wonder men dare trust themselves with men.
> Methinks they should invite them without knives:
> Good for their meat, and safer for their lives:
> There's much example for't. The fellow that sits next him, now
>> parts bread with him, pledges the breath of him in a divided
>> draught, is the readiest man to kill him. 'T'as been proved. If
>> I were a huge man I should fear to drink at meals
> Lest they should spy my windpipe's dangerous notes.
> Great men should drink with harness on their throats.

A crack of thunder made us all jump — thunder and bombs being closely allied in the ears — and a great wave of rain swept over us. My audience chose to retreat under the tarpaulin, suddenly alarmed by the prospect of getting wet. Brian and Glen, now disrobed, came out of the trees and began a farcical dance in the style of Isadora Duncan. The Nackeroos, now that the threat of Shakespeare had been removed, lost their fear of the rain, and followed Brian's and Glen's movements until all seven of them were prancing about the clearing in a grotesque, naked parody of modern dance. I stood watching from just inside the tarpaulin, my top hat still sitting firmly on my head. On the far side of the camp, Isaiah and Ngulmiri, standing well away from each other, observed what must have seemed to them to be an outbreak of madness. At one point, Fulton detached himself from the group and placed his hand on my arm.

'Come on, Will. It's fun.'

Not wishing to reinforce any misconception he might have about my being standoffish and stuffy, I stripped, and launched into an exaggeratedly interpretative routine. I found myself laughing along with everyone else, and this time of prancing in the rain, in the middle of nowhere, remains fixed in my memory as being amongst those rare and uncomplicated moments of pure happiness.

When the rain had passed, the camp became a quagmire, and there was nothing for it but to surrender to the inevitability of being filthy. It is amazing how quickly all the appurtenances and inhibitions of civilisation can fall away. A muddy hand wiped on a thigh, or rubbed through the hair, becomes clean enough. A body, however, simply becomes a palette on which different shades of dirt, grease, mud, sap, and even blood, mix, dry, and flake off, or stubbornly adhere.

In the late afternoon, Charlie left us.

The rations were unpacked and examined, and each man went about his appointed tasks. Andrew Battell was gripped by a fierce bout of shivering, and sat wrapped in his bedding in the impossible humidity. Fulton tinkered with the new radio-charger, Rufus began assembling bits and pieces for dinner, and Nicholas Ashe took each of their weapons, stripped them down, and cleaned them. Isaiah and Ngulmiri stayed close to the horses. I wandered over to where Isaiah stood and asked him whether he thought the Japanese could successfully invade this part of the world. He shook his head.

'Croc get 'im.'

The idea that Australia's best defence was an ancient reptile didn't inspire confidence.

'You and Ngulmiri don't talk. Different language?'

Isaiah shot a quick glance in Ngulmiri's direction.

'Taboo, boss. He married wrong way. Very bad.'

I thought of telling him that Brian had, in my opinion, married 'wrong way' too, but that I still spoke to him. When I looked from Isaiah to Ngulmiri I felt there was more there than I was capable of grasping, so I held my tongue. Whoever Ngulmiri had married, the problem went deeper than choosing a dull, vapid, vulgarian, as Brian had done.

'Fires now, boss.'

I walked back with him into camp and he began to set half-a-dozen fires in a circle around a central fire. The fires weren't for cooking—Rufus was busy concocting some sort of fried-rice affair over a primus stove—so I surmised that they were to provide smoke to keep mosquitoes and sandflies at bay, at least temporarily. Beside each fire he laid a bundle of damp branches. All day I'd been swatting flies, sandflies and mozzies, the last two in annoying but not overwhelming numbers. I knew this would change at dusk, and dusk was fast approaching.

'Put your pants on, boss. Shirt, too.'

I took his advice, went to my kit, and got dressed. Rufus called out that I should put on two shirts and two pairs of pants.

'Are you serious?' I asked.

He shrugged.

'These fuckers can skewer you through thick cotton, mate.'

There was a scurry in the camp as everyone hurried to cover every bit of his skin. We all donned mosquito gloves and our netted hats, and pulled thick socks over the cuffs of our trousers. I felt suffocated by my own clothes, but when the insects arrived I saw that there was no alternative if one was to remain sane. The fires were lit and a pall of smoke raised. We ate our meal inside the circle, although Isaiah and Ngulmiri took their food to their grass shelters and ate it there. The food was palatable, and Rufus's bread was excellent. It was closely examined and given the thumbs up.

'You're a bloody good cook,' Fulton said, and indeed Rufus had managed to coax flavour out of his mixture of rice, bully beef, dried vegetables, and herbs. I realised that the 'Herbs For Victory' campaign actually meant something. For each mouthful I lifted the netting that covered my face and, despite the smoke, which greatly reduced but didn't entirely eliminate the mosquitoes, one or two of the creatures would zip in and find my cheek or neck. I wondered if Isaiah and Ngulmiri fared any better in their shelters.

'Why don't Isaiah and Ngulmiri stay and eat with us?' I asked.

''Cause they're fuckin' niggers, mate,' Nicholas Ashe said. 'They shouldn't even be eating our rations, I reckon. They should find their own fuckin' nigger food.'

'We'd be rooted without them,' Rufus said.

'We'd be rooted without the horses, too,' Ashe said, 'and I don't want to eat with them, either.'

'Surely they're entitled to rations,' Brian said. 'And pay.'

'They get paid,' Ashe said sourly. 'Five bob a week and nigger twist.'

'So they get paid in a week what we get paid in a day. That doesn't seem fair to me,' I said.

Ashe made a farting noise with his lips. 'Fair? You know what's not fair, mate? The left-hand side of a black gin's bum. That's what.'

'What's "nigger twist"?' Brian asked.

'Tobacco,' Rufus said. 'It's rolled up like a stick of liquorice.'

It was a strange sensation talking to figures whose faces weren't visible and whose individuality was obliterated by their head-to-foot coverings. Nothing, however, could obscure the vitriol that seeped from Nicholas Ashe whenever he referred to the 'niggers'. It became clear in the course of the conversation that he held in his dark heart a particular detestation for white men who married Aboriginal women. 'Combos' he called them. He'd only heard rumours that there were white women who'd taken up with Aboriginal men, but this seemed so outrageous a proposition that he'd assigned it to the status of myth.

'Where are you from?' I asked at a break in a diatribe about some bloke he'd met who'd turned out to be a half-caste, and nobody knew, and he'd actually bought the bastard a beer.

'Brissy,' he said. 'Couldn't wait to get out of there.'

Ashe's attitudes didn't seem to bother anyone else, and the only conclusion I could draw from this was that Ashe's feelings were accepted as reasonable, or not so unreasonable as to be worthy of comment or dispute.

Andrew Battell took to his bed as soon as he'd eaten the few mouthfuls he could manage. The shivers had passed and been replaced by sweats, so his clothes must have been torture.

'There's nothing we can do,' Fulton said. 'He doesn't want

to be evacuated. We just have to wait for it to pass. We've all had a dose.'

There was a great deal of praise for Brian's and Glen's little magic act, and it was agreed that Brian made a satisfactory woman. No mention was made of my contribution. It had been cut short by the rain, so any legitimate judgement was impossible anyway. There was talk, too, of how close the Japanese were, and there was no doubt at all expressed about their intentions. Invasion wasn't a matter of 'if,' but 'when'. This certainty wasn't good for the nerves.

'I wouldn't trust the niggers up here as far as I could throw them,' Ashe said. 'They've had contact with the bloody Japs for years.'

'But why would the Aborigines want to be invaded by the Japs?' I asked.

'Dunno. Maybe they think the Japs will give them better tobacco. Who knows what they think, or even if they think.'

The fact that both Isaiah and Ngulmiri were within earshot was of no importance to Ashe. He didn't credit them with feelings worthy of even the most grudging respect. He was of the view that, 'You wouldn't watch what you said in front of a dog, so why should you worry about the blacks?'

'It's a clear night,' Fulton said. 'We might be able to pick up Tokyo Rose.'

'I don't want to hear that shit,' Ashe said.

'So go to bed,' Fulton said, and for the first time I heard in his voice a note that suggested the camaraderie between them might be fragile. I was anxious to talk with him about the three deaths that had so alarmed Army Intelligence in Melbourne. I'd have to do this discreetly because it was important that Fulton not know that the real purpose of this visit was to unmask a murderer, not raise their morale with vaudeville. Until I had a clear idea about what was going on up here, I didn't want to expose Fulton to any unnecessary danger.

Glen, Brian, Rufus, and I brought smoking branches under the tarpaulin while Fulton fired up the battery-charger and settled himself in front of the radio. It would be a long night of transmitting and receiving for him unless the skies remained clear and free from electrical storms. The FS6 was capable of voice transmission over relatively short distances, but this was only used in emergencies, the outgoing signals being too easy to intercept and track. All other transmissions were done in ciphered Morse, which demanded great accuracy. Enciphering and deciphering were skills I couldn't master. Fulton, however, was obviously at home with the FS6. He tinkered and fiddled until a woman's voice broke out of the static.

'Tokyo Rose,' he said. 'It's not always the same person.'

I was expecting a sultry, come-hither voice designed to lure men to their deaths. Instead, a rather flat, almost officious, voice with an American accent told us, as if it were a news broadcast of an irrefutable truth, that the Empire of Japan considered the troops in northern Australia to be prisoners of the Japanese already.

'We guard you with our bombers,' she said matter-of-factly, 'and General Tojo sends his regards and gratitude to the Australian government, which feeds you until our soldiers arrive.'

There was a moment of static, and Glen laughed—no one else did—and then she was back.

'Australian soldiers, you are lonely where you are. Your girlfriends are not so lonely. Nice American soldiers look after her. Maybe they'll marry soon. Boys in Darwin, ask the

American soldier if he knows your girlfriend. Ask him how she is going. He knows.'

The transmission was lost.

'Cunt,' Rufus said.

'Surely no one's going to fall for that,' Glen said.

'If you're tired, shit-scared, and miserable,' said Fulton, 'and you hear it often enough, you start to think about it.'

Certainly, Tokyo Rose had done something to the mood of the evening, and we left Fulton to his transmissions and his smoke-screen, and decided it was time to turn in.

'Check your bedrolls,' Rufus said. 'Just in case. Snakes and scorpions. And when you hear Ngulmiri call out, don't panic. He's just letting any blackfellas who might come by know who he is and what his country is. It's an etiquette thing, and stops any trouble.'

As I walked in my heavy clothes towards my date with scorpions, I realised that my dream of lush, benign rainforest was now comprehensively deceased. I carried a smoking branch with me, and when I reached the coffin of cheesecloth that Brian had erected for me, I gingerly lifted its edge and shone my torch through a cloud of mosquitoes to check if anything serpentine had crawled in. There was nothing there, so I waved the branch about to drive out any insects that had rushed into the space, and quickly stretched out on the bedroll, the branch still in my hand. The cheesecloth was thick—so thick that it wasn't transparent—and smoke soon filled the small void. At least it had the desired effect of clearing out the mosquitoes, and I was able to release some of it when I tossed the branch away.

I waited for a minute, and, when I was sure I was alone, took off the cumbersome hat with its netting, and the gloves. I'd been strongly advised, however, to keep all my clothes on, however stifling it became; given that the cheesecloth excluded even vigorous breezes, I thought I might die of heat exhaustion or smoke inhalation.

When my head touched the bedroll it became apparent that it was wet. The cheesecloth wasn't waterproof. My clothes were wet, too, as they soaked up the bed's moisture. I was suddenly so tired that I didn't care. I couldn't, however, ignore the insistent whining that began close to my ear. By now the smoke had seeped out from a tiny breach in my defences, and at least one mosquito had found the hole and gained entry. And then another; and another. I slapped at them, put my hat and gloves back on, and wondered why I'd ever thought this operation was a good idea. Ngulmiri, who was on horse-tailing duty, began calling out his name and some other words in his language. He did this several times. I was glad we'd been warned about it because I found it alarming and spooky. I fell asleep thinking that a few short weeks before I'd been luxuriating in an unpatriotically deep, hot bath. Still, I thought ruefully, that had turned out rather badly. Perhaps, starting from such a low base, this experience might improve, rather than decline. As if.

It rained heavily during the night, so heavily that water and mud flowed freely under and around my bed. I awoke so thoroughly saturated in rain and sweat that it was as if I'd spent the night submerged in a pond. It was just daylight, and when I raised the corner of the cheesecloth I saw that no one else was yet stirring. Through the filmy gauze of the hat netting I noticed the cheesecloth around Andrew Battell's bed bulge as a body pressed up against it. He must be getting up, I thought. A figure, dressed as I still was, and unrecognisable, emerged and stood up. His hands were briefly exposed and, as he looked down at the low, elongated tent-like covering, he slowly put his gloves on. To my astonishment, he then lifted the edge of his netting veil and spat. Why would Andrew Battell spit on his own bed? He was feverish, it was true, and the cloth's inability to secure a decent night's sleep might well provoke an irrational attack against it.

I lay back down, put my hands behind my head, and waited until the Nackeroos decided the time was right to get up. Having accepted that there was nothing I could do about the water, I even managed to doze, and it was a deep, reviving doze, which I was shaken out of by Brian.

'We're leaving,' he said.

There was bustle in the camp. Rufus was busy preparing ersatz scrambled eggs, using powders of various kinds, and Isaiah and Fulton were loading the FS6 onto horses—it took four horses to accommodate its bits and pieces and, from the strain apparent on Fulton's face as the accumulators were loaded, it was clear that they were very, very heavy. The horses couldn't possibly be expected to carry these for more than a couple of hours without relief. This explained, I suppose, the extraordinary number of remounts required to service only four Nackeroos. The tarpaulin had been taken down, and crates and boxes gathered into the centre of the camp, prior to loading or discarding.

I packed up my things quickly and, following the lead of the Nackeroos, I wore long sleeves and trousers. This wasn't going to be a day for wandering about naked in Eden.

At some point it was noticed that Andrew Battell's little tent hadn't been packed away.

'Get up, you lazy bastard,' Nicholas Ashe called, but without rancour. Battell's dengue fever gave him some leeway, temporarily, in the pulling of his weight. All the others had either been in his position already or knew that they would inevitably be so at some stage. There was no reply from Battell's tent.

'Maybe he's off having a shit,' Rufus said.

We ate, and final preparations for departure were made.

'Why are we leaving?' I asked Fulton as I forced the barely edible egg-matter down.

'Last night, Platoon HQ recalled us. Fair enough, too. We've been on patrol for weeks now. It's going to take us a couple of weeks, maybe, to get back to Flick's Waterhole.'

He pulled out a Fighter Guide map, with hand-drawn additions, and showed me what lay ahead. It was a maze of water courses and swamp.

'It doesn't seem logical to me,' I said. 'Flick's Waterhole is south of Company HQ. Why don't we go straight there, to Roper Bar?'

'We're not just going home, Will. We're mapping all the way. We mapped a route on the way up here, so we know where there's grass and water for the horses, and where the going is impossible. With the Wet settling in now, things will have changed, so we'll go back pretty much the same way and see what's what. It's going to be bloody hard work, and without the blackfellas we couldn't do it.'

'Maybe Nicholas Ashe needs to appreciate that a bit more.'

'Nick's all right, Will.'

He said this in a way that precluded further discussion, so I let it go, supposing that camaraderie forged in difficult conditions had dulled my brother's decency. Brian's words about our having separate fathers echoed suddenly in my mind, and I looked at Fulton's profile with some concentration. Family resemblance isn't a reliable marker of paternity or maternity; but, even so, I thought I detected, in the general shape of his head and in the way he held it, a decided difference from either Brian or me — and it wasn't just that he was younger. He wouldn't grow to look like us. No. He'd grow to look like someone else entirely.

Nicholas Ashe appeared and declared that, as we were ready to leave, it might be a good idea for someone to wake Andrew Battell. This time he sounded irritated, as if he'd been prepared to make allowances up to a point, but that point had now been reached and passed.

'All right,' Fulton said, 'I'll wake him and help him with his kit.'

He began by standing outside Battell's cheesecloth tent and calling his name. There was no reply, so he pulled the material back to reveal Battell apparently asleep, although not wearing his mosquito hat. Fulton was about to shake him when he drew back and said, 'He's dead.'

We hurried over and stared down at Battell's face. His eyes were open and lifeless but, appallingly, maggots had already been deposited in their corners and in his mouth, and they crawled and wriggled as they sought purchase to feed.

'How did the flies get in?' Brian asked, and at that moment it seemed like a more important question than how Battell had died.

'Maybe he went to the dunny and left a gap,' Glen said.

'Yes, he did,' I said. 'Just after dawn. I saw him leave his tent.'

As soon as I'd said it, I realised I'd made a terrible mistake because, as if to prove my skills as a detective hadn't deserted me, I was struck at that moment by the knowledge that the person leaving Battell's tent at dawn wouldn't have been Battell, but his killer. I'd just alerted this man to the fact that he'd been seen, and this put my life at considerable risk, especially in a landscape where there were a million ways to die — and all of them could look like an accident.

'What do we do?' Rufus asked reasonably.

'The first thing to do is to radio someone and tell them,' I said, 'and then we should try to figure out how he died.'

'We know how he died,' Fulton said sharply. 'Dengue. And I know it sounds hard, but we're not unloading and reloading the radio. We can do that tonight. It's not going to make any difference.'

'Well, I think we should check to see if there might be any other cause of death,' I said quietly, but firmly. Brian caught the determination in my voice, and realised that I might have reason to believe that Battell's death was suspicious.

'We have to do that,' he said. 'For the family.'

'You're going to do an autopsy here, are you?' The small, unexpected sneer in Fulton's voice was unfamiliar, in the true sense of that word.

'No,' Brian said calmly, 'but we can check for things like snakebite.'

'Or stab wounds,' I said sharply, unable to resist the small shock such frankness might provoke in the murderer, and signalling at the same time that he needn't think I was going to be as easy to dispose of as the feverish Andrew Battell.

Fulton shook his head and looked puzzled. 'Fine. Do whatever you like, but I don't want any part of it. Nick and I will dig a grave. Charlie Humphries can bring some people around to collect the body later.'

Glen, Brian, and I dismantled Andrew Battell's bedding arrangements and exposed his body to the open air. This was going to be unpleasant. Only his face was visible, but the blowflies were already crowding on it, above it, and around it. Without speaking, we set about removing his clothes. Brian took off his boots and socks, and I undid the buttons on the two shirts he'd worn to bed. In only a few minutes the corpse lay naked in the dirt.

While Glen waved a branch about to shoo away the flies, Brian and I looked closely at the body. Corporal Battell had several nasty sores on his legs, and his chest was pocked with impetigo. There were dozens of mosquito and sandfly bites—some of them merely welts, others angry, inflamed mounds—and many open sites of infection. If a snake or scorpion had bitten him, none of us was sufficiently experienced to confidently identify the puncture marks. I knew that Corporal Battell hadn't suffered the misadventure of venom.

I forced myself to look at his head. Glen was ostentatiously looking away, and I didn't blame him. There was no sense of the living Corporal Battell in this pale, rigid, fly-struck face. I reached out and gingerly moved the head slightly by pushing against the chin. A few dislodged maggots fell onto my hand, but the gorge rising in my throat subsided when I saw the raw burn of a ligature mark around his throat. Unmistakably, he'd been strangled, swiftly and brutally, and by a pair of hands that were experienced and strong.

'Have you found anything?' Glen asked, still resolutely avoiding looking at the body. I caught Brian's eye and nodded in the direction of Corporal Battell's throat while saying, 'No. Fulton was right, I think. Dengue fever.'

Brian and I wrestled Corporal Battell into one of his shirts, and raised the collar to disguise the scar. Then we put one pair of his trousers back on and squeezed his feet into his shoes. I covered his face with his spare shirt, and reassured Glen that it was now safe to look.

'I just can't stand maggots,' he said. 'It's like a phobia. It's not the body.'

'You finished?' Fulton said, and his tone implied that he thought we'd done something unnecessary and inappropriate. Brian stepped forward and said quietly, 'We had to check, Fulton.'

Fulton shrugged, but Brian's words had mollified him. I knew that if I'd spoken the same words, the effect would have been different. I was reminded that I was an outsider in my family, condemned by my putative resemblance to my father — a man to whom I was never close and whom I never really knew, or liked particularly. It seemed unreasonable and unfair that I should inherit familial disdain simply because my father's death put him beyond personally expressed disapproval. It's strange that the mind permits such ruminations even at times when one might expect the attendant drama to drive them out. Even then, as I was helping carry Andrew Battell's murdered body to the prepared grave, I couldn't prevent the intrusion of irrelevant domestic tensions.

The grave was shallow and water had pooled at its bottom, but we had no choice other than burial. We couldn't sling the corpse over the back of a horse and take it with us to Flick's Waterhole, and the only other option was to place the body on a platform above ground, as was the tradition amongst some Aborigines, or so Rufus said. I'd already lost sight of the man who was Corporal Andrew Battell, so I felt no guilty pang when I started to think that a dead body is an inconvenience at the best of times, let alone in a situation like this.

We put him in the earth and covered him over. Fulton hammered in a rough bush-timber cross, and we observed a minute's silence. No eulogy was delivered. As Fulton noted, the details of Battell's life were unknown to them. The most that could be said was that he did his job, that he was a bit dour, and that he was sick for much of the time. He wasn't known to have said anything really amusing, and he'd never mentioned a girlfriend or family. It was acknowledged that his natural reticence might have been increased by the debilitating effects of dengue fever.

'We should go now,' Fulton said, 'and get some distance in before it gets too hot.'

He seemed to have assumed authority, and no one resented it. And so we began what would become the longest two weeks of my life.

Chapter Six

GOOD MEDICINE

I NEEDN'T HAVE WORRIED about having to ride on one of the horses. The weight on their backs, and the oppressive heat, meant that we walked beside them. Fulton said that we'd be lucky to do twenty miles a day.

During the first hour of our exodus we passed through tall grass over terrain that was flat, and it wasn't very arduous. When the grass gave way to trees it was necessary to watch the horses carefully. Several of them attempted to divest themselves of their loads by squeezing between two trees, in order to dislodge the protruding weights. One of the horses succeeded, and time was lost as it was reloaded and disciplined into walking on. With surprising suddenness we found ourselves in dense scrub—a species of low-growing and prickly wattle—and the good sense in wearing protective clothing became clear. The Nackeroos seemed to know where they were going, which was just as well, because if someone had spun me around I'd have had no idea what direction I was facing.

Around midday we came to the first of many streams we'd have to cross. It was wide, but it didn't appear to be flowing very rapidly. In the dry months, Rufus said, this creek didn't flow at all. I found this astonishing as the volume of its flow gave the impression of permanence. Isaiah's experienced eye declared it shallow enough to permit fording without the horses having to swim. They stretched out along the creek's edge, and lowered their heads to drink.

No one saw the crocodile until it was too late. It rose from the water, its jaws agape, with the awful and monstrous precision of its kind. The horse that was its target, one of the few with nothing on its back, raised its head too slowly to avoid having its face clamped between the jagged vice of the reptile's jaw. A brutal twist knocked the horse off its feet and, flailing and whinnying, it was dragged into deeper water where, in a matter of seconds it was silenced. The only sound we could hear was the thrashing of the crocodile as it repositioned its grip and headed for the opposite bank. There was panic amongst the remaining horses, and they bolted. Stunned by the force of this thing which had erupted from the creek, I stood rooted to the spot, staring at the place where moments before a stocky Waler had stood drinking.

'The horses!' Nicholas Ashe yelled. 'Get the fucking horses!'

It took an hour, but all the horses were rounded up and assembled again at the edge of the creek. The thickets of ti-tree and wattle had served as a natural barrier against a free bolt, so none of the mounts had made it very far.

We were all shaken by the incident, and the knowledge that we had no choice but to cross the creek made me quake in my boots—literally. I could feel my ankles knocking against the high leather.

'Boots off, boss,' Ngulmiri said, and made a sucking noise to indicate the effect of thick mud. Very few words were spoken as we began the crossing. Having been given a rifle, I felt marginally less terrified, and my fear was soon replaced by sharp, insistent little stabs of pain as razor-like shells bit into the untempered soles of my feet. All I could think of was infection, and this took my mind off predation.

When we were a safe distance away on the far side, and in drier country where crocodiles were unlikely to lurk, we stopped, stood close together and, inexplicably, began to laugh. While Isaiah and Ngulmiri watched the horses, which grazed on a good swathe of Mitchell grass, we boiled a billy of tea and dunked army biscuits in the hot, bitter brew.

Late in the afternoon we came upon an immense billabong, its surface alive with countless thousands of water fowl—chiefly magpie geese and Burdekin ducks. The horses were watered with vigilance, and we all swam briefly in, for me, a confusing blend of relief and fear. Afterwards, Nicholas Ashe shot three Burdekin ducks—an action that took no skill. Firing a shotgun into so dense a flock was bound to get results, although he dropped the chestnut-and-white birds at our feet with the flourish of a sharpshooter. They were rather beautiful creatures, I thought, with pink legs, and bills the colour of pale flesh. Isaiah was told to pluck and gut them, and he did so, close to a fire he'd built so that maggots mightn't be deposited on them even while he was dressing them for the pot. (The cooked ducks were greasy in the end, and I decided that the next time they were on the menu I'd take charge of their preparation, and engage either Isaiah or Ngulmiri to help cook them carefully.)

The tedious work of unloading the horses was done quickly, and methylated spirits was rubbed into their backs — a measure taken to harden their skin. The radio was set up, and Ashe volunteered to man it. It was impossible to say if the temperature dropped as the sun set because, again, we were dressed in multiple layers.

I was assiduous in applying disinfectant powder to the cuts and abrasions on my feet, and both Brian and Glen followed my example. The three Nackeroos didn't bother — their hardened feet might have suffered less than ours.

Without my noticing, both Isaiah and Ngulmiri had constructed low, paperbark shelters over which they'd thrown a good covering of grass. They took turns horse-tailing throughout the night, constantly swatting at mosquitoes with the amputated wings of the Burdekin ducks, and crawling between shifts into their relatively insect-free grass and bark domes. We suffocated again under cheesecloth, and during the night I was disturbed by the eerie and unsettling bellowing of crocodiles.

The following morning I woke to discover that the boots I'd foolishly left outside my covering had been fly-struck and, having no way of knowing whether I'd removed all the maggots from the recesses of the toes, I was obliged to put my feet into them and hope that there weren't so many that they'd be squashed into a foul mousse.

The morning's walking was uneventful, if arduous, broken only by the passing overhead of a noisy, creaking flock of glorious, red-tailed black cockatoos, too numerous to count.

It rained not long after we'd moved on from lunch. It was another ferocious, obliterating downpour which created flows of water around our feet that might easily have been mistaken for the overflow from a nearby river. I was reassured by the Aborigines' and the Nackeroos' calm maintenance of an even pace forward that we weren't going to be swept away by a wall of water rolling over us.

When the rain stopped, the air became so thickly humid that it was difficult to breathe. I was looking down at the ground, following the heels of Brian's boots in front of me and allowing my mind to wander in the direction of Fulton's paternity — an absurd and pointless indulgence when I knew that I was in the company of a murderer, and determining the murderer's identity ought to have been my paramount concern. I'd had only the briefest of conversations with Brian the previous evening for, despite there being so few of us, we were never far enough from each other to make conversation of a sensitive nature possible or safe.

The real reason, probably, for my pondering the question of Fulton's paternity was that I was vaguely ashamed to discover that its uncertainty made it easier for me to accept that he must be amongst the suspects. After all, there wasn't a wide field from which to choose. I'd eliminated the Aboriginal men — I couldn't imagine either of them suiting themselves up in someone's gear (and where would they get it from anyway?) — so the only possible suspects were Fulton, Rufus Farrell, and Nicholas Ashe. I established a hierarchy of likely culprits, with Ashe at its head, Rufus Farrell some way down, and Fulton only on the list because he was present at the time of the murder.

I looked up and watched Fulton walking beside a horse several feet in front of me. He must have felt my gaze because he turned around and smiled at me. I wonder, I thought, if I actually like you, now that I'm not obliged to. But I rejected this as mean and irrational. We did have the same mother, after all, and our mother's features were unmistakably present in Fulton's handsome face, obscured though it was by his dark beard.

'Boss!' Isaiah called from the front of the line of horses. 'Crash, boss!'

We moved up and saw, a short distance away, the wreckage of an aircraft. Almost simultaneously, the air was tainted with the foul smell of something dead. Ashe instructed Isaiah and Ngulmiri to stay with the horses and to take the opportunity to shift the accumulators onto a fresh remount. The six of us cautiously approached the mangled aircraft, hearing the unmistakeable murmurings of blowflies smug and secure in the convenience of their find.

'Is it a Zero?' I asked.

Rufus shook his head.

'It's American. A B25 Mitchell bomber.'

'How many people would have been on board?' Brian asked.

'Three. Pilot, navigator, gunner.'

Our noses and ears told us that there were no survivors, and from the shattered wreckage it was obvious that no one could have walked away. It was Rufus who clambered up and peered into the cockpit.

'Two blokes here,' he said. 'Sort of.'

Glen, who'd wandered away a little, called, 'Body over here!'

I saw him discreetly vomit. I went across to where he was, and found there the charred and bloated remains of an airman. He must have been thrown clear on impact. It wasn't possible to determine his age or to discern any features that were recognisably human. If it weren't for the burnt and tattered remains of his flying suit, I mightn't even have been sure that what lay before me was a creature of my own species.

'This must have happened days, maybe even a week, ago,' I said. I placed one hand over my nose and mouth, and retrieved the dead man's dog tag, which had dropped into his chest cavity and balanced there on a piece of exposed rib, scorched and tarnished against that white protrusion. I poked at what remained of his clothing with a stick, but could find no other identification. If he'd been carrying a wallet or a photograph, it had been burnt into ashes indistinguishable from the ashes around it. At least his family would know what had happened to him. He was doubtless a young man in his early twenties; soon, somewhere far way in America, a telegram would be delivered, and someone would be reduced to inconsolable days of inexpressible grief.

We buried the three airmen in the sludge that was the earth. The two who'd remained strapped in the cockpit came away in ghastly sections. They, too, had been badly burned; one of them carried a wallet that had somehow survived, but all it contained was a small photograph of a young man with his arm around the shoulders of a severe, older woman — his mother, we presumed, unless, as Ashe crassly noted, he was sexually attracted to the elderly.

Fulton put their dog tags in his pocket and, because there was nothing else we could do, we went on our way, having been delayed by death yet again.

The terrain began to change, so subtly that it was only when I looked behind me that I realised we'd been climbing a gentle incline. The landscape stretched out at our backs in an endless expanse of red, brown, and yellow ground, daubed here and there with smoky greens.

I contrived to fall in beside Brian at the rear of the group, temporarily out of earshot of the others. 'At least we know the intelligence about suspicious deaths up here was right,' I said.

'Battell's the fourth, right?'

'The fourth we know about, and we're down to three suspects. We both need to be very careful, Brian. Me especially, now that he knows I saw him leave Battell's tent.'

'And you have no idea who it was?'

'The only part of him that was visible was his hands, and I was too far away to see if there was anything distinguishing about them.'

We were speaking quietly, but Brian lowered his voice even further to say, 'You mean two suspects, don't you? We can eliminate Fulton, surely. He's our brother.'

'Apparently that's only half true. What else don't I know about him?'

Brian dismissed the question with a wave of his hand.

'He's our brother, Will. What does it matter if he's lucky enough not to have our father's blood running through his veins?

'And whose blood does run there?'

The look Brian gave me was eloquent in his assessment of me as being simple-minded.

'Are you serious, Will? It's Peter Gilbert, of course. How could you not know that? How could you have lived in the same house I did and not know that Dad barely acknowledged Fulton? Fulton would have been, what, five when Dad died? I was just a kid, Will, but I didn't see Dad so much as speak to Fulton.'

'He knew? Dad knew that Peter Gilbert and Mother were having an affair?'

'He knew. I don't think he cared particularly. He was a cold bastard.'

My instinct was to defend the man to whom I was regularly compared. My will had been subjected to the enervating humidity, and I couldn't summon the energy to do so. In truth, I couldn't recall much, if anything, about our father that would generate a fond reminiscence. I couldn't accuse him of overt cruelty—he never struck me, and I don't recall him ever raising his voice. Nevertheless, my strongest memories are of outings calculated to frighten, appal, embarrass or, worse, bore me, and all undertaken with the cruel pretence that they were celebrations of my birth.

My silence must have discomposed Brian, or perhaps he thought his remarks about our father had offended me, because he said, 'You're not like him, Will. Not really. I think he was probably kindest to you.'

'This is a strange place to be talking about our father.'

Brian laughed.

'I can't think of a better one.' He paused. 'But you do look like him. I think that's why Mother doesn't like you.'

This startling little aperçu was delivered as if he were repeating a fact so immutable that it had declined into a truism. I was wrong-footed by it, and I could think of nothing to say. He took my silence this time to mean that I could find no objection to his observation.

'Ashe seems the more likely of the two, doesn't he?' Brian said.

'The three.'

'All right, the three. Ashe still seems the most likely.'

I agreed with him, and said so, but cautioned against allowing a prejudice against Ashe to obscure details that might implicate Rufus or Fulton.

'Frankly,' I said, 'I don't like Ashe, but if there's one thing I've learnt since becoming a private inquiry agent, it's that the key to the murder lies in the relationships between those around the victim. We have no idea how things stood between Rufus and Battell, for instance. Did they know each other before they became Nackeroos?'

'Given that this is the fourth death, trying to find a personal motive might be misleading.'

I agreed with him. Four deaths in a secret army unit like the NAOU looked more like politics than the mundanity of jealousy, rage, or revenge.

'Should we speak to Glen about this?' Brian asked.

'No. It was made clear to us in Melbourne that you and I are the only people privy to this information. I don't doubt that Glen can be trusted—I'm sure that they wouldn't have sent him up here if they didn't have confidence in him—but our instructions were unambiguous, and designed to protect him. You haven't told him anything, have you?'

'Of course not,' he snapped, and I was reminded that it didn't take much to fan that little ember of resentment between us into a flame.

The column came to a halt—not suddenly, but gradually. The pace at which we were moving precluded any movement having the weight of suddenness. Ngulmiri, it transpired, had seen a bee. This didn't immediately strike me as a compelling reason to stop. By the time we'd made it to where Rufus and Fulton were standing, Ngulmiri had taken off in pursuit of the insect.

'Sugarbag. Sweet, that one,' Isaiah said.

He and Ashe stayed with the horses. The rest of us followed Ngulmiri's darting form to the base of a spindly tree. He shimmied up it, and plunged his hand into a busy hive.

'My god,' I said, 'won't he be stung?'

'They're native bees,' Rufus said. 'No sting.'

In no time at all, great chunks of oozing honeycomb were gathered onto pieces of bark and, although I was reluctant at first to try it, one mouthful was enough to convince me that the ferocity of this frightening land was softened by the comfort of unexpected and sublime sustenance. We took a generous quantity back to Ashe and Isaiah. It had to be eaten on the spot — we didn't have any way to store it, and it wouldn't have survived the greedy attention of flies anyway.

Ngulmiri collected a sticky supply of black wax from the hive, as well as honey, and I was surprised when he applied this to his cheeks and ripped out his growing beard by its roots. Brian, thinking of his next performance perhaps, smeared a small amount on his own stubble, and when he couldn't bring himself to rip it off, Ngulmiri stepped in and deftly removed it. Brian let out a yowl, and refused any further depilation. He was left with an irregular patch of bare skin on his chin, from which pinpricks of blood seeped. I told him that he should disinfect the area unless he wanted to run the risk of developing impetigo. Ngulmiri laughed at his squeamishness and, with the help of a mirror, returned his own cheeks to the desired glabrous state, leaving his goatee untidy and untouched. For good measure, he dabbed the beeswax on his chest and made that hairless as well. It was a revelation to me to observe that human vanity is not confined to what I'd been raised to know as civilisation.

There was more rain that night, and black spots of mould were erupting on shirts, trousers, boots, and bedding. Even Brian's satin sheath, which he'd folded tightly and packed carefully, was under attack. Ngulmiri again disturbed my sleep by calling out at intervals, and the disconcerting howling of dingoes made the horses whinny with alarm. I had by now become relatively used to the conditions, and resigned to the fact of being wet, hot, and frequently weak with exhaustion

The following morning, Glen asked, 'What day is it?'

Fulton, who'd been up late again sending signals, said that it was Sunday, 1 November.

'It's my birthday,' Glen said.

'I'll make you a loaf of birthday bread,' Rufus replied.

'What's the difference between birthday bread and ordinary bread?'

Rufus shrugged. 'It's made on your birthday. You can have ersatz birthday eggs for breakfast, too, if you like.'

'I'm twenty-eight years old,' Glen said to no one in particular, sounding like someone out of Chekov.

'And never been kissed?' Ashe said.

'You're not volunteering, are you Ashe?' I was pleased to note the dismissive little edge in Glen's voice, as if he disliked Ashe as much as I did.

We'd been walking that morning for a couple of hours when I noticed a painful spot on my calf; then, as soon as it had made its presence felt, every step increased the nuisance, until my trousers assumed the abrasiveness of a rasp. At morning tea I rolled up my trouser leg and found an angry, red swelling, unpleasantly responsive to the slightest pressure. Fulton looked at it and diagnosed an ulcer.

'It's not an infected bite,' he said. 'Too big. It's not good, Will. Ulcers up here are a bastard to treat.'

The rest of that day's walk was agony as my whole world shrank to the dimensions of the putrefaction bubbling in my leg. So distracted was I that I paid scant attention to the landscape we were passing through, and by day's end I could barely recall it at all. After dinner, which I forced down, I thought I was becoming feverish, and retreated early to the hideous chrysalis of my bed. I didn't announce that I was ill. Andrew Battell's killer mustn't know that I was in any way vulnerable. I barely slept, and when I did I was plagued by dreams of lepers: a small group of them were shuffling towards me, their arms outstretched in a welcoming gesture of acceptance. Waking from these fitful sleeps offered little relief, for the rain was falling not with soothing coolness but with hammering aggression, and I couldn't shake the anxiety that the swelling in my leg wasn't an ulcer after all, but the first sign of disfiguring leprosy.

When I looked at my leg in the morning, the ulcer had formed a pus-filled crater. I dusted it with disinfectant powder and bandaged it carefully, using a frugal length from the supply we'd brought with the rations. This turned out to be pointless, as we'd gone very little distance before we were knee-deep in runnels of water and mud. My discomfort was soon so apparent that Fulton suggested I ride one of the horses and, as there was no danger of it breaking into a gallop, I said I'd give it a go. The ulcer, however, was in precisely the wrong place for sitting astride a horse. It rubbed viciously against its flank, and I had to dismount almost immediately. Nicholas Ashe helped me down and expressed sympathy. He wanted to know how bad it was, and asked if he could take a look at it. Suspecting that he was determining how weak I might soon be, I told him that I was fine really, and that I could certainly walk without assistance.

I noticed that Brian stayed close to me for the rest of that day, and that night he suggested that we swap beds, so that if anyone made an attempt on my life he'd find himself grappling with a robust Brian instead of me. I found this gesture unaccountably moving, and I had to turn away from him to prevent his seeing that my eyes had filled with tears—a surge of emotion I put down to my rising fever.

The sky on Tuesday morning was heavy and dark. I pulled the filthy bandage away from the suppurating ulcer and could barely bring myself to look at the pulpy mess it revealed. The inescapable fact was that my leg was rotting. I could smell it. Isaiah passed me and looked down at my calf.

'Piss on 'im. Fix 'im up short time.'

'What do you mean?'

'You piss on that one. Good medicine. Start. Wait a bit, then piss on 'im.'

He rolled up a trouser leg and pointed to a small, shiny scar.

'Fixed that one up, you bet.'

It was a measure of how desperate I'd become that, far from recoiling from this bizarre therapeutic advice, I was prepared to do exactly as Isaiah suggested. I was a little wary of accepting uncritically the idea that the accumulated wisdom of thousands of years might come down to urinating on one's own leg; but I'd run out of options, and that made this one viable. I wasn't, however, prepared to do it in the public gaze, so I hobbled out of sight, took off my boot and sock, exposed the ulcer and, standing on one leg, directed the mid-stream flow onto it. It was excruciating. Doing this several times a day was going to require a very particular kind of discipline.

That day's walking was relatively easy. We crossed a large expanse of open ground, broken here and there by the perpendicular of a ghost gum, its trunk bone-white against the blue-black of a heavy sky. On their way up from Flick's Waterhole, the Nackeroos had buried a cache of tinned food and fuel near one of the gums, and we ate from this rather than further deplete the fresher rations. Towards nightfall we came upon a wide billabong, aflame with lilies. It would have been a vision of paradise were it not for the smoky haze of mosquitoes that floated at its edges. Unfortunately, we were obliged to spend our nights near water to allow the horses to drink. Without this necessity the evenings might have been almost tolerable.

I'd treated my ulcer three times in the course of the day and, although I wasn't expecting a miracle cure, I was expecting something. It didn't seem to me to be any better. Indeed, it was appreciably worse. I couldn't think clearly—the pain was now so relentless and awful that it obliterated the possibility of reflection and deduction. Brian told me that he'd spent the day observing Nicholas Ashe and Rufus Farrell, and hadn't noticed anything about either of them that was diagnostic of a potential for multiple murder. I became impatient with him—a shortness that came from my pain—and pointed out that psychopathy wasn't a nervous tic that would manifest itself while a man was walking beside a horse. I apologised immediately, and reminded myself that Brian hadn't had my experience in pursuing the murderously inclined.

I wouldn't have thought it possible that the rain of the previous night could be equalled, let alone surpassed. The chest-rattling thunder and white blasts of lightning may have made it seem more extreme, but the force with which it fell and fell that night was staggering. There was a distinct possibility that we'd drown in our beds.

It was still raining at dawn, so breakfast was peaches. Building a fire was impossible, and Rufus wasn't prepared to wrestle with the primus stove under these conditions.

Fulton complained that the rain and the electrical interference had made telegraphy difficult, and that he'd spent much of the night trying to unravel static. He was jumpy, and said that there was an unusual amount of radio traffic, as if something serious was unfolding. He said he recognised the touch of the operators he usually had contact with, and that the bloke at Roper Bar was stabbing the Morse with uncharacteristic urgency.

'They're dots and dashes,' Brian said, expressing precisely what I wanted to say. 'How can you tell anything from that?'

'I can tell,' he said simply. 'Morse is a language, and it has nuance.'

I'd been astonished to hear the word 'pejorative' echo across the Timor Sea, and I was only marginally less astonished to hear 'nuance' uttered here, wherever 'here' was.

I became conscious in the course of this conversation that there'd been a noticeable diminution in the pain radiating from the repulsive crater on my calf. I looked at it: although it still seemed angry and proud, there did appear to be a less extravagant crème anglaise of pus at its centre. My spirits rose, and as we walked out of the night's bivouac, despite the ground having dissolved into a foul mousse, I was confident that I wouldn't find the day as difficult as the day before. My optimism would turn out to be misplaced.

Glen's voice struck the first discordant note.

'Fuck,' he said. 'Fuck, fuck, fuck,' as he attempted to secure straps on one of the horses. He held up his fingers and flexed them. They looked perfectly normal to me, but Glen insisted that they'd swollen to grotesque proportions.

'This happened in New Guinea,' he said. 'I swell in the heat. They're useless, just bloody useless. They're not fingers, they're balloons.'

Given that there didn't seem to be any discernible injury or infection, his fury at his newly clumsy digits struck me as self-indulgent.

'Try pissing on them,' I said.

The disgust on his face was almost comic, but understandable.

I hadn't shared with him the secret of Isaiah's urine therapy, so my terse suggestion must have sounded callous. We were all a little on edge, our nerves tautened by the possibility that the Japanese had launched an invasion during the night. Conversation was rendered impossible as the rain intensified, and the going was so slow that staying where we were, I thought, would have been the sensible thing to do. Fulton was anxious not to lose a day, and to get to Flick's Waterhole as soon as possible. I suspected that he'd heard something amongst the previous night's static that he was keeping from us.

Late in the morning our bedraggled convoy was halted by a wide, swiftly flowing creek — that, at any rate, is what Fulton called it. It's a measure of how frayed my temper had become that I found this designation irritating almost to screaming point. Any sensible person would have called this a river. It wasn't a creek, I held, if crossing it could kill you.

The roar of the water now competed with the rain, and instructions had to be shouted. The horses knew that they'd be expected to swim, and they were dangerously jumpy. Fulton stripped off his clothes and entered the water.

'It's fast,' he called.

When the water reached his shoulders I could tell that it was an effort for him to keep his footing. In the centre he was obliged to swim a few strokes to get over the deepest point, but despite being a strong swimmer he was carried several feet downstream. From the look on his face when he found his feet again, I could tell that swimming against the current had used considerable reserves of his energy. I wasn't a strong swimmer — I was capable, but not strong — so watching Fulton hadn't been reassuring. To my surprise, he returned, and when he'd recovered his breath he said, 'It's do-able. The horses should be fine.'

The plan was to ride one and lead one, and the expectation

was that the process would take at least a couple of hours, with each of us swimming back to collect the remaining horses.

Urging the Walers into the flow was surprisingly straightforward. I felt secure astride my mount, and it and its companion experienced no difficulties. This was true for all the horses in the first group. But I found returning to the crossing point both strenuous and frightening. The fact that I survived it had nothing to do with skill, and everything to do with luck. It was almost as if the creek took a breath just as I reached the deepest part, and the current eased sufficiently to allow me to swim without being swept downstream.

It was when we were taking the second group of horses across that disaster struck. I'd made it safely to dry land and looked back in time to see a great surge of debris-laden water rise like a liquid escarpment and fall with hideous force on Brian and the horse he was riding. They were pushed with astonishing speed out of reach and out of sight. The creek resumed its steady flow, and the sense that it had chosen Brian out of us all was inescapable. It took a moment to fully comprehend what had happened. We were agape. I looked at Fulton foolishly, as if I thought that he should be doing something to retrieve Brian. Despite the beard and the hairy chest, his rain-soaked face betrayed him as the young boy he still essentially was. His eyes were shocked and desperate, and he watched the water with impotent despair.

I scanned the banks. Glen and Ngulmiri were yet to cross. Any attempt to follow Brian on dry land would be frustrated by the thick scrub that grew along the creek's edges. The openness of our crossing point was the exception, not the rule. All this I took in in a matter of seconds. My decision to enter the creek and allow it to carry me in the direction it had thrust Brian had nothing to do with courage. It was more like rage—an irrational anthropomorphising of the creek into an entity whose bullying indifference to decency needed to be challenged. It was anger, not love, that propelled me into the brown swell.

I swam to the middle, and was immediately and efficiently relieved of the need to swim, except for an occasional stroke to prevent myself from tumbling out of control. The Nackeroos were soon lost to sight, and the folly of what I'd done struck me forcibly even as I struggled to remain buoyant.

I had no idea how far downstream I'd been carried. The inexorable, terrifying, and impersonal force of the water made time and distance meaningless, unless some witness on the bank were able to say, yes, he drowned at precisely this moment and at that spot. Even though I wasn't struggling against the flow, I was struggling with it, and I knew that exhaustion was close.

Then, by chance, I saw Brian. Water had washed into my eyes, and the grit in it had forced them closed. I opened them for the briefest of moments, and saw his body caught in a tangle of overhanging branches. Bizarrely, his horse stood on the bank nearby, its load intact. Using reserves of strength I didn't think I had, I pushed myself out of the deepest part of the creek and found my feet. The walk against the current in the shallows wasn't dangerous, although every step sank into mud, and every withdrawal sapped more of my energy.

When I reached Brian there was something so inert in his attitude that I thought he must be dead. He was stuck fast in a web of thin and whippy branches; I couldn't see what exactly was supporting his weight, so I assumed a sharp, sturdy bough must have skewered him somewhere. With trepidation, I touched his chest and looked closely at his face. He was bleeding profusely from a head wound, and his expression was hidden by blood.

I stood, paralysed by sudden grief, and I was vaguely aware, too, that somewhere in amongst the maelstrom of my emotions lurked the dread of having to tell Mother where, and how, he'd died. I knew that she'd hold me responsible, and that from that moment I'd be subjected to a kind of emotional excommunication. I bowed my head and closed my eyes, and when I looked up I found myself staring into Brian's open eyes. The relief I experienced at that moment is the closest I have ever come to ecstasy. With the power that comes with madness, I wrapped my arms around his waist and dragged him into the water. Perhaps if I'd been a bit more careful he wouldn't have suffered quite such severe lacerations on his back. He was semi-conscious and confused, but I managed to manoeuvre him to the small, clear area where his horse still stood. It hadn't wandered anywhere because there was nowhere to wander. We were hemmed in by thick, sharp shrubs—so thick as to appear impenetrable.

Brian sat with his head between his knees. The rain pounded his back, sending pink rivulets of blood into the mud where his buttocks rested. He finally raised his head and said, 'Bloody hell.'

Having come close to death, and having been pulled from its jaws by his own brother, one might have hoped for something grander, or more edifying.

'You're all right,' I said, and told him what had happened.

'And you jumped in after me?'

'You needn't sound so surprised. Of course I jumped in after you.'

He nodded, and his eyes reddened.

'Thanks,' he said quietly.

I was suddenly embarrassed by what threatened to be an upwelling of emotion from him, and said, 'I have no idea where we are, or how we're going to find the others, and this rain is driving me mad.'

'At least it keeps the flies and mozzies away.'

He was right about that. Without the rain it would have been impossible to prevent a blowfly strike at the site of the ulcer on my leg; and with blood oozing from various cuts and abrasions on his body, Brian would have been more fly than man.

'How far do you reckon we are downstream?'

'No idea,' I said. 'I think I was probably in the creek for fifteen minutes before I saw you. We must be at least a couple of miles from where we were. Maybe more.'

'So if we follow the creek back, we'll be right.'

I looked over his shoulder at the dense vegetation.

'Easier said than done. We'll be cut to pieces crawling through that stuff.'

Brian pointed to the horse, and reminded me that our costumes were in the packs on its back. He'd wear Glen's suit, and I'd wear mine. It would be a black-tie crawl to safety. We had no choice, though. However absurd it might look to be wandering through this wilderness dressed as if we were on our way to an opening night, the alternative of walking through it naked was out of the question.

We knew the going wouldn't be easy. What we didn't know was that it would be almost impossible. The bushes didn't part accommodatingly as we pushed into them. Their roots, trunks, branches, and mean little leaves resisted our advance. It was the necessity of bringing the horse with us that made us abandon a route close to the creek and to deviate away from it through scrub that allowed us to pass. We thought if we kept within earshot of the rushing creek we'd be right, but we'd barely gone any distance at all when what was rain and what was creek became uncertain and, finally, indistinguishable.

Wherever we came upon a clear passage we took it, relieved to be moving forward. We stopped after an hour's trek, and I climbed a spindly trunk to get some idea of the lie of the land. The tree was only slightly taller than the undergrowth, and ahead, behind and side to side, all I could see was an endless vista of low-growing green, with here and there a protruding tree. There was no sign of the creek, and when I climbed down I realised with dismay that I could no longer be certain whether it was to our left or our right. I hoped Brian's sense of direction was better than mine.

'I can't see a thing from up there. It's all the same. Do you have any idea where the creek is?'

'I've been following you. My head is killing me. I haven't been concentrating.'

'Well, here's something that might focus the mind. We're lost.'

'They must be close,' Brian said.

'That depends on whether we've been walking towards them or away from them.'

'Haven't we been going in one direction?'

'No, Brian, we haven't, and that's not my fault.'

'All right, all right, keep your tuxedo on. I'm sure we're vaguely heading towards them. Besides, surely someone will come looking for us.'

I had no confidence at all that this would happen. The Nackeroo's assumption would be that, if either or both of us had survived, we'd find our own way back to the group. Our only hope would be if Fulton was prepared to risk the further splintering of his already depleted party by allowing Ngulmiri or Isaiah to search for us.

We were stuck on the horns of every lost person's dilemma. Do we stay where we are or do we move on? We agreed that remaining in one place, particularly this place, would lead to the discovery some years hence of the two best-dressed skeletons in the Territory. Our only hope was to move.

'I don't suppose there's any food in those packs?' I asked.

Brian shook his head.

'Our costumes, Glen's props, odds and ends.'

'If the horse isn't carrying any food, it might have to become food.'

'You know we look ridiculous, don't you?'

'I think we might be facing bigger problems than the incongruity of our appearance, 'I replied. 'We should keep moving.'

The rain intensified until I thought it might be possible to drown standing up, on land. We walked in the only direction open to us, and we'd both become so disoriented that the only direction we could safely eliminate as not being one in which we should be headed was up.

Time ceased to be measured in minutes or hours, and became instead manifest in the gathering strength of hunger pangs, and weakness in the limbs. Nightfall took us by surprise. The world went from grey to black with almost an audible thud. We were still hemmed in by scrub, so there didn't seem any point in tethering the horse. We didn't bother unpacking it, and allowed it to wander our narrow demesne searching for whatever grass it could find.

'I don't like this,' Brian said. 'This is the most hungry I've ever felt in my entire life.'

It wasn't possible to light a fire, and we were obliged to lie as comfortably as we could in the mud. The distraction of conversation was denied us by the incessant drumming of the rain. Sleep was a remote likelihood, but I was so exhausted that it came upon me in spite of everything; as I slipped into a semi-conscious slumber, I marvelled at the body's ability to adapt, however reluctantly, to the hostile demands of its immediate surroundings. Even through my intense discomfort I was grateful I wasn't cold, and that the mosquitoes had been suppressed by the rain. If we'd been subjected to their harrowing attacks I think I might have lost my mind.

Brian and I awoke almost simultaneously to the ferocious droning of mosquitoes. It was dawn, and the rain had ceased. Instinctively we plastered mud on our faces, hair, and hands. The mozzies still swarmed noisily around our heads, but we were protected to some extent from their vicious little probes.

'I'm starving,' Brian said—a statement, as I told him, which could be added to the many redundant remarks he'd made in the course of his life.

'Where's the horse?' he said suddenly.

Not wishing to trade further in the obvious, I confined myself to a straightforward expletive which sufficiently covered the fact that the horse was unequivocally gone. So we stood in our tuxedos, caked in mud, hungry and horseless—and then it started to rain again.

'What day of the week is it, Brian?

'Thursday, I think.'

'Thursday, 5 November.'

'Should that mean something?'

'It's the anniversary of our father's death.'

'Like I said, should that mean something?'

'Why do you hate him?'

'I don't hate him. If I hated him, I'd celebrate his death. I barely remember him. I think what I feel is indifference, but even if I'd loved him, I'd swap all my memories for a piece of toast.'

It was Isaiah who found us. We'd been walking for a few hours, and the rain had eased, although the dark, ponderous clouds were a guarantee that more would fall. We'd come across some fruiting trees, but as we'd been warned in our training that some berries could kill or blind a careless forager, we resisted the temptation to ease our hunger. We filled our bellies with water, which gave us no energy but which went some way towards alleviating the nagging pain of an empty gut.

We were resting in an open patch of scrub, saying nothing to each other — only too aware that the situation was a desperate one — when Isaiah stepped from behind a bush and said, 'Hey, boss.' It was as if he'd materialised from the earth itself, and my first impulse was to crawl on my hands and knees and kiss his feet in gratitude. Not wishing to offend him, I settled for vigorously shaking his hand. Brian grabbed him by both shoulders and kissed him on each cheek — a continental gesture that took Isaiah entirely by surprise.

He'd brought bully beef, which we wolfed down without dignity or grace, and he told us that the horse had found the Nackeroos, and that he'd followed its tracks to where it had bolted, and then followed ours to where he'd found us. This seemed a miracle to me. I couldn't see how any tracks could survive the conditions.

'Easy one, boss,' was all he said.

By late afternoon, we'd rejoined Fulton, Ashe, Farrell, Pyers, and Ngulmiri. They laughed immoderately at our appearance. However, I was relieved to see that they were all still alive, and that the murderer amongst them hadn't seen fit to further reduce their number. Yet.

Three more nights and four more days of enervating, torturous walking brought us, on Sunday, 8 November to Flick's Waterhole—One Platoon HQ. The fact that it carried the moniker 'headquarters' inevitably created in my imagination the notion of something substantial and well-equipped. When Fulton told us that we were only a couple of hours shy of it, I couldn't refrain from picturing an oasis of comfort and civilisation.

My first impression was dispiriting, to say the least. We approached it through a veil of rain and along a track glutinous with mud. It was difficult to determine the extent of the camp. There were three quite large tents—rectangular and solid, in the American way—and there was a thick, healthy growth of trees that spoke of good, permanent water. I'd had just about enough of water by this stage so, while appreciating its influence on this corner of the Northern Territory, I longed for the evaporative fury of a fierce sun. Although the ulcer on my leg was responding well to my eccentric and repellent therapy, my feet had begun to feel soft and pulpy as if they were beginning to rot, and there was a painful gripping in my intestines that threatened to erupt into diarrhoea. This battery of discomforts dulled my ability to see at a glance that Flick's Waterhole, while not a resort, offered considerably more amenity than the section camp we'd left at West Alligator River.

We reported to a Lieutenant Linden, the platoon commander, in his commodious tent. He'd already been apprised by radio of Andrew Battell's death, and had had ten days to absorb it, which may explain his curt expression of condolence—perhaps he was merely pragmatic about the absence of anyone who might reasonably be expected to require condolences. He did his duty by acknowledging a fallen comrade, and moved quickly to the more pressing matter of informing us that we'd be required, after only a day's rest, to return to A Company HQ at Roper Bar, some eighty miles north of Flick's Waterhole. Road transport was out of the question: trucks couldn't negotiate the track without sinking up to their axles. The thought of more walking made me want to weep, but any notion that the order was a capricious one was dispelled when Lieutenant Linden said that there was every expectation that Port Moresby would fall to the Japanese, and that military strategy suggested that the Nackeroos at Roper Bar would form the frontline of troops on Australian soil. Sixteen of the twenty Nackeroos at Flick's would be returning with us.

Glen, despite his swollen fingers, immediately suggested that we put on a performance. Lieutenant Linden thought this was a splendid idea, and said that the rough sleeping-quarters, with its tarpaulin roof, would provide an ideal space. He asked us how much time we would need. Two hours, we thought, should be enough time to scrape the mould and mud off the weary tuxedos; and Brian, of course, had to shave many days' growth off his face. A fully bearded femme was too grotesque to contemplate.

The Nackeroos who crowded into the bush-timber structure that constituted their dormitory were a ragged lot. Their clothes hung off them in tatters, and their faces were barricaded behind beards of varying extravagance. They pushed the bush bunks to one side and surrendered to the magic of Glen Pyers, illusionist, and his beautiful assistant. At such close quarters, and with limbs disfigured by bites, scratches, and sores, Brian sensibly decided to play his part for laughs, and so successful was he that laughter rolled up and down the half-mile length of the waterhole. The

Aboriginal horse-tailers, of whom there must have been at least six, would have heard this laughter from their position away from the tents. They hadn't been invited to attend the concert.

Glen's fingers were troubling him, because he fumbled one trick—something I'd never seen him do. But he turned it to his advantage and created a comic bit out of it.

With such a well-primed and generous audience, I was sure it was safe to risk one of the more obscure but delightful speeches from *Cymbeline*. It became apparent, not long after I'd begun, that the people before me were leaning forward, not to ensure that not a syllable was lost, but in expectation that at any moment the joke would be delivered. When none came, the energy in the room—if this clumsy shelter could be called a room—drained away, and all they could lavish on me was desultory applause, and a collective regret that packing for tomorrow's departure forbade a second soliloquy. The thuggish Nicholas Ashe had the gall to suggest that I should do my pieces first.

'That way,' he said, 'Glen and Brian would be a reward for having to listen to you, rather than you being a punishment for having enjoyed them.'

I didn't give him the satisfaction of a reply, but firmed him up as the chief suspect in the murder of Andrew Battell. You may imagine, therefore, my confusion and disappointment when, four days later, he was found at Roper Bar, seated under a tree, the back of his head blown out, his pistol in his hand. It was assumed he'd taken his own life—men had gone troppo up there before and almost killed themselves, or someone else, before being invalided out to Brisbane or Townsville—but I knew that Nicholas Ashe hadn't taken his own life. In death, he held his gun in his right hand, and Ashe was left-handed. It seemed unlikely to me that his final act would be a demonstration of ambidextrousness.

PART TWO

Chapter Seven

ROPER BAR

THE ROPER RIVER COILS AND UNCOILS for more than two hundred and fifty miles from where it rises to where it spills into the Limmen Bight in the Gulf of Carpentaria. The Roper Bar is not a pub. It is a point some eighty-seven miles from the sea at which it is possible to cross the river from side to side and at which it is no longer possible for substantial boats to proceed up its length. At some time a police station had been built on the southern bank of the river, and this was large enough and sufficiently well-constructed to accommodate the cookhouse and several offices. Signal and troop quarters were purpose built, and the area was dotted with tents and shaggy huts draped in paperbark. When we arrived, three days after leaving Flick's Waterhole, Roper Bar was a busy place. The fact that Roper River was the most obvious, and most convenient, point at which the Japanese might attempt an incursion into the Australian mainland leant the camp at Roper Bar an air of something like controlled panic. Well, not panic exactly, but an expectancy and permanent alertness that made men prone to being easily startled and to have the appearance of having been deprived of sleep.

We straggled into the encampment at three o'clock on Thursday, 12 November: a date seared into my mind with the permanence of a psychic tattoo. This was not just because it was the day before Nicholas Ashe died, but because it was the day on which I lost my faith in the power of Shakespeare's verse to make strawberry jam out of pig shit.

A Company HQ at Roper Bar was under the charge of a man named Lieutenant Jenkinson, and as he had only recently taken up the position and was facing a degree of surly hostility from men who preferred the previous OC, he was most anxious that we take their minds off their troubles poste haste. A performance was scheduled for that very afternoon.

The audience was quite large—at least sixty men—and amongst the faces were a dozen dark, Aboriginal ones. Brian decided that he could put sufficient distance between himself and the front row to create his impressive illusion of femininity. His wig was beginning to look a little tired, having suffered the rigours of this extremely wet Wet season, but he thought it would do if he hid its ragged sections under a digger's hat. Fully made up, with the hat pulled jauntily down on one side, the effect was more than adequate. It was almost beguiling. The audience certainly thought so. With a generous blindness to his undepilated forearms, they laughed and whistled their approval, and he and Glen performed their routine smoothly and with a precision of comic timing that would have set audiences on their ears in London or New York. Glen's dexterity was unaffected this time by his swollen joints, and the whole performance was top hole.

I thought I'd made a sensible decision in replacing obscure Shakespearean gems with crowd pleasers like Hamlet's 'To be or not to be' and Henry V's 'Band of brothers.' I began with my back to the audience, and when I faced them, ready to intone Hamlet's meditation on life and death, I'd produced a virtuosic flow of tears. Given Hamlet's state of mind, I thought this was a not-unreasonable interpretation. The audience, so swift in embracing Brian's and Glen's tomfoolery, were at a loss how to respond. They obviously had failed to grasp that this was acting, and saw only a grown man in a tuxedo sobbing his way through some of the most beautiful lines in the language — lines that were largely, it seemed, incomprehensible to them. What kind of education leaves a person ignorant of 'bare bodkins' and 'fardles'?

I paused at the end of the speech to collect my breath, wipe my eyes, and mop my streaming nose. I'd given them a magnificent display of a racked and tortured man. An audience with even a scintilla of sensibility would have needed a moment to compose itself as well. The only discomposure I could detect amongst them was barely controlled sniggering and the spectacle of a number of fellows whose heads were bowed in what I could only resentfully interpret as embarrassment.

I was tempted to give them a piece of dire doggerel, which no doubt they would have lapped up with the gusto of a dog eating its own vomit, but I felt an obligation to expose them to the great rallying call of Harry Hotspur. Here, surely, they would find some resemblance between their own situation and the outnumbered English. In a practical demonstration of courage in the face of overwhelming odds, I decided to move amongst them as I spoke. The verse tumbled from me, the movement to the crescendo of 'For England, Harry and Saint George,' unstoppable and electrifying. For a few moments I *was* Henry V.

To this day, I'm not sure who it was who hit me. At some point in the speech I placed my hand upon a Nackeroo's shoulder—a little touch of Harry—and squeezed it in what any normal person would have felt as a fraternal gesture of solidarity and comfort. In a blur of movement, whoever it was leapt to his feet and slammed his fist into my face. I reeled back and fell awkwardly into a soldier who wasn't pleased to receive my weight. He pushed me away with unseemly roughness, so that I fell forward into the chest of a brute who steadied me by grabbing the front of my tuxedo before placing his greasy plate of a hand over my face and shoving me with such force that I felt something tear in the muscles of my neck. I crashed onto the ground on my back. I lay winded and in a state of mild shock. Around me there was an unhurried dispersal of the audience, as if the assault they'd just witnessed was of so little moment that, as soon as it was done, their attention was directed elsewhere. My well-being, and the savage injustice of the attack, were of no interest to them whatsoever. One or two men even stepped over me on their way to whatever duty they were due to recommence. It was Nicholas Ashe who helped me to my feet.

'You need to learn how to do something useful, mate. Can you juggle?'

'No,' I said calmly. 'I do not juggle. I don't ride a unicycle, I don't swallow swords, and I don't balance crockery on a stick.

I'm an actor, not a member of a travelling freak show.'

I said this more to soothe my own feelings than to educate Ashe. He greeted my words with a derisive little snort and walked away, but not before tossing the word 'fairy' in my direction. I took a step after him, and became aware that the slightest movement of my head to the left or right caused an excruciating bolt of pain to run through my body. I stood, rigid, and gingerly experimented, now oblivious to the movement of soldiers about me. My neck couldn't possibly be broken. I was fairly certain that a broken neck would be rather more discommoding than whatever damage I'd sustained.

'Don't worry about it,' said someone behind me. I would have turned my head to acknowledge the speaker's words, but I was obliged to slowly turn my whole body. To my astonishment, the speaker, his hands on his hips, and a broad smile on his face, was Archie Warmington.

'I thought you were rather good, Will. Really. I could see exactly what you were trying to do.'

He lit one of his aromatic kreteks and offered one to me. I declined by shaking my head, and very nearly passed out in the process.

'I think the fellow who hit you first was drunk on a bit of NT champagne.'

'Champagne?' The possibility that champagne might be available at Roper Bar was so singular that it momentarily drove out any curiosity I had felt about Archie's presence.

'Not real champagne, of course,' he said, in that beautifully groomed accent of his. 'The sad and desperate stir a teaspoon of Salvital into a glass of methylated spirits, and knock it back while it's still fizzing. It does awful things to people; makes them deaf to poetry, apparently.'

'What are you doing here, Archie?'

He expelled a cloud of clove-scented smoke into the air.

'People who know these things think I'll be more useful here than at Ingleburn.'

He put his arm around my shoulder and propelled me towards the cookhouse.

'You need a cup of tea.'

'I'm just about ready to try the methylated spirits.'

'Oh, come on, Will. I'm sure that's not the worst reaction you've ever had.' He paused, and considered the unfortunate and logical extension of his observation.

'I'm terribly sorry, Will. That wasn't quite what I'd intended to say.'

'I must reluctantly admit, Archie, that the glories of Shakespeare's verse have proved to be damp squibs beside the explosive appeal of a man in a dress.'

'Ah,' he said, 'Brian,' and he looked at me with great sympathy. 'Brian, of course, has the rare gift of glamour. The rest of us are merely lumbered with varying degrees of ability.'

Not belonging to any specific platoon, Brian, Glen, and I drifted about the camp at Roper Bar and found a spot to call our own. Neither Brian nor Glen mentioned the incident that had effectively immobilised my neck, but they did express sympathy for the obvious pain I was in. I read their silence on the matter not as discretion, but as the impious acceptance that violence against my person was the proper, acceptable, and inevitable consequence of my performing. Fortunately, the pressing issue of a murderer amongst us occupied my mind so fully that all else seemed trivial, and I didn't press for further comment.

As always with Glen, wherever a group of men gathered he

saw an opportunity to relieve them of any money or valuables they might be carrying. He went off in the direction of the cookhouse, wearing only a pair of ragged shorts and carrying a pack of cards. A Nackeroo with only a watch to wager would be asking somebody else for the time before Glen was through with him.

'Archie being here is a surprise,' I said to Brian.

'I thought he might turn up. He hinted at it back at Ingleburn.'

'He didn't mention anything to me.'

Brian looked at me in a way that came perilously close to condescension.

'Well, why would he?'

'Why would he mention anything to you?'

'Why wouldn't he?'

This conversation was doomed to plunge us back into pointless childhood bickering.

'Fine,' I said. 'Obviously, learning how to walk in heels encourages confidences.'

'That's not all it encourages,' he said, and laughed. He narrowed his eyes at me, daring me to satisfy the curiosity he knew he'd piqued. I'm always reluctant to play into other people's hands in this way. I can't bear to offer them their smug, little victories so easily. Which isn't to say that Brian wasn't right on the money about my curiosity. Only it wasn't just curiosity, exactly. It was more like astonishment, disbelief and, it grieves me to say, a small stab of distaste, which a psychiatrist would no doubt have diagnosed as deeply resisted jealousy. It wasn't. I mention it only to dismiss it.

'Ashe is our man,' I said firmly, signalling that whatever the nature of the relationship between Archie Warmington and my brother, it was of no further interest to me. 'There is not a single appealing quality about Ashe.'

'Didn't you warn me just the other day not to let prejudice blind one to the facts?'

'His repellent personality is a fact. He's so careless about disguising his personal ugliness that he's exposed himself as capable of any outrage. His complete lack of remorse for anything he says or does is chilling.'

'I'm willing to go along with you up to a point, but I think we're going to need stronger evidence than his indifference to your acting before we can present him to Army Intelligence.'

'He's killed four people, Brian. This isn't about a bad review.'

I didn't storm off, but I left with pointed vigour, and headed for the latrines. These were a short walk into the scrub. Situated amongst saplings, they offered no privacy of any kind. Half-a-dozen bisected oil drums sat over a narrow pit of some depth—at least twelve feet, I calculated. The smell wasn't as bad as I'd expected—the pit had been recently set alight, and the pungency of burnt oil suppressed more offensive odours. I understood why some men called them 'flaming furies.' There were two Nackeroos perched on drums when I arrived, airily blasé about their grunting, straining evacuations. They were chatting amiably, and said 'Gedday' when I joined them. Not wishing to appear sheepish or coy, I dropped my trousers and sat beside them.

'You're that actor bloke,' one of them said. Obliged by my neck injury to stare ahead, I said, 'Yes,' and smiled warmly. The smile, of course, went unseen, and I was conscious that my rigid, forward-facing posture might be misconstrued as pomposity or rudeness. Before I could explain that my inability to turn towards them was the result of pain, not snobbery, one of them said, 'Well, fuck you. You were shithouse anyway.'

They both stood up and, with one or two further words of criticism, they left. I think it was the injustice of it, but the words of these two young men—words that might never have been uttered had I been able to look at them—cut me more deeply than a bad review in the London *Times* might have done. I prayed that no one else would come along. Within seconds, two more Nackeroos arrived.

'I can't look at you,' I said, pre-empting any trouble. 'I'm not being rude. I've hurt my neck.'

'What makes you think we'd want you to look at us, your majesty,' one of them said, and they both laughed until their laughter and flatulence merged into a hideous symphony. I couldn't wait for this day to be over.

I slept quite well that night. The meal we ate was comparatively acceptable, and the rain held off until almost dawn, even though thunder rolled and clapped intermittently. It wasn't long after breakfast that the news that a Nackeroo had shot himself passed through Roper Bar with the speed and efficiency of an urgent telegraph message.

'Who? Who was it?' everyone was asking, and people started naming this person or that, as though they might be likely candidates—a telling reflection on the number of highly strung men in the camp.

Archie Warmington found us and, indicating that we were to ask no questions, led Brian, Glen, and me to a place on the far side of the latrines. Fulton and Rufus Farrell were there before us. I wasn't immediately sure who the figure slumped at the base of the thin tree was. His head was thrown back, and his features were distorted by the shattering passage of the bullet that had ripped through the roof of his mouth and exited through the crown of his head, taking much of his skull with it.

'It's Ashe,' Fulton said. 'Must've gone troppo. Didn't seem the type, though.'

'They never do,' Archie said. He crouched in front of Ashe's body and stared at it.

'Did anybody hear anything last night?' he asked.

'I doubt it,' Glen said. 'This is a long way from camp, and there was lots of thunder.'

Archie nodded.

'Still, we should ask around.'

No one disputed Archie's assumption of authority on this matter. His age, his manner, and his rank meant that we all deferred to him as a matter of course.

'You were the last group to have anything to do with Ashe,' he said. 'Does this death surprise any of you?'

Rufus cleared his throat. 'If you'd asked me yesterday if I thought Nick Ashe would ever top himself, I'd have said no. But look at him. He's still got the gun in his hand, so now I think, yeah, why not?'

It was only then that I noticed the pistol, and noted as well that the left-handed Ashe was clutching it in his right hand. I held fire, knowing full well that the person who'd shot Nicholas Ashe was either my brother Fulton or Rufus Farrell. I stole a glance at each of them. Both had shaved off their beards, and their youthfulness suddenly struck me as the ideal blind for ruthlessness. It now seemed so obvious. The real world here was reflecting the great tradition of murderers in fiction in which the least likely is almost always the most likely. The only difficulty was in determining which of the two was the least likely. They each had a claim on that position.

Archie made a quick assessment in favour of suicide. There

was certainly no evidence that Ashe's body had been dragged from elsewhere to its final position, although the heavy early-morning rain would have washed out any marks. The gun was cold, suggesting it had been used some hours previously and, as far as I could tell, the body was free of insect infestation, due no doubt to the rain.

'His family needn't know the truth,' Archie said. 'The news will be bad enough without adding to it. They'll be told he was hit during a strafing run by a Zero. It's better for them to hate the Japs than to hate us for letting this happen.'

I was shocked by Archie's matter-of-fact dismissal of the truth as an inconvenient threat to the morale of Ashe's family. He noticed.

'This bothers you, Will?'

'I think that the truth should be told. Yes.'

He nodded.

'But we don't know what happened here. We don't know the truth of this.'

'We know he wasn't strafed by a Zero,' I said evenly.

'He's dead. I want to find the kindest lie. If I tell his parents that he committed suicide, or even that he might have committed suicide, I'm passing on an uncertain assumption, which is a species of lie. Whatever I say, whatever approach I take, leads to the one indisputable fact I do know—that Nicholas Ashe is dead. Knowing exactly how he died is of no use to his family. If they believe he died being a soldier, then they've been lied to, yes, but they've also been given a gift.'

This was pure sophistry, but I could see that those around me had swallowed it whole. Archie Warmington dropped a notch or two in my estimation.

That Ashe had taken his own life had been accepted by everyone at Roper Bar by lunchtime. In the closed world of the Nackeroos, it had also been accepted that this fact should remain at Roper Bar.

Ashe's death had put something of a dampener on the camp, and Glen, with uncharacteristic sensitivity, decided to postpone any further dexterous swindling. This meant that I couldn't get Brian alone to discuss how we should proceed, and I could see that he was as anxious to discuss it as I was. I caught his eye when Glen insisted that they practise an illusion which he'd felt hadn't gone as smoothly as he'd liked during their last performance. They wandered into the scrub, and I sat making a desultory attempt to stitch together my increasingly ragged army-issue shirt.

'Poor Cinders,' Archie said, and sat beside me. He lit a kretek. 'This is beautiful country, don't you think?'

'There are a lot of creatures that live in it that rather take the shine off it.'

'Are you talking about insects, or me, or both?'

I put down my needle and thread.

'I wasn't talking about you, Archie. I didn't like Nicholas Ashe, and I'm sure the family that produced him is as unpleasant as its progeny, but they do have a right to the truth, even if the truth is that we don't know for sure whether he took his own life or not.'

'It's the "or not" that's a bit of a worry, isn't it?'

I suddenly wondered whether Archie had been briefed by Army Intelligence, despite our having been told that Brian and I were the only two privy to the situation up there. If he was with Intelligence I'd let him show his hand before revealing mine. I'd look unreliable if I shared sensitive knowledge before being cleared to do so. It was essential that I proceed on the assumption that Archie was precisely who he seemed to be — a senior officer, albeit a rather odd one, in the North Australia Observer Unit. Nothing more and nothing less.

'Yes,' I said. 'The "or not" is awkward because murder seems an extraordinary thing, even in the middle of a war.'

'He was well-liked, I believe.'

'Not by the Aborigines.'

'And not by you.'

'I wasn't suggesting that he was killed by one of the Aborigines.'

'And I wasn't suggesting that he was killed by you. I'm actually pretty sure it was suicide, and I think we should leave it at that.'

'Fine,' I lied. 'I've got no argument with that.'

There was silence between us for a few moments. When he next spoke, Archie's voice was almost wistful.

'I wish I had my paints here. I'd like to get these colours on paper.'

'You paint?'

'I try. Watercolour. I picked it up in Bali. I was there in the thirties, at a place called Ubud.'

'I can't say I've ever heard of it.'

'It's just a place, but a beautiful place. There was an artist there who was a friend of mine. Walter Spies. He taught me how to paint.'

'Are you any good?'

He shook his head and stood up to leave.

'No. No good at all. An amateur, and not a gifted one.'

'What were you doing in a place like Bali?'

'Another time, Will. I actually came here to pass on a set of orders to you, Brian, and Glen. I'm afraid it's a rather awful assignment.'

'I'm learning all about degrees of awfulness.'

'This will take you into a sphere of awfulness you couldn't have imagined. You're being sent to a place called Gulnare Bluff. You'll only be there for a few days. The blokes who are there already have been in place for a couple of weeks, and that's about as much as anyone can stand. The relief platoon will pick you and them up on Monday.'

I was secretly glad to be getting away from Roper Bar for a while. It would allow the embarrassment of the assault on me to recede.

'Rufus Farrell is going with you. He's replacing a bloke out there who's sick as a dog and has to be evacuated. You get along with Rufus all right, don't you?'

'Of course. He's a decent fellow.'

The neutrality of my answer was a response to the unexpectedness of the question—or was I reading something into it that wasn't there?

'When do we leave for this ... what was it called?'

'Gulnare Bluff. In about two hours.'

'More walking, I suppose. Endless, endless walking.'

'The first bit is a boat trip, but you have to walk in and— I won't lie to you—it won't be easy. You'll need to be down at the dock at fourteen hundred hours.'

He was about to leave, but I raised my hand to stop him. I stood up carefully.

'Why are we being sent there?'

'Lieutenant Jenkinson is concerned that the men who are out there are getting jumpy. It's boredom mainly, but the interminable waiting and watching can shred a man's nerves. A bit of entertainment might be just the tonic they need.'

'I don't think they see Shakespeare as a tonic, unless it's the cod-liver-oil variety.'

'Break them in slowly. Do some fluff, and throw in a snippet at the end. They'll sit still if they know it's only for a minute or so.'

'I've never really equated Shakespeare with administering a needle to the arse. Just clench the buttocks and it'll all be over before you know it.'

Archie took a final, deep drag on his kretek, and dropped the butt into the mud at his feet.

'Just friendly advice, Will. This time you won't have to compete with Brian. He won't be wearing that dress at Gulnare Bluff, believe me.'

He touched his finger to his right eyebrow in farewell, and headed towards the converted police station. I hadn't got Archie Warmington's measure. Not by a long shot.

Chapter Eight

GULNARE BLUFF

THE BOAT THAT WAS TO TAKE US at least part of the way to Gulnare Bluff was called *The Hurricane*, a 35-foot fishing vessel that looked like it had weathered several hurricanes in the course of its life. Brian, Glen, Rufus Farrell, and I came aboard and were confronted by several boxes of supplies—I knew this meant that we'd be carrying them some distance over land. I tested the weight of one and found it alarmingly heavy. There were already several men on board, including an Aboriginal fellow with the ludicrous name of Mordecai—further evidence, if any were needed, of the wretched and deadly touch of the missionary.

We sailed down the Roper River for more than eighty miles until it widened into the estuary that spilled into Limmen Bight. Keeping as close as possible to the dense mangroves that grew along its edge, we chugged around the coast until we reached the Phelp River. Here we turned in and tied up at a jetty that earned the name only because it was a structure that jutted some way into the river. The trip took four hours, and although I tried to engage Rufus Farrell in conversation, he seemed unusually reticent. If he hadn't assumed the position of prime suspect I would have said that Nicholas Ashe's death had affected him badly. When I asked him outright how he felt about it, he set his mouth firmly and said, 'I don't want to talk about Nick's death.'

During the trip I jotted down as many lines as I could remember from various bits of poetry, good and bad, that I'd accumulated over the years, including, God help me, almost all the verses of the dreadful 'The Tay Bridge Disaster' by William McGonagall, Scotland's most embarrassing literary gift to the world. It was a cruel irony, but having been appalled to discover just a few months before that it was thought to be high art by a member of my acting troupe in Maryborough, and having privately judged that member to be brainless, I was now reduced to trotting it out for the edification and entertainment of culturally starved troops. If there wasn't already something in the Geneva Convention about reciting McGonagall to a captive audience, perhaps there ought to have been.

There were three soldiers on the jetty, and each of them was dressed in the now familiar mosquito hat and gloves. It was clear that one of the men was ill. He was sitting with his head between his knees while his companions stood on either side of him. We put on our protective clothing and off-loaded the supplies. The ailing Nackeroo was helped aboard, and both his helpers returned to the jetty. Introductions were made, but they were pointless as no one was recognisable beneath his clothing.

'The blokes out there'll be bloody glad to see you,' one of these fellows said. 'Anything to break the monotony.'

Although this was an assessment of our potential that skated close to damning with faint praise, we acknowledged it graciously.

'So where is this Bluff?' I asked.

'That's it over there, mate.' He pointed into the distance to a dark shape rising on the horizon, barely visible in the gathering gloaming. 'And between here and there, there's nothing but mud.'

I'd walked through a lot of mud since arriving in the Northern Territory, but nothing like this. We sank into it up to our knees with every step we took, and the unwieldy ration box on my shoulder, coupled with an inability to move my neck, made me think that I simply didn't have the physical stamina to reach the Bluff. The foul stink that was released with each footfall weakened both my resolve and my endurance further.

'If any of you blokes is thinking about quitting, forget it,' said the Nackeroo who'd done all the talking so far. Clearly, he was speaking from experience. '*The Hurricane*'s already left, so you can either stay here for the night or find the energy to keep going. If you want my personal opinion, you'll be equally comfortable whatever you decide.'

His companion gave a little chortle of approval at his mate's witticism, and we plodded on. There was no possibility of considering the implications of Nicholas Ashe's death. Detection and deduction require a clear head. They are not easily managed in a world of stench, exhaustion, pain, and despair. I was glad of the mosquito hat, and not just because it protected my face. It also hid from view an astonishing swelling of tears. These began first as gentle weeping, and escalated into sobs which shook me from head to foot. I'd never experienced anything like it, and I felt as well a terrifying dread of what might lie beyond, of what might happen when the sobbing stopped. Was this a nervous breakdown? I was rescued by the words, 'We're here.'

This turned out to be only partly true. 'Here' was certainly solid ground, but the observation post was one hundred and forty feet up the Bluff. This part of the walk seemed initially to be a breeze, as our feet weren't sucked into the earth, but the incline soon became almost as deadly as the mud.

When we finally arrived at the place where the Nackeroos were camped, the air was thick with smoke. There was no wind, so the smoke hung, suspended, providing merciful respite from mosquitoes that were the size of hornets. Having moved a considerable distance beyond the end of my tether, I took in nothing around me, and slipped into my cheesecloth cocoon, indifferent even to the possibility that Rufus Farrell might try to kill me during the night. Eternal sleep began to feel like an attractive option. However, temporal sleep, despite my state of collapse, proved more elusive. I actually prayed for rain, just to silence the incessant and nerve-destroying whine of the super-mosquitoes. I was constrained, too, to sleeping on my back—any attempt to adjust my repose being met with a sharp and painful reminder that the walk across the mudflats had done nothing for my neck.

Dawn broke with a clap of thunder and a downpour. I was miserable. The only aspect of my life that was going even remotely well was the ulcer on my leg. Remarkably, it had almost healed, leaving an unsightly but small depression on my calf. Whether it had responded to Isaiah's recommended therapy, or whether my generally robust constitution had done the trick, I can't say. All in all, though, I didn't think I'd be taking Isaiah's advice back to Mother as a remedy for her corns.

The rain eased and then stopped altogether. There were six men stationed at Gulnare Bluff, and as soon as I got up and began moving around I could see the advantage of the location. It was a kind of hell, but it offered clear views of Limmen Bight, the estuary, and a good way up the Roper River. If this was where the Japanese intended to land, they wouldn't do it unnoticed. It was pointed out to me that Gulnare Bluff wouldn't go unnoticed by the Japanese, either. They would assume it was manned and would subject it to heavy bombardment. The awful fact of the matter was that a posting to the Bluff was potentially a death sentence—a grim truth that played on the nerves as savagely as the sandflies and mosquitoes. The men at Gulnare Bluff scanned the horizon with fierce concentration twenty-four hours a day. It was a strange and debilitating exercise.

Over breakfast that morning, we met three of the Nackeroos. Each lifted his veil briefly and grinned. The two who had brought us across the mudflats were on top of the Bluff, at the signals station, so we had yet to see their faces.

'Good to see ya,' one of them said. 'Ya gunna have a bit of trouble singin' and dancin' up here, I reckon.'

It was obvious that we were going to have a lot of trouble doing anything at all. I couldn't see how Glen could manage his illusions with the impediment of his mosquito gloves; and yet taking them off, even for a short time, was inadvisable. When it was explained that the entertainment planned for them was in the way of magic tricks and recitation, one of them said, 'No worries. We'll get a good cloud of smoke going for you.'

Smoke was the Nackeroos' best friend; if we were to survive at Gulnare Bluff, we'd have to learn how to live with it and in it. Even going to the toilet meant gathering a bundle of green leaves, and generating enough smoke to make it bearable.

'You don't want a sandfly bite on your knob,' one of them said.

After breakfast, we were taken to the top of the Bluff where the signallers sat in a ditch, sheltered from the sun and rain by a tin roof. It was referred to as a 'hut'. Inside, two men sat with the FS6 radio in a pall of smoke rising from smouldering vegetation in tins. I ducked in for a moment, but the temperature was killing. It was decided that at lunchtime Rufus Farrell, who'd already seen our act, would take over the signalling, and for a brief period only one Nackeroo would maintain the watch while the remaining four Nackeroos had their morale lifted, or merely interfered with, as the late Nicholas Ashe would no doubt have described it. At least with Rufus in the sig hut, no one would be in immediate danger of being murdered.

Glen, Brian, and I discussed what we might do. It was decided that Glen would do a few simple sleights of hand, but nothing that required Brian's assistance. Brian would revisit the Geebung Polo Club, having made such a success of it with the lepers.

'And what will you do?' Glen asked, unable to completely expunge the snideness from his tone. I had no choice but to hand him a small victory.

'I thought I might do 'The Tay Bridge Disaster'. It might get a few laughs.'

'It's not Shakespeare, is it?'

'It's McGonagall,' Brian said. 'Are you sure, Will?'

'Shakespeare is too much for their simple minds, so perhaps his polar opposite will be more acceptable.'

Glen's tricks went over well, as they always did, and Brian's rendition of the Paterson poem was greeted with enthusiastic applause from the audience of four. When my turn came, I removed my mosquito hat and, adopting a thick and entirely convincing Scottish accent, introduced myself as Mr William McGonagall, the greatest poet to emerge from the industrial squalor of Dundee.

'It is my melancholy duty,' I began with mock gravity, 'to commemorate in verse the terrible night that the Tay Bridge fell doon.'

As the poem progressed, its absurdities tumbled one upon the other until almost every verse provoked a decent laugh. When I rang out the final couplet:

For the stronger we our houses build,
The less chance we have of being killed

I experienced the most pleasing sensation, hearing cries of, 'More! More!'

I had no more McGonagall in my repertoire — a situation I intended to address as soon as we returned to Melbourne — and although I was sorely tempted to sneak in something more worthy while they were still well-disposed towards me, I took my bows and handed back to Glen, who asked for more smoke, and sat amongst the four, performing card tricks. Brian and I took the opportunity to move some distance away where we could discuss the pressing matter of our now seriously diminished list of suspects. Before we began, Brian said that he'd never heard the McGonagall performed before — he'd only read it — and that he thought I did it extremely well. I thanked him, and complimented him in return on his mastery of the 'Geebung Polo Club'. There was an exchange of fraternal warmth between us, and I might have asked him about Archie, but I suspected it would spoil the moment, so I said instead that we had to face the grim reality of having only two people at our disposal who might be guilty of multiple murder — and one of those people was our brother.

'I've been thinking about it,' Brian said, 'and I've got no doubt at all that Nicholas Ashe was murdered — his gun was in the wrong hand, for a start.'

'Yes,' I said hurriedly, not wanting Brian to think he was alone in noticing this. 'I saw that straight away.'

'I don't think we can rule out the possibility that the man who killed Battell and the man who killed Ashe were different people,' Brian said.

'Even if he was an accomplice, he was an accomplice of either Rufus or Fulton.'

Brian thought about that for a minute.

'Yes, there is that. It's possible, though — I agree it's unlikely, but it's possible — that the deaths aren't related in any way. What if one of the blackfellas killed Ashe?'

I shook my head.

'Unlikely.'

'Based on what? If I were a blackfella I wouldn't mind having a go at someone like Ashe.'

'We're getting distracted. We know three blokes were killed before we arrived. Army Intelligence put us where they knew the next deaths were likely to occur — and they did occur. There's no need to consider any possibility other than the one we were sent to investigate. I agree that either Rufus or Fulton might have an accomplice, but that doesn't let them off the hook. One of them killed Battell. That much we can be sure of, because there were no accomplices at the West Alligator camp. Of course, Fulton may in fact be Rufus' accomplice, or vice versa.'

Brian made no reply. I'm sure he was wrestling with the terrible possibility that Fulton was not the harmless and decent companion of his childhood, but a dangerous and violent psychopath.

'He's only a half-brother, Brian.'

He lifted the netting around his face so that I could see his furious expression.

'That doesn't make him half a brother, and I don't think Mother considers him to be half a son.'

'All right, all right. Point taken. I was only trying to say that there might be elements of his personality that flow from an unknown source.'

Brian spluttered his disdain.

'Flow from an unknown source? What's that supposed to mean?'

'What do we know about Peter Gilbert's background? Who knows what's lurking there?'

'And what can you tell me about *our* father's background, and what's lurking there? Not much, I'll wager. I certainly couldn't. I don't even know if he had any siblings, and I certainly never met his parents. I assume he had some. They were our grandparents, and we never met them. Don't you think that's odd?'

'Odd is not the same as psychopathic.'

'Now you're being ridiculous. You think Fulton has inherited a tendency to kill people from someone in his father's family?'

I recognised the absurdity of it as soon as it was uttered.

'I'm just trying every angle, Brian. What we have to do is set a trap, with one of us as the bait.'

'That would be you,' Brian said rather too quickly. 'After all, you're the one who saw the person kill Andrew Battell, and you were seen. There's a motivation for disposing of you right there. He'd have no reason to kill me.'

Brian's reasoning made hideous sense.

'Fine. I'm willing to be the bait. I wasn't attempting to manoeuvre you into it.'

'I didn't say you were. I was just pointing out the obvious advantage of putting your life in danger, rather than mine. As it were.'

'Our problem, of course, is that we don't know the reasons behind any of these deaths. We need to know something about the previous three, and find the thread that binds them.'

We agreed on the importance of this, but were uncertain how to achieve it. We knew that all three earlier deaths had been of Nackeroos from A Company, and we assumed that they'd taken place at Roper Bar, or in a platoon to which either Fulton or Rufus was attached. I thought that it shouldn't, on the face of it, be too difficult to ask a few questions that would elicit useful responses. We had to be careful, of course, not to arouse suspicions about our investigative role.

'Archie Warmington must know something about these deaths,' I said. 'Even if he was in Ingleburn when they happened, he would have been told blokes had died, but not necessarily that they'd been murdered.'

'True. I'm sure most people up here just put each of them down to illness or accident, but not murder. Army Intelligence suspects murder, though, which means that they must have someone up here feeding them information.'

'So why do they need us?'

'Because whoever it is isn't in a position to find out the identity of the killer. Do you think Archie is Army Intelligence?'

'You'd be better placed to know about Archie than I would, Brian.'

He didn't bite, but simply repeated his question.

'There's certainly more to Archie than meets the eye,' I said. 'If he's not Intelligence, he's more than a humble Nackeroo. When we get back to Roper Bar, I think you should ask him a few questions—in a quiet moment.'

With his veil down, I couldn't determine his reaction. All he said was, 'If Archie is Army Intelligence, he already knows about us. If he's not, he's too smart not to work out that something is up if I start questioning him.'

'I wasn't talking about an interrogation—just an innocent question dropped into a conversation at an appropriate time.'

He shrugged, which I took to mean that he agreed.

In the afternoon we gave the Nackeroos some relief from watching, and took their place. After only half-an-hour I'd had enough. My arms ached from lifting the binoculars, and my head pounded from the glare and concentration. How did these men do this for hour upon gruesome hour? In the dry season, we were told, the mozzies and sandflies weren't quite so bad, but thirst could drive a man mad. There was no water on Gulnare Bluff—it had to be brought across those stinking mudflats, and the ration was inhuman. At least in the Wet it could be collected daily. We wouldn't have been sent across to entertain them in the Dry. There wouldn't have been sufficient water to support such a luxury.

A squall blew in at about three o'clock, and visibility became poor. This didn't provide any respite from watching. I squinted into the sheets of rain, suddenly terrified that the Japanese might take this opportunity to launch an assault. I almost convinced myself that I could see something, and was about to call out, but when I looked again it was gone.

Rufus Farrell had been in the sig hut since lunchtime. When a Nackeroo came to relieve me I clambered into the ditch beside him. The smoke was suffocatingly thick, but at least it was possible to remove the stifling hat and netting. He was neither sending nor receiving when I joined him, and he seemed grateful for the company.

'Give me the Alligator River any day,' he said. 'This place is a serious shithole.'

I laughed companionably, eager to reassure him that he had nothing to fear from me.

'I'm sorry that I asked you about Ashe's death earlier, Rufus. That was thoughtless of me.'

'Don't worry about it. I was just a bit shocked by it, that's all — the suicide thing. I can't imagine ever wanting to do that.'

'How old was Ashe?'

'Nick? He was about my age, I reckon. Twenty-two. Why?'

'It's just too young to die, that's all, let alone like that.'

Rufus scratched at the stubble on his cheek, and shot me a sideways glance.

'I don't reckon he killed himself,' he said. 'I reckon someone shot him and tried to make it look like suicide.'

He waited to see what effect these words would have on me. I watched his face carefully.

'What makes you say that?' I asked calmly. He met my gaze, then shrugged and looked away.

'Dunno.'

I leaned towards him and whispered, 'I think you're right, Rufus. I think someone murdered Nicholas Ashe. I know someone murdered Nicholas Ashe.'

He nodded but was wary, almost afraid.

'His gun was in the wrong hand,' I said. 'That was a careless mistake.'

Rufus began to cough. Had I just pointed out an error he wasn't aware he'd made?

'We should tell someone,' he said.

'I wouldn't do that, Rufus. They'll think it was you.'

A look of genuine fear crossed his face.

'Why would they think it was me?'

'Because I'd have to tell them that I think it was you.'

He looked stricken. Before he had a chance to reply, I put my hat back on and said through the netting, 'I know Andrew Battell was murdered, too. I know that for a fact.'

I climbed out of the sig hut, absolutely confident that Rufus Farrell was a shaken man. If he was innocent he'd do nothing beyond resenting my implications and hating me for them; if he was guilty I was in no doubt that, within a very short space of time, perhaps even in the next few hours, he'd try to kill me.

The meal that night was a particularly disgusting mix of Devon and rice. Devon was, ostensibly, pressed meat. It was greasy and rank, and my mouth felt furred and violated for hours afterwards. Bully beef was prime rump by comparison. Rufus Farrell ate with us, along with two other Nackeroos. The obliterating nature of our clothes meant that I never formed any clear idea of the identities of the men on Gulnare Bluff. It was like living in a bizarre harem where we were all obliged to conform to the wearing of strange hijab. Rufus was seated on my left, but if any of the other three changed places I wouldn't have been able to tell them apart unless they spoke. It was almost as if one of Glen's small illusions — which pod conceals the pea — had manifested itself in human form.

'Got any stories?' one of them asked.

In a moment of pure inspiration I said, 'I've got a story. It's about a murder.'

I felt, rather than saw, Brian turn towards me, and I fancy that I felt Rufus Farrell flinch.

'Go on then,' he said.

'It happened in Denmark a long, long time ago.'

I sensed Brian relax, and I told the story of *Hamlet*. They were quiet and they listened, and no one tried to hit me — something I now took as the measure of the success of a performance. I hope I don't sound too smug if I say that I retold the plot with considerable effect, lingering particularly over Hamlet's ploy to expose Claudius as the killer of Hamlet's father. I used the words of the text sparingly but tellingly, and by the play's end, when all the corpses had piled up, I'd managed to achieve a tiny part of my dream — to bring Shakespeare to a place where he'd never been brought before. It wasn't exactly the exciting production I might have hoped for, but it was a start. The only hint that the concentration of one of the Nackeroos might have wandered was his query as to whether or not any of this had made it into the papers.

We sat for a little while after the conclusion of the story and made small talk. The squall that had blown in earlier had hung about, dousing us intermittently with showers. Now it settled into steady rain that grew progressively heavier until conversation became impossible below the level of shouted remarks into another's ear. There was no point trying to sleep under sopping cheesecloth, so we sat with our backs against trees, imagining that the sparse leaf-cover offered some protection from the rain. At least we were able to remove the hats, and we stripped off our clothes as well. It was a blessed relief to feel cool and momentarily clean.

When the rain eased, and then stopped altogether, we put our saturated clothes back on and crawled into the cover of the cheesecloth. I'd become familiar with, and almost indifferent to, the rank smell of mould. I'd also become inured to sleeping in wet clothes, although I had no intention of sleeping that night.

I expected Rufus Farrell to make a move, and he wasn't going to catch me off-guard. Brian, whose sleeping kit was only a few feet from mine, was also on watch, having been briefed by me about my encounter with Farrell in the sig hut.

It seems extraordinary, given that my life may well have been in danger, that one moment I was reflecting on the possibility of changing my public performances from pure Shakespeare to enacting tales from Shakespeare, and the next I was so soundly asleep that the gunshot, when it came, initially formed part of an elaborate dream, the details of which I don't remember.

It was the second shot that woke me. In a panic that didn't run entirely out of control on account of the sharp pain in my neck, I crawled out from under the cheesecloth into the mud. I could see Brian flailing under his, and gave silent thanks that my injury made flailing impossible. It was raining slightly, but the wind was strong, and the general noise of trees and shrubs being whipped by it exacerbated the fear that was running riot through my body. Brian was soon beside me, along with Glen. The darkness was so complete that I couldn't see beyond a few feet. If Rufus Farrell was standing a short distance away with a gun pointed at me, I wouldn't have known; and I was too unnerved to make the logical assumption that if I couldn't see him, he couldn't see me either. We instinctively stayed close to the ground and remained silent. A word was as good as a flare in revealing where we were. Somewhere off to the right, where the Nackeroos slept, there was a panicked cry. At first it was a yowl of terror, and then it coalesced into words.

'They're here! They're here! The fucking Japs!'

Another shot was fired, and another cry went up. I felt my guts turn to water. So this was it? We'd been surprised in our sleep. The Nackeroos on watch must have been killed already, otherwise they would have put up some resistance, and there would have been more gunfire to alert us. Had they had their throats slit by an advance party? Still we didn't move. I could hear Brian panting. In the darkness there was the sound of running feet and a voice called, 'Hold him down! Hold him down!' An incoherent roar came from someone's mouth, followed by a gunshot and a yelp of pain. It was Glen who first surmised what was happening, and he leapt to his feet and disappeared in the direction of the commotion. Whimpering reached us, and the low murmur of several people talking. Glen returned quickly.

'The bloke named Baxter's gone troppo.'

We'd been introduced to this man, but I'd only seen his face briefly, once. He was the silent one who'd come with us across the mudflats.

'He thought he saw a Jap in the camp. The silly bastard's gone and shot himself in the foot.'

We crossed to where Baxter lay on the ground, writhing in agony. Rufus Farrell was there, and two of the Nackeroos. One must have remained on watch, and the other in the sig hut.

'He's been edgy for days now,' said one of them. 'We should've had him taken out.'

'He could've killed me,' Rufus said. 'That first shot missed me by a bee's dick.'

'So it was you he saw moving around,' I said. 'What were you doing?'

I knew what he'd been doing. He'd been heading for my bed—probably knife in hand, or maybe he'd intended to strangle me, just as he'd strangled Battell.

'I was going to the dunny,' Farrell said.

Baxter moaned. I knelt beside him and told him that he was all right, that he'd hurt his foot, but that he wasn't badly injured. This didn't seem to calm him down. Whatever light there was gathered in the wild whites of his eyes, and he glared at me as if I were an object of immense horror.

'Jap cunt!' he shrieked, and spat at me. It took all of us to restrain him after that. He jerked and pushed and convulsed until exhaustion and loss of blood calmed him. By then, dawn was slowly turning the darkness into a pellucid grey.

'Is there any morphine?' I asked.

'Yes, mate,' one of them said sarcastically, 'and the nurses' quarters are just through the scrub there.'

I didn't take this personally. We were all shaken by what had just happened. I reminded myself that I was the oldest person there by a long way, and I had an obligation to assert some authority over this mess. No one else seemed capable of doing anything practical.

'We need to see how much damage he's done, and we need to stop the bleeding. There must be a first-aid kit here.'

In the growing light I saw that no one was wearing his hat, and for the first time I got a decent look at these Nackeroos. The sarcastic young man, who nodded when I mentioned the first-aid kit, looked about twelve years old, although he must have been at least twenty-one. His straw-coloured hair was plastered to his skull, and needed cutting. Manhood was creeping into his brown eyes before appearing anywhere else on his face.

'Get it!' I said fiercely, and he obeyed without demur. The other Nackeroo was probably the same age as the boy soldier, but he'd matured more rapidly. His cheeks and chin were dark with stubble.

'Put your knees on his shoulders and, Glen, I'd be obliged if you sat on his chest. Brian, grab his good leg. I'm going to take his boot off.'

The blood drained from Glen's face, and I thought he was going to faint.

'Don't you dare faint,' I said. 'I need you to hold him down.'

He straddled Baxter and sat with his back to me.

'No. The other way. I want you to lean forward and press down on his thighs. When I take his boot off he's not going to like it.'

'I'm not going to like it, either.'

'Close your eyes and try not to be distracted by his screams. His legs need to be held still.'

Baxter's boot wasn't going to come off easily. As soon as I'd undone the laces, it became apparent that the army had issued him with a size that was too small for his feet; he must have suffered awful blisters while his feet gradually stretched the leather to accommodate them. My first attempt to remove the boot resulted in a violent and not unreasonable reaction to the agony it caused. I suspected that the bones at the top of the foot had been broken. There was nothing for it but to plough on, and to pay no heed to Baxter's appalling cries of pain.

I wrestled and worked the boot away from his shattered foot. When it finally came, Baxter's cries intensified as if the leather had somehow been containing the worst of the injury. His sock, crusted with mud and blood, had almost become one with his flesh. He mustn't have changed his socks since his posting at Gulnare Bluff had begun. As I peeled the wool away, I still couldn't see how much damage had been done. I needed water. The young Nackeroo had by this time returned with the first-aid kit, and I sent him away to fetch a can of clean water. I had no idea what I was doing or even what needed doing. The only thing I could think to do was wash the wound, sprinkle disinfectant powder into it, if there was any, and bind it with a bandage.

When the water arrived I sponged the foot as gently as I could, trying not to press down around the point of the bullet's entry. It looked a mess. I thought it might have been a nice clean hole. Whatever ammunition he'd used had blasted an ugly entry wound and an even uglier exit wound. A sprinkle of powder and a length of bandage weren't going to do much for Baxter. It was better than nothing, though, so I opened the battered first-aid tin, hoping to find something I might use. The only thing in it was a bandage that was black with mould, and the pointless barrel of a needle-less syringe. There wasn't even any Aspro. I looked at Brian.

'It's a pity that dress isn't here,' he said. 'We could've used strips of that.'

Baxter had quietened down, and he began to slip in and out of consciousness.

'Can I get up?' Glen asked. I noticed that his eyes were tightly shut, and I imagined that they been shut throughout Baxter's ordeal.

'We have to cover the wound,' I said. 'It's going to be tough enough stopping flies from blowing it without making it easy for them.'

'Maybe it'll keep raining,' Glen said weakly.

'Maybe he's got a clean pair of underpants in his kit,' said the older-looking Nackeroo.

'Did you see the state of his socks?' I replied. 'I really don't think this bloke's underpants should be anywhere near an open wound.'

Brian suggested we find a clean-ish piece of cheesecloth from his bedding and cut it up. He did so, and washed it, even though it was already sopping wet. At least it made us feel as if we were doing something vaguely related to antisepsis.

Baxter lay almost motionless, moaning in the most unearthly and disconcerting fashion. I was sympathetic, but I wanted desperately for him to shut up.

Rufus Farrell had made himself scarce. There was no reason

for him to remain with Baxter or with us, but I knew that he'd absented himself in order to avoid further questions about his movements—movements that had led to Baxter's dreadful injury and to the inadvertent saving of my life.

'Someone needs to sit with him,' I said, and addressed the young man who'd fetched the first-aid kit. 'What's your name?'

'Smith,' he said. 'John Smith.'

'Unusual name. You must get people asking you to spell it all the time. You sit with him, John, and talk to him. Keep reassuring him that he'll be all right, and keep the flies off his foot.'

Roper Bar had been radioed about Baxter, and the decision was made to change the personnel at Gulnare Bluff one day early. *The Hurricane* would arrive that afternoon, with five fresh Nackeroos. Rufus Farrell was to remain as the sixth. When they arrived we'd head back, somehow carrying Baxter with us. To this end we improvised a stretcher, using thin bush-timbers and the remains of his cheesecloth bed covering. It was strong enough to support his weight and, with a man on each of the four pole ends, we thought it wouldn't be too onerous transporting him across the sucking mud. It wasn't going to be easy, but we agreed we could manage it. There was, in any case, no choice.

Rufus Farrell took up his position in the sig hut while the others took turns to maintain the watch and gather their equipment ready for departure. Glen, for whom the whole Baxter incident had been surprisingly traumatic (despite his protestations, I was certain he was phobic about the sight of blood), volunteered to watch the horizon until the relief party arrived. Proximity to Baxter made him queasy. This allowed Brian and me the luxury of uninterrupted conversation.

'It's Farrell,' I announced. 'He took the bait, no doubt about it. If Baxter hadn't started shooting at him, I'd be a dead man.'

'I wasn't asleep, Will. I'd have stopped him. Were you asleep?'

'It isn't strictly relevant whether I was asleep or awake. The point is that Farrell was on his way to try to silence me.'

Brian must have sensed that I was in no mood to brook disagreement because he didn't offer an alternative explanation for Farrell's movements. Even so, just in case he was thinking of an alternative, I added firmly, 'The dunny story doesn't wash. Where were the smoking leaves he'd need? Nowhere.'

'That's true. I hadn't thought of that.'

'So now we have a bit of a problem. Farrell is going to stay here with five unsuspecting Nackeroos. He's already killed five. What's five more?'

'We have to warn them.'

I thought about that for a moment, and knew how ridiculous it would sound to make such an extraordinary accusation against a Nackeroo to members of his own unit—it would be dismissed out of hand. Otherwise, in the unlikely event that they believed us, I couldn't see them waiting for the law to take its course.

'However we feel about this,' I said, 'when you get right down to it, we don't actually have any evidence that would stand up in a court of law or a court martial. Our certainty counts for nothing. All we can do is try to convince someone with influence, like Archie Warmington, that Rufus Farrell needs to be arrested and investigated.'

'So we just leave him here?'

'I don't think he'll try anything. He knows now that I'm on to him.'

'Should we at least tell Glen?'

'Absolutely not—not till we're back at Roper Bar anyway. I don't want him going off half-cocked here and confronting Farrell. This has to be managed delicately. With Archie's help, we should be able to find out about the previous deaths and maybe collect some compelling evidence. Without it, we're sunk. All Farrell has to do is deny it.'

The essential truth of this struck me so forcefully that I felt a surge of something like despair. What kind of evidence could we gather?

'This isn't going to be easy,' I said. 'The trail of earlier deaths is well and truly cold, and Farrell's been clever. Unless someone saw him, I'm not sure how to nail him.'

'You saw him kill Andrew Battell.'

'I saw him after Battell was dead. I didn't actually see him strangle him, and I couldn't swear under oath that the figure was Farrell. Of course it was Farrell; we know that, but a barrister could tear my testimony to pieces in minutes.'

'It's a relief it's not Fulton, at any rate. I reckon we should bring him in on this. He might know something, and not know how important it is.'

Brian was right. The person most likely to provide good information about whatever ties there were between Ashe, Battell, and Farrell—and probably the other three—was Fulton. Now eliminated as a suspect, he'd been elevated to the status of a witness. He may well have noticed, or overheard, something that seemed obscure and meaningless until he reconsidered it in the light of these deaths. Any good private-inquiry agent will tell you that the solution to a crime is frequently to be found in an insignificant, easy-to-overlook detail.

'We'll get Archie and Fulton together as soon as we get back, but under no circumstances are we to let slip that we're working for Army Intelligence, even though it would probably help our credibility.'

'You needn't say it like that—like you think I'm going to give us away.'

I sighed ostentatiously.

'That's not what I meant, Brian. I wasn't having a go at you. I was thinking out loud more than anything. Christ, you're touchy sometimes.'

'Yeah, well, you have a way of bringing out the best in people.'

Any further discussion along these lines was mercifully terminated by the arrival of the men from Roper Bar. They entered the camp in the now familiar anonymity of their protective gear. Two of them had been there before. The other three weren't reticent about expressing their first impressions, and swore with a kind of fatigued gusto.

When everything was in order for our departure, Baxter was placed on the stretcher, and his four fellow Nackeroos took the first turn at carrying him out of the camp. The descent to the mudflats was hard going, and it took some ingenuity and enormous strength to prevent Baxter from being tipped onto the ground. He was silent and still, having retreated into an open-eyed stupor that might have been shock or madness. The temporary cessation of rain made the going a little easier, but it meant I was deputised to keep the flies away from his foot. The cheesecloth bandage was wet with blood, and ripe for fly-strike.

There was very little talking as we negotiated the decline, all our concentration being required to keep our footing and to keep Baxter as level as possible. When we finally reached the stinking mudflats it was almost a relief, and we stopped to rest a moment before beginning the horrible crossing. Brian and I took one end of a pole each, while two of the Nackeroos said they'd keep their places. Each sucking step, with the weight of the stretcher dragging us down, was agony for my arm and for my neck. I thought I could manage, but a searing spike of pain across my shoulders was followed by the sickening dizziness that I knew from experience to be the prelude to passing out. It happened so quickly that I didn't have time to warn the other bearers. I simply dropped my end of the pole and collapsed into the mud. I can't have been unconscious for more than a few seconds; when I came to, I saw that Baxter had been pitched into the mud, face first, and that the Nackeroos were scrabbling to free him and put him back on the stretcher.

'He's not dead, is he?' I heard John Smith say, and I assumed he was talking about me.

Brian was leaning over me, and in my half-waking state I felt him fumble through my shirt to check for a heartbeat. When I gurgled incoherently, he lifted my mosquito veil—an action I considered careless and thoughtless. My face was immediately attacked. I suppose this had the remedial effect of bringing me around quickly, and I struggled to my feet.

'You gave us a fright, mate,' one of the Nackeroos said. 'There was a young bloke, real young he was, who had a heart attack crossing these flats. I thought you might have been another one.'

'I'm sorry,' I said rather sheepishly.

Glen, ungraciously, I must say, took my place and we continued. Even without the burden of the stretcher, I found myself several times on the brink of collapse, and it took every last shred of willpower to keep going.

The Hurricane was waiting for us at the small jetty, and I couldn't have been happier if she were the Queen Mary.

Doubtless the trip back was perilous, being undertaken in darkness. The weather held, which was a mercy, and the captain seemed to know these waters well, so we lay on the deck unconcerned, grateful to be rid of the cumbersome hats and gloves. The going, however, was very slow, and because we hadn't left the jetty until quite late, it was dawn before we approached the landing place at Roper Bar.

'There seems to be a welcoming committee,' Brian said.

Archie Warmington was standing on the bank, flanked by two Nackeroos neatly dressed in their best World War One cast-offs. Each of them held a rifle.

We filed off *The Hurricane*, and Baxter was taken to get medical attention, although he wouldn't get proper treatment until he was evacuated to Katherine. Glen, Brian, and I approached Archie.

'What's all this?' Glen asked. 'It looks like you're expecting the bloody governor-general.'

Archie didn't smile. He turned to me and said, with measured gravity, 'Private William Power, I regret to inform you that you are being placed under arrest for the suspected murders of Corporal Andrew Battell and Private Nicholas Ashe.'

The two uniformed Nackeroos took an arm each. Too stunned to move or speak, I was only vaguely aware that my hands were being forced behind my back and handcuffed.

'I'm sorry, Will,' Archie said. 'I have to follow orders. I'm sure there's been some mistake, but we've received information that leaves us no option but to place you temporarily under guard until the matter is cleared up.'

Brian's mouth dropped open, and Glen stared at me in a way

that suggested he always knew there was something murderous about me. My mind cleared suddenly, and I said, 'Rufus Farrell. That's where your information came from, isn't it?'

'I'm not at liberty to say,' Archie replied.

I was led to an area of freshly cleared ground, fenced around with coils of barbed wire, which had thoughtfully been set up in the mottled shade of a few trees. My hands were released, and I was told to enter through a small opening. One of my guards came in with me and, to my dismay, attached a small length of chain to my ankle. He twisted the barbed wire shut as he left. He didn't say a word. This was to be my prison, at least for the moment.

I had to hand it to Rufus Farrell. He was smarter, or more cunning, than I'd given him credit for. In the distance, I saw Brian and Archie wander off together into the scrub.

Chapter Nine
FROM BAD TO WORSE

THE WEATHER DIDN'T CONTINUE FINE. It's not called the Wet for nothing, and this wet season, although still in its meteorological infancy, was muscling its way into the record books. There was no shelter in my little compound. There was some consolation, however, in seeing that the guard had no shelter either. I hobbled over to him.

'We're both prisoners,' I said.

He looked at me and raised his eyebrows.

'No,' he said, 'we're different.'

'We're not, you know.'

He laid his rifle on the ground and performed two energetic star jumps.

'I can do that,' he said. 'That's one difference.'

He picked up his rifle and turned his back, no doubt secretly pleased at this taunt.

I could see that there was very little movement in the camp, the rain confining most people to whatever covered spaces they could find. I wasn't cold, but wet, clinging clothes are never comfortable, and this exacerbated the outrage that was growing within me at being snookered in this way by Rufus Farrell. It would be the briefest of misunderstandings, but it would buy Farrell time, and who knew what that might mean? I felt most keenly the humiliation of standing in chains, in the pouring rain, on public display. Farrell must have radioed Roper Bar with the absurd information that he'd uncovered the truth about Battell's and Ashe's deaths; and whatever he'd said, it must have been sufficiently convincing to warrant my arrest—and he'd managed it in Morse. I had to give him full marks for his signalling ability.

I don't suppose I was chained and confined for more than an hour. Archie reappeared with two men in tow, this time dressed only in shorts.

'I see the formal part of these proceedings is over,' I said.

Archie indicated, after the rolling back of the barbed wire, that the chains around my ankles were to be removed.

'I'm sorry, Will. We had to go by the book.'

'And it took you a full hour to discover that Rufus Farrell was covering his own arse by lying to you.'

'If I were you, Will, I wouldn't say another word.'

I quelled the anger that might have led me to say something I might have regretted, and began to walk away from Archie and his companions. One of them placed his hand solidly on my chest.

'I think you've misunderstood something,' Archie said. 'You're still under arrest. We're taking you to be questioned. Tomorrow you're being transferred to Katherine for more detailed questioning.'

'This is too absurd!'

'Not another word, Will.'

I had no trepidation that this matter might go badly for me — how could it? — so I entered the former police station more curious than alarmed. As one section of it had been turned into a cookhouse, the unsavoury odours of military cuisine penetrated its corridors and the small office to which I was taken. A man, younger than I, and rather short, stood up from behind a desk. I knew he was taking his role as inquisitor seriously because he was wearing a shirt. It was filthy and sweat-stained, but it was undeniably a shirt. He saluted Archie, who returned the favour. Archie closed the door to the office, and the three of us stood in awkward silence.

'I'm Captain Dench. Major Warmington you know already, I believe.'

He motioned me to sit down.

'This is all irregular and difficult, and frankly I haven't got a clue how to deal with it, so I'm batting you to Katherine. They can sort it out.'

'May I say something?' I asked.

'I wouldn't,' said Archie. 'I'd keep my powder dry. I wouldn't be digging the hole you're in any deeper.'

I was tempted to draw attention to the inelegant mixed metaphors, but the look on Archie's face was so severe that it stopped me.

'No,' I said. 'No. This has gone far enough. Two men have

been murdered, and the man who murdered them is at Gulnare Bluff, probably dispatching a few more Nackeroos even as we speak. Now, I'm sorry if you find this irregular and difficult, because it's really very simple. Andrew Battell was strangled. I *saw* the man who did it. Nicholas Ashe did *not* shoot himself. He was left-handed. Rufus Farrell was on the point of killing *me* last night. Are you following me so far?'

Neither Archie nor Dench spoke.

'Brian can confirm all of this.'

'Who's Brian?'

'It really inspires confidence to know that you've come here so well prepared, Captain. Brian is my brother.'

Dench looked at Archie, who nodded. Archie's inexplicable silence aroused great agitation in me.

'Why don't you say something, Archie? You know this is ridiculous. You know it. What's going on here? What's this about?'

'It's about murder, Will. Or so you and Rufus Farrell say.'

'And Brian?'

'And Brian, of course, but I'd expect him to support his older brother. He's loyal — an admirable quality.'

'He has many attractive qualities, but of course you know that already.'

'He did warn me that you might turn ugly.'

Captain Dench had lost the thread, so he interrupted.

'We're not taking Private Farrell's word as gospel. The reason you're not leaving for Katherine until tomorrow is that he's being fetched from Gulnare Bluff now. No one's happy about it, I can tell you — *The Hurricane* has more important things to do than waste a day going back there. He'll be going with you to Katherine.'

'All right,' I said. 'That's a relief.'

'The situation is this, Will,' Archie said. 'Rufus Farrell says that you more or less told him outright that you'd killed the two men.'

I scoffed.

'He understood that he was next. He also pointed out that no one had died until you arrived. Not evidence, I grant you, but quite a coincidence.'

I almost let slip my knowledge of the earlier three deaths, and that would have revealed me as being other than an actor. But this knowledge would be my trump card, to be produced only if Farrell's testimony somehow placed me in danger.

'On the other hand, you say Rufus Farrell is the culprit—and Brian concurs—and although your evidence, as I understand it, seems highly circumstantial, it can't be ignored. Until a proper investigation is undertaken, it's pretty much your word against Farrell's. This matter will be dealt with by the military and not the police. The NAOU is a unit that must not be exposed to publicity at this vulnerable point in the war.'

'I have no objection to that. My own experience with the police, and their powers of deduction when it comes to murder, has been less than awe-inspiring.'

As soon as I'd said this, I wished I hadn't. Captain Dench pounced on it.

'You've been involved in murder investigations in the past?'

'Some,' I replied, and added this to the list of things I'd rather not have said. Dench's incredulity was epic.

'Some?'

'It's irrelevant. I'm not saying another thing.'

'I wish you'd taken my advice about that at the start,' Archie said.

'I do have just one question,' I said. 'Is Rufus Farrell under arrest?'

'Yes,' Archie said. 'You and he will be treated in precisely the same way. Arrest isn't quite the right word, though. You're both under guard, pending an outcome.'

'You used the word "arrest" down on the wharf.'

'Yes, it was lazy of me. I don't have the power to arrest anybody but, as there are no provosts here, we have to take the military law into our own hands from time to time.'

Captain Dench, who was observing me in a subtly different fashion since my slip about previous murder investigations, informed me that I was to be confined to that room until the jeep's departure the following morning.

'You won't have any visitors. The advice from Katherine is that you are to remain isolated, especially from your brother Brian and …', he checked a note in front of him, 'Corporal Glen Pyers. He's a magician, I believe.'

He said this with an unmistakable sneer. I felt obliged to defend Glen against the slur.

'He's a fine magician, as a matter of fact.'

'Nevertheless, unless he can walk through walls, you won't be seeing him. A guard will be posted outside the door, and if you need to go to the toilet he'll escort you. I can assure you, Private Power, that we won't be idle while you're cooling your heels here.'

I presumed he meant that some attempt was being made to gather evidence. I didn't like their chances of finding anything significant.

Archie spoke. 'I should warn you in advance, Will, that between here and Mataranka you won't be under armed guard. We can't spare the men and, like I say, we don't have any provosts here anyway.'

I indicated that the absence of a guard was perfectly understandable, and neither here nor there as far as I was concerned. Archie cleared his throat.

'The road between here and Mataranka isn't good, and you'll be bloody lucky to get through without getting bogged.'

I wasn't sure where this traffic report was headed.

'The thing is, Will, that you and Farrell will be shackled.' He paused. 'Together.'

My eyes opened wide in disbelief.

'You have to see it from our point of view,' Archie said quickly. 'At some point you're going to have to push the vehicle. If you were shackled individually, one of you might try to make a run for it, however awkward that might be. We don't want the driver to be worried about keeping an eye on you both. If you're locked together, you'll keep an eye on each other.'

'You're going to chain me to a murderer?'

Captain Dench very smartly said, 'Maybe we're chaining Private Farrell to a murderer.'

I offered him a withering look.

'If he kills me, I suppose you'll think it's an efficient solution to the case.'

Dench shrugged.

'It would certainly be strong evidence in favour of your innocence.'

Throughout this interview Captain Dench had been growing in confidence. He'd been uncomfortable at first, but now he was beginning to enjoy himself.

'When this war's over,' I said, 'you should think about being a policeman. They need smarmy, oily little bastards like you.'

'Funny you should say that,' he said airily. 'I wanted to be a copper before the war. I was told I was too short.'

He said it defiantly, daring me to make a remark that might justify a physical response from him. Archie intervened.

'I think that'll be all for the moment, Captain Dench.'

Dench obediently got to his feet, saluted, and left the room.

'He's a good man, Will. If it'd been anyone else he'd have put you on a charge for insubordination. Brian did say you had a special gift for making enemies.'

He said it lightly, and smiled, and was gone before I could reply.

My bedding had been brought to me, and I spent a comfortable night — possibly my most comfortable since leaving Ingleburn. It gave me petty pleasure to demand to be taken to the latrines well after midnight and, despite the ghastly prospect of being chained to Rufus Farrell for many, many hours, when I returned to the room I slept soundly, oblivious even to the buzzing of a few mosquitoes.

At daylight I was taken from my room and obliged to wait beside a jeep that had seen better days. If this crate made it to Mataranka it would be a miracle. If the engine even turned over, I thought, I might have to reassess my religious beliefs. My hands were cuffed in front of me by a Nackeroo who said nothing, and on whose neck sat a tick. I didn't draw his attention to it, which was mean of me, but my Good Samaritan urges were at a low ebb. I couldn't see the wharf from where I was standing, but I assumed *The Hurricane* had arrived and that Rufus Farrell would soon join me.

When I first caught sight of him, walking towards me between two formally attired Nackeroos, it struck me how young he was. As he came closer it was evident that he was nervous, as well he might have been, knowing that in a short time he could be facing a firing squad. I didn't know if successful court martials led to execution; but as I watched Farrell, I thought a traitor's death an appropriate end for him. A man, however young, who had killed other men had very little to offer the society that spawned him.

He looked tired and oddly vulnerable, so that when he was pushed close to me—he had to be pushed—I felt no fear of him. Our legs were chained, and a shackle attached that joined us at the ankle—my left and his right. His hands were cuffed in front of him, in an identical fashion to my own. By now a small crowd of curious gawkers had gathered. Neither Brian nor Glen was amongst them. I imagine they'd been instructed to stay well away.

Our driver arrived, and he'd been well chosen—he was tall, thick-set, and had the stern, humourless face of a preacher or an executioner. I knew that I would certainly be reluctant to annoy him, in case he tried to preach at me or kill me—a distinction without a difference. Getting into the open jeep was difficult, and required a level of cooperation that neither Farrell nor I was initially willing to exercise. We were helped by our driver, who simply shoved us into our seats, indifferent to the pain and discomfort this caused. I was more fortunate than Farrell. I saw that the metal clamp around his ankle was so forcefully dragged along his flesh that it made it bleed.

Once seated, we were unable to prevent our legs from touching, and it made me almost physically ill to realise that this was the touch of a killer. It was a small, forced intimacy that felt to me like rape. I looked straight ahead—not only because I still couldn't turn my head from side-to-side, but also because the thought of looking at Farrell was so abhorrent that I was certain I'd throw up the meagre and unpleasant breakfast I'd recently eaten.

Within a few minutes of leaving Roper Bar we were in the familiar wilderness of sparse forest, cut through by the rough and inadequate road we were on. The tyres of the jeep threw mud at us in spatters as it tossed and rocked its way through sodden potholes and over fallen branches. Even if I'd been tempted to say something to Farrell, the noise of the engine would have required me to shout, and I certainly had no intention of shouting remarks at him.

An hour into our journey we became bogged for the first time. The driver ordered us out and instructed us to push. Farrell was uncooperative, and it was difficult to maintain a sensible rhythm to our movements. He dragged his leg heavily, without waiting until I was ready, and the consequence was that the process was made more difficult than it needed to be. At first I thought it was deliberate, but I soon realised that his anxiety about being hobbled with the one man who knew the truth about him was leading him to make involuntary attempts to pull away from me — each of them frustrated by the chains that bound us. When we did manage to get behind the vehicle and push, it came free from its bog quite easily, and we continued the journey.

Over the next few hours we crossed several streams, and became bogged twice. It took us more than half an hour to free the vehicle on the second occasion. There'd been no conversation since leaving Roper Bar, apart from the instructions given by the driver.

We stopped for lunch near a slow-moving creek. The air was humid and oppressive, and my clothes, ragged and filthy, stuck to my body with sweat. Farrell and I wordlessly came to an agreement about walking, and made it to the edge of the water without incident. We washed our faces, and drank until the awful feeling of dehydration had been banished. Our driver stripped off his clothes and lay full length in the centre of the stream, allowing it to flow over and around him. This was a luxury denied to Farrell and me. The most we could achieve was filling our cupped hands with water and emptying the dripping contents over our heads and down the front of our shirts. I leaned far enough forward to put my head under water, but thought better of it at the last minute. With the driver several feet away, it could have provided Farrell with the tempting opportunity to drown me.

After we'd crossed the creek and driven for a few miles, the rain began to fall in earnest, and our progress was slowed as the jeep slid and skidded over the suddenly treacherous track. The rain intensified to the point where visibility was practically zero, and the track began to resemble a flooded creek bed. It was clear that there'd be no let-up for a very long time. This was a monsoonal downpour, not a brief shower.

To my consternation, the driver seemed determined to plough ahead, but it turned out that he was looking for a track off to the side. He must have been very familiar indeed with this route, because even in good weather I wouldn't have been able to distinguish one section from another. He, however, turned the jeep into what looked to me like a thick patch of scrub, beyond which was a rudimentary, badly deteriorated, and now liquid track. It fell away quite steeply into an unexpected depression. It wasn't quite a ravine, but the decline was sufficiently severe to ensure that the jeep's slide down into it was steady.

Our momentum was constant and not alarming. I certainly didn't feel in any danger — which is why, when the jeep's right front wheel struck a tree root, I was jolted out of something of a reverie. The jeep tipped perilously, came down heavily, and went into a gut-churning slide. The driver wrestled with the wheel to no avail and, before I knew exactly what had happened, Farrell and I were thrown clear in a tangle of painful, wrenching limbs. I don't think I lost consciousness, but perhaps I did, because I have no memory of hitting the ground. I recall uttering a small cry and then being aware that I was lying on top of Rufus Farrell in a dreadful parody of the missionary position, staring down into his surprised eyes.

As soon as he'd established that he was relatively uninjured, he began clawing at me and shoving me away simultaneously, a combination of movements that spoke volumes for the confused state of his mind. I rolled off him, and he tried to scrabble to his feet. This was extremely difficult to do so long as I remained lying down—the tugging of the shackle at my ankle was terrible.

'Wait!' I said. 'Give me a chance to stand up.'

He didn't offer any assistance, and it took a moment to adjust our positions so that we could both stand comfortably.

'Are you hurt?' I asked.

He seemed astonished that I was speaking to him. He leaned his torso away from me and said, 'I don't think so. Winded is all.'

I moved all my limbs gingerly and discovered that I, too, was unhurt.

There was no need to wonder what had happened. The jeep was upside down, and as there was no sign of the driver we knew that he was pinned underneath.

'What's his name?' I asked.

'No idea,' said Farrell, and he began calling, 'Driver! Driver! Are you all right, mate?'

There was no answer. We weren't able to see under any part of the jeep—it had sunk in mud up to its doors.

'He could be drowning under there,' I said.

We tried valiantly to tip the jeep over, but it wouldn't budge. Farrell suggested we look around for a fallen sapling. We found one. All hostilities between us were temporarily suspended, and we were able to move efficiently and use the sapling as a lever to raise the side of the jeep a few inches—high enough to see that the driver was indeed pinned underneath.

'All right,' Farrell said. 'One big effort, and this thing should roll onto its side.'

We heaved, and with very little resistance the jeep did as Farrell predicted. The driver was face down in the mud, and when we pulled him away it became obvious that he wasn't breathing. Farrell cleared the driver's nose and mouth, and attempted to resuscitate him. I thought it was hopeless. Farrell breathed into his mouth again and again, in a kind of desperation as if his own life depended on saving the life of this man. A religious person might have declared the sudden choking and spluttering that ensued a miracle.

However, when I looked down at the driver's lower body, the miracle of his survival was tempered somewhat by the nature of his injuries. Something was terribly wrong with the angle of his legs, and the top of his trousers had been torn away to reveal a bloody crush of bone and flesh where his right hip ought to have been. Having awoken him from death, Farrell had awoken him to a world of pain and, if he survived, condemned him to life in a chair. He didn't cry out, though, and seemed oblivious to the destruction of his legs. He looked vaguely at us and sank into unconsciousness.

'Well done,' I said, and meant it.

'Where are we?'

The thick rain meant that the only way to find out was to explore the immediate area on foot. There was nothing we could do to help the driver, apart from construct a clumsy lean-to of leaves and bark to keep the worst of the rain out of his face.

'He was coming down here for a reason,' I said. 'We should follow the track to the bottom.'

'Don't try anything,' Farrell said. 'I'll kill you if I think you're about to try anything.'

'I don't doubt it. You have plenty of experience.'

'I don't know what you're talking about. Just don't try anything.'

'Don't *you* try anything either, Farrell.'

We stared at each other, our faces streaming with water. Farrell's expression was a curious mixture of belligerence and nervousness. I manufactured a look of uncompromising steeliness, and it had the desired effect of making him drop his eyes. Being only a few inches apart, I could see small muscles jumping in his neck and jaw.

We walked the short distance to where the track levelled out, and found the remains of what would once have been an insubstantial hut, constructed on all sides of corrugated iron, hammered to a skeleton of bush timbers. One or two pieces of iron had fallen to the ground, but the roof was intact so that, although the weather moved freely through the structure, the ground inside, while soggy, had not suffered the inundation of the area around it.

'We can't carry him down here,' I said. 'His whole lower body's been crushed.'

'Well, we can't leave him up there.'

The pounding rain made thinking difficult.

'We can't do anything with these bloody handcuffs on!' I yelled, my frustration boiling over. 'He must be carrying a key.'

'It wouldn't be in one of his pockets. He'd have hidden it somewhere in the jeep, just in case either of us had any ideas about overpowering him.'

I calmed myself down.

'If we drag him by the shoulders, and hope he stays out to it, we probably won't do any more damage than has already been done.'

Farrell nodded, and we made our way back to the jeep.

The driver was heavy, and having to walk backwards, in unison, was tricky. Farrell slipped over once and took me with him. The driver's head thudded into the mud, which provided some cushion, I suppose. I slipped over next, and the consequences were repeated. When we eventually began moving successfully I tried not to think about what was happening to the driver's body as it bumped and twisted over the uneven ground. Mercifully, he remained unconscious.

When we'd laid him in the hut, Farrell said it was probably used by the Nackeroos as a supply cache, and that, somewhere nearby, cans of food and maybe medical supplies would be buried. It didn't take long to find them. Behind the hut, a less than artfully arranged bundle of thick sticks indicated that the cache was buried beneath.

'We need to be bloody careful,' Farrell said. 'Some bastards rig these with a grenade, just in case an Abo finds it and decides to help himself.'

'I'm not hungry,' I said.

'There might be morphine for the driver.' He began peeling the sticks away one by one.

'If one of these was wired to the grenade pin and we pulled it, we'd be history.'

'Do grenades work in the wet?'

'Are you serious?'

'No. Desperate.'

My whole body began to shake.

'For Christ's sake, keep still,' Farrell hissed. He leaned forward and removed another stick with his cuffed hands, and then another. The world swam before my eyes and, unable to do anything about it, I fell into a faint. The remaining sticks rose to meet me as I collapsed on top of them. I heard Farrell scream, and disappeared down the well.

I must only have been out for a matter of seconds because, when I groggily came to, Farrell was sitting down, his shackled leg pulled away from me, his face drained of all colour, and he was panting hysterically. He suddenly began to laugh.

'No grenade,' he said.

I wanted to be sick, but I'd suffered enough humiliation in front of Farrell for one day, so I suppressed the urge.

My fainting did nothing for my image as a hard man in Farrell's mind, and he grew in confidence before my eyes. Almost pushing me out of the way, he began digging with his hands. The earth came away easily in great, gloopy dollops, and a tin box was revealed about one foot down. We pulled it out and opened it. There were several unlabelled tins of food and a box of ammunition, but no medical supplies. We helped ourselves to a few tins, and roughly sloshed the mud back over the box. It was beginning to get dark, and the realisation that we'd be spending the night there, chained together, with a critically injured man for company, made me uneasy. If I fell asleep, Farrell could make his move. Of course, being attached to a dead man would be something of an inconvenience for him, but I was sure he'd simply find a way to hack off my foot and free himself from the burden of my corpse.

Inside the hut, the rain was amplified by the iron, and it swept in when the wind began to rise. The flimsily attached sheets rattled and clattered, and the ominous, wet slap of leaves outside announced that this was to be more than just another monsoonal dump. It had all the makings of a fierce storm. The driver groaned, which was unsettling, and his groans swelled into a horrifying aria of agony. We moved across to him and restrained him. The whites of his eyes showed in the last of the light, and in them I saw naked terror.

'It's all right, mate,' I said uselessly, somehow hoping that the word 'mate' would do instead of morphine. His mouth opened and closed, and he squeezed his eyes shut before releasing a roar so shocking and so loud that we were pushed back by it. He slumped into an open-eyed stupor, his breathing laboured but strong. God help him, I thought—he's not going to die.

We were both badly shaken by the driver's ordeal.

'We need to eat,' I said, as if this might restore some calm.

'And how do you suggest we open the tins?'

'This bloke must have a knife at least.'

When I said this I felt Farrell stiffen, as if the mention of a weapon offered an opportunity. It was too dark now to see whether or not the driver had a knife on his belt—I hadn't noticed one earlier.

'We need to check him,' I said.

This simple task was made complicated by the obvious uncertainty about what the person who found it first would do with it. We solved this by running our hands over the driver's body in the same place at the same time. It was both ludicrous and disgusting fumbling about in the blood and pulp of his midriff. There was no knife. We agreed to go outside, clean our hands, and search the jeep. Perhaps the key to the handcuffs might turn up, too. This was much more difficult than expected and, as the wind became more violent, it was also frightening. Having been caught in a cyclone in Maryborough I had no wish to revisit the experience.

A great, hot scribble of lightning ran across the sky, and in the surgical whiteness of its light I saw Farrell's stricken face. I'd seen that look before on other brontophobes. When the thunder crashed about us he jerked involuntarily and waved his cuffed hands in a circle as if he might conjure an axe or a club with which to defend himself against its force. More thunder exploded, and the sky became alive with great veins of lightning forming an almost continuous display. I'd never seen an electrical storm of this magnitude. In any other circumstances, it might have been magnificent; here, it reinforced our vulnerability, and filled me with dread.

We searched the jeep cursorily, both of us nervous about being out in the open. I was worried about being struck by lightning; Farrell, it seemed, was worried about dying of thunder. We hurried back to the hopelessly inadequate shelter of the hut. I failed to mention to Farrell that I'd discovered a knife, caught between the front seat and the side door of the jeep. It was mere chance that my hands had found it and not his, and in his distracted state he hadn't noticed that I'd managed to drop it down the front of my shirt. It was a sleight-of-hand of which Glen would have been proud. In one quick motion I feigned scratching an itch on my neck, and dropped it through my open collar. It slipped down and sat where the shirt was tucked into the trousers. Now at least I had something with which to defend myself, and I was prepared to go hungry rather than tell Farrell about it.

The constant washes of white light and chest-rattling peals of thunder conspired to drive Farrell and me into a corner of the hut. The rain blew in and the ground was saturated, but I think Farrell felt safe hunched at the place where two flimsy walls met. I sat with him, having no other choice, and I almost felt sorry for him. The storm had unmanned him. The Wet season must have been a nightmare for him. I wondered, indeed, if it had driven him mad, and that his crimes weren't symptoms of his insanity. He put his head between his knees, and his body was eloquent in speaking for the trauma he was undergoing.

The wind now howled, and in a burst of light I saw that the driver's mouth was open and that he was screaming; but his screams were lost in the general cacophony. We must have been sitting in our corner for half an hour when Farrell leaned into my ear and shouted, 'I need a piss!'

We stood up. I thought he'd do it where he stood, but he indicated that he wanted to do it outside. I was surprised, but grateful. We took just a few steps away from the hut, and were astonished by the force of the wind. Farrell fumbled at his flies and I looked away. A shriek of metal put my teeth on edge, and I turned back to Farrell to ask him to hurry up. Just then, an extended and brilliant wash of lightning exposed the horror of what had happened in an instant. Farrell's torso, his hands still holding his penis, swayed, stunned into remaining upright, despite his head having been cleanly sliced from his body by the guillotine of flying roof-iron. His trunk, teetering uncertainly, was peculiarly expressive of a profound surprise. It collapsed at my feet.

I closed my eyes against the unspeakable thing that had just happened—closed them against the gouts of blood that were pumping from Farrell's arteries. When I opened them I couldn't bring myself to look around for his head. The thought of it staring at me in a sudden flash of illumination was so disturbing that I resolutely kept my eyes straight ahead. It was only when I began to walk away that I realised I was still attached to Rufus Farrell.

This was a situation unique in my experience, so a solution didn't immediately present itself. I couldn't remain standing in this tempest, so I half-dragged, half-carried Farrell's decapitated corpse back into the hut with me. A gap in the roof showed where the guilty piece of metal had clung. Because I didn't know what else to do, I sat down in the corner—so numb that I didn't flinch as, one by one, the remaining sheets of iron were prised from the hut's frame by the wind's fingers, and thrown into the night.

For hour upon hour, the three of us sat or lay, exposed to the furious elements in the scrawny timbers of the hut picked clean of all protection by the hammering wind. I discovered that when the human mind is deluged with fear and despair, and yet survives, it enters into a dull acceptance that grotesque extremes are somehow not just normal but right and proper. Which is why I decided to use the knife I'd secreted to cut Farrells' foot off, above the point at which the shackle encircled it.

Having made the decision, I knew I had to do it immediately. If I waited I'd lose my nerve, and it was an action suited to the violence of the storm—it felt almost like it was part of it. It proved to be a difficult task. I rolled up his trouser leg and began sawing. The blade met the resistance of bone quickly, and no amount of sawing with the heavy but blunt knife was going to sever the foot. I eventually managed it with brutal chopping motions. When the final thread of tendon came away, a rush of bile pushed its way up from my gut to my mouth, and I began to sob. The violation was made no less obscene by the fact that this was the body of a murderer.

As if to perform some sort of penance, I crawled across to the driver. His eyes were open, staring at Farrell's corpse, but unseeing, I supposed. He'd stopped screaming, although his mouth was moving soundlessly. I put my ear to it to hear what he might be saying, but all I could pick up was the faint susurration of weakly expelled breath. He couldn't last much longer.

The wind dropped, the rain became a benign patter, and the lightning played across the sky silently. I can't now understand how I did it, but I slept until the dreadful whine of mosquitoes woke me to a dim dawn and to a rising brightness that would reveal the hideous reality of the night's work. I glimpsed Farrell's head, and scrambled to my feet, anxious to remove myself from it and from the shape that I knew to be the rest of him.

In daylight it was an easy walk to the upturned jeep, and when I reached it I was surprised to see an Aboriginal man standing by it. He was wearing shorts and carried no weapons, and the sight of me with my hands cuffed and with a chain trailing from one leg must have so alarmed him that he took off before we could exchange a single word.

For want of anything better to do, and to keep my mind off what lay behind me, I searched the jeep thoroughly, hoping to find a key to my manacles. I found nothing that was useful — no gun and no key. There was a roughly drawn map of what I recognised as the route in and out of Roper Bar, with side tracks along which caches of food, ammunition, and petrol had doubtless been stored. There was, however, no indication of which track was which, and no way of knowing which of the lines represented our current position. There was also a log book. I didn't linger, but returned quickly to where the driver lay.

I averted my eyes from Farrell, and tried to shoo away the flies that had settled amongst the ruins of the driver's legs. I could see that, if he wasn't soon to become more maggot than man, I'd have to build a smoking fire. There was no problem finding wet vegetation, but dry kindling was scarce, and I didn't have any matches. I checked the driver's pockets, and found in one of them an expensive-looking cigarette case — thin, gold, and beautifully tooled — that didn't fit the bulk and demeanour of the driver at all. It was the kind of object that I would have expected Archie Warmington to have about his person. I opened it to find half-a-dozen cigarettes and a dozen-or-so matches. There was also a striking-pad machined into the back of the case. An inscription in the lid read, 'To Clarence. Always. Always. Always. Always.' Despite Oscar Wilde's dictum that it is an ungentlemanly thing to read a private cigarette case, I found this strangely affecting.

Without kindling, I had no choice but to use the map and pages from the log book to create a fire that was all smoke and no flame. It was minimally effective, but when the last pages of the log book had caught there still wasn't a sustainable blaze. I would have to sit by Clarence and swat the flies away. First, though, I opened a can with the knife and ate its contents, which were foul strips of cabbage in a sour liquid that might once have been vinegar. I sat by Clarence and prayed for rain.

The rain didn't come but, a few hours later, with a grinding of gears and a complaining engine, a Ford V8 truck did. It stopped at the jeep, and two Nackeroos got out. I stood up and called to them. One of them was carrying a rifle, the other a pistol and, as they came towards me, both weapons were pointed at my chest. I was offended by the implication—although, on reflection I understood that the sight of a manacled, shackled man with a headless body nearby and a bloodied, wounded soldier at his feet was not, perhaps, encouraging.

The conversation that ensued was limited to a barked command that I step away from Clarence. A brief reconnoitre of the ghastly scene was so distressing for one of them that he was sick. The other one looked at me warily and with barely contained hatred, as if he held me personally responsible for the bloody mayhem. When his lips began quivering, and after he'd struck me sharply across the face, I realised that he did, in fact, hold me personally responsible. I was about to upbraid him when he stuck the barrel of his pistol in my mouth.

'If you say one word, just one, I'll blow your murdering, fucking brains out.'

I didn't doubt him, and made no move to challenge the hopelessly incorrect conclusion to which he'd jumped. He ordered me into the back of the truck, and when I'd clambered up into it he followed and tied my already restrained hands to a metal strut. It wasn't him I had to convince of my innocence, so I settled my nerves by breathing deeply and telling myself that everything would be fine as soon as the people in Katherine were presented with my testimony.

Considerable time elapsed before I saw the newly arrived Nackeroos again and, when I did, one of them—the one who'd been sick—appeared at the back of the truck with Clarence slung across his shoulders. The other jumped up into the truck and, as carefully and tenderly as he could, took Clarence and laid him down on the floor. Although moving Clarence would only have compounded his injuries, there was no other option. They placed him as far away from me as possible. When they collected Rufus Farrell's corpse they weren't quite so careful. They wrapped his head and foot in sacking, but had none to spare for his torso, which they deposited rather closer to me than I would have preferred. They did, however, treat his body with great respect. All their contempt they reserved for me.

The trip to Mataranka was torture for Clarence, who was bumped and jarred and jolted, first into a frenzy of screaming and then into blessed unconsciousness—blessed for both of us. I've never been able to hear the evidence of another person's pain without sinking into a white-knuckled, sweaty swoon. I thought everything would be better when we reached Katherine. It wasn't.

Chapter Ten

BROCKS CREEK

THE OFFICERS IN KATHERINE had been expecting a jeep carrying two prisoners, each of whom had declared the other the killer of two Nackeroos—the deaths of whom had not, prior to these mutual accusations, been counted as suspicious. They were certainly not expecting a truck, in the back of which was a distressed actor, the dismembered pieces of one Nackeroo, and the crushed remains of another. From the look of dismay on the face of the officer who peered in at us, I could tell that this was going to take some sorting out.

Clarence was dealt with first, of course. He was carried on a stretcher to whatever makeshift medical facilities were available — there, I hoped, to be pumped full of morphine. Rufus Farrell was removed next, and I certainly understood the disgust and horror on the faces of the men who took him away. No one said anything to me. I was left sitting in the back of the truck, subject to the stares of passing Nackeroos. They weren't kind or even curious stares. They were hateful and antagonistic, as if the word had been passed around that I was the killer of their comrades and, worse, that I'd mutilated one of them. I began to feel very afraid that rough justice might take precedence over the rule of law. I knew very little about military law but, as it was my only hope of release and exoneration, I had high hopes that it functioned rationally.

Eventually I was taken to a small tent inside a square of barbed wire. It contained a chair and a palliasse and nothing else. It was just high enough to stand up in, and it was intolerably hot. I did think that someone should have informed me about what was going on, as a matter of courtesy if not of law. Psychologically, it was unsettling to know nothing — which I suppose was their point. By the time someone arrived to talk to me I'd worked myself up into a mild panic, so that my demeanour must have appeared slightly maniacal.

The man who entered the tent was informally dressed. If he'd gone to any trouble at all it was to put some pants on, but nothing else.

'I'm Lieutenant Murnane,' he said, 'and I've drawn the short straw and been told to fill you in on what's happening.'

'Are you a lawyer?'

'No, mate. In civilian life I'm a tram conductor.'

'They've appointed a tram conductor as my defence?'

'I'm just here to tell you what's up, not to defend you. Some other poor bastard'll have to do that. Do you understand?'

My eyes must have had a wild, dissociated look in them.

'Of course I understand,' I snapped.

'OK. In a little while you'll be taken across to a tent and there'll be three officers there who'll ask you a whole lot of questions and decide whether or not to hold a DCM.'

'A what?'

'District Court Martial. In a minute some food will arrive, and by the time you're finished they'll be ready for you.'

The food tasted fine, and it was only afterwards that I realised that it had probably been spat in or despoiled in some other way. The tent where I was to be questioned was spacious and open on one side. The furnishings were ad hoc—a table, a few chairs, a crate, drums, and boxes. Lieutenant Murnane sat me in a chair facing the table, and left me. I was alone for only a few seconds. A guard was posted at the entrance to the tent. Three men who were neatly, formally dressed in the best of Nackeroo clobber came in and sat behind the table. After arranging some papers he'd brought with him, the man in the middle spoke first.

'You are Private William Power?'

I nodded.

'Please respond verbally.'

'Yes. I am Private William Power.'

We'd got off to a bad start. My tone was faintly sarcastic, which wasn't the effect I was after at all. Each of the three men exchanged a brief, telling glance.

'I'm Major Purefoy. The gentleman on my right is Major Hunt, and the gentleman on my left is Captain Collins. We want you to understand, Private Power, that this is neither a court nor a court martial. We're here to ask questions and to try to establish just what the hell is going on. It's informal, although notes will be taken. This is the first stage in what might turn out to be quite a lengthy process.'

'It doesn't sound very legal to me,' I said. Again, my state of mild panic invested my tone with an undesirable quality — this time, of churlishness.

'This is the NAOU, Private Power, not the Melbourne Club. We deal with things in our own way. But I assure you that it is perfectly legitimate.'

The man who said this was Major Hunt, who was sitting closest to the open side of the tent. Grey light from the thickly overcast sky fell across his face and accentuated the pitted legacy of acne.

'Think of this as a conversation rather than an interrogation,' said Major Purefoy.

'It already feels like a conversation with menaces,' I replied.

'All right, let's move past this pointless sparring and proceed. My understanding is that the deaths of two of our men, Corporal Andrew Battel and Private Nicholas Ashe, were at first assumed to be the result of dengue fever in the former case and suicide in the latter.'

He waited for an acknowledgement that this much was true.

'Yes.'

'While you were posted on Gulnare Bluff, according to information radioed to Roper Bar by Private Rufus Farrell, you led him to believe that you had in fact killed the two men and that you were waiting for an opportunity to kill him as well.'

I was so shocked to hear this calumny spoken out loud that all I could manage was a splutter.

'You'll have your chance in a minute, Private Power. Now, Private Farrell's account is very different from your own. According to the radio messages we've received, you claim that Private Farrell is the guilty person, and that you actually saw him strangle Corporal Battell at the platoon's West Alligator River camp.'

He paused again.

'Is that more or less the situation?'

'Yes.' I decided the details were better left until later.

'Roper Bar HQ decided that they were unable to settle the issue and decided to send the two of you here. Understandably, they're a little distracted by the imminent Japanese invasion, and don't have the resources to spare on a case like this—and frankly, Private Power, neither do we. Be that as it may, here we are.'

'The "we" doesn't include Private Rufus Farrell though, does it?' said Major Hunt. 'Private Rufus Farrell is conveniently dead.'

'I had nothing to do with Farrell's death,' I said between clenched teeth. My panic was rapidly metamorphosing into anger.

'Cut himself shaving, did he?' he sneered.

Major Purefoy put a hand on Hunt's arm.

'We'll get to the circumstances of Private Farrell's death later. Let's just establish Private Power's role in the earlier deaths first. Could you briefly outline for us what that role was?'

I needed to tread carefully here. I had a responsibility to Army Intelligence to keep secret their part in placing Brian and me in the NAOU. I was keenly aware of how territorial different sections of the military were, and I didn't want to create unnecessary tension between Intelligence and the Observer Unit. I began calmly.

'I am an actor, and my brother Brian, who is also now a performer, and a man named Glen Pyers, who is a magician, were sent here, via the Third Division Concert Party, as a troubadour unit, charged with bringing some entertainment to soldiers in remote, isolated areas.'

'And what do you do?

'I recite Shake … I recite and tell stories.'

'I believe there is a third brother.'

'Fulton, yes. We were sent initially to where his platoon was stationed on the West Alligator River.'

I sensed that the three investigators thought this a bit odd, as if the meeting of three brothers signified something sinister. I pre-empted them.

'There's nothing suspicious about the posting. The army, in its wisdom, saw it as merely a pleasant coincidence, and they certainly had no objection to the three of us making contact. They saw it as an opportunity to add something more to the morale-boosting intention of the whole exercise.'

'You think the army believed it would give everyone a warm glow to hear about the touching reunion of the three of you?'

Major Hunt just couldn't help himself.

'No,' I replied evenly. 'It was a happy coincidence, and that is all. And not that it's any of your business, or relevant, but the fact is that I don't get along particularly well with my youngest brother, so you can forget about warm glows.'

They each jotted something down.

'We arrived at the West Alligator River to find Fulton, Nicholas Ashe, Rufus Farrell, Andrew Battell, and two Aboriginal men. Battell was ill and quite weak. I can't say I detected any animosity amongst them — except Ashe's hatred of the Aborigines, which everyone else either tolerated or endorsed. They made no effort to challenge him, at any rate. We arrived on Thursday, and the platoon was ordered to break camp and return to Roper Bar on Friday. Very early Friday morning, just on dawn, I saw someone stand up from Battell's mosquito netting. At first I thought it was Battell, but whoever it was took the trouble to lift the mozzie veil and spit into Battell's bed.'

'And this was Rufus Farrell?'

'I know now that it was. At the time, his face was obscured by his hat.'

'And what did you do then?'

'I stayed in my own bed and slept.'

'You say you'd just witnessed a man being killed, and you went back to sleep.'

'No. It was only in retrospect that I knew Battell had been strangled at that time. I thought the figure was Battell himself.'

'And why would he spit in his own bed?'

'He was feverish. I thought he might be expressing his loathing for the cheesecloth. It is appallingly uncomfortable under it. I don't know. I had no reason to think that anyone other than Andrew Battell would be standing up from that bedding.'

More notes were taken.

'How did you discover that Corporal Battell had died?'

'It was Fulton who discovered that. We were ready to go, and Corporal Battell hadn't left his bed. They hadn't insisted that he help pack up because of the dengue fever. Fulton pulled back the cheesecloth and tried to wake him, but he was dead. It was immediately decided that he'd died of dengue. I thought there might be more to it than that, and said that we should check for other causes.'

'Why would you do that? It seems a strange thing to do.'

'Look, apart from acting, I'm also a private inquiry agent in civilian life, and I suppose I'm naturally suspicious. You don't need a higher degree in geometry to draw a line between an unidentified man spitting on a bed and the appearance of a corpse in that bed.'

I hoped that the revelation that I was a private detective would suffice to explain my insistence on an examination of Battell's body. I wasn't willing at this point to explain that the suspicions had been fuelled by prior knowledge of deaths in the NAOU. None of the three officers said anything, but they continued to scribble notes.

'It was still possible that Battell had died of a snakebite, or a scorpion sting, or something other than dengue. Fulton was unhappy about checking the body, but we did it anyway, and it took no time at all to see that he'd been strangled. There was bruising around the neck.'

'So you reported this to the others immediately?'

I could see where he was going with this.

'No, I didn't. I now knew that one of them had killed Battell, but which one? My investigative experience led me to hold fire, allow everyone to think that I'd found nothing unusual, and to wait and watch for the culprit to make a mistake.'

'But your brother ...' he checked his notes, '... your brother Brian knew.'

'Oh, yes. He saw the bruising.'

'Anyone else?'

'No. Glen didn't look at the body, and nobody else did either.'

'So Rufus Farrell could only have known that Corporal Battell had been strangled if he'd done it himself, or if you'd told him?'

'Precisely.'

'Precisely indeed. Did you tell him?'

I could have, and perhaps should have, lied at this point. I didn't.

'Yes, I told him. I told him that I knew that Corporal Battell had been murdered. I was laying a trap for him, knowing that if he knew that I was on to him, he'd try to silence me.'

'I see. Do you think radioing his fears to Roper Bar was an efficient means of silencing you?'

'He intended to kill me, but was stopped before he could do it.'

Captain Collins spoke for the first time. His voice was light, and his gaze was so direct and unwavering that it made me uncomfortable. I had the feeling he was looking for physical flaws in my face.

'You say you had no firm idea who the culprit was at West Alligator. How did you discover that Rufus Farrell was guilty?'

It was a simple question, and I thought my answer would be strong, but it came out sounding vague and unconvincing — even to me.

'I believed at first that Nicholas Ashe was the most likely culprit because he was violent.'

'Violent?'

'Well, rough.'

'You thought he was a murderer because you didn't care for his manners?'

'If you'd known him, you would have been unsurprised if he *had* been guilty. As it happened, his death ruled him out of contention. This meant, of course, that either Fulton or Rufus Farrell must have been responsible. Farrell mentioned that Ashe was holding his gun in his right hand — the wrong hand for it to have been suicide. I'd noticed this, too, but I suspected that Farrell hadn't been observant as I had, but that he'd known because he'd put it there, and realised afterwards that he'd made a mistake.'

Major Purefoy interrupted.

'Ashe and Farrell had been in the same platoon for quite some time. Wouldn't he have known that Ashe was left-handed? Isn't it far more likely that a newcomer might make such a mistake?'

'An unobservant newcomer, possibly. I'm not unobservant.'

There was a flurry of scratching pens.

'I hadn't ruled my brother Fulton out as a suspect. I'm not so sentimental as to suppose that the blood relationship was proof of innocence. But, by degrees, almost by instinct, I came to know that Rufus Farrell was the murderer, and I told him so, which is why he countered by accusing me.'

'To be frank, Private Power, it strikes all of us that there is something to be said for Private Farrell's observation that the deaths of these two men corresponds very neatly with your arrival.'

The x-ray gaze of Captain Collins caused me to break cover.

'That would make sense only if Corporal Battell and Private Ashe were the only two Nackeroos to have died recently in A Company.'

The effect of this statement was remarkable. I'd expected them to acknowledge that there had indeed been three previous casualties, and to demand to know how I could possibly be aware of them. Instead they looked puzzled, and Captain Collins said, 'Corporal Battell and Private Ashe are the first fatalities in any of the units of the NAOU. I can assure you that if three men had died in A Company, our company, we'd have heard about it'

I'd produced my ace too early. Their surprise seemed genuine, though. How was it possible that these deaths had filtered down to Army Intelligence in Melbourne, but been kept from NAOU Command? It wasn't possible. Something was radically amiss. None of them was interested in pursuing the claim of three prior deaths. They were far more interested in hurrying to the facts surrounding Rufus Farrell's macabre passing.

'Did you kill Private Farrell?'

I wasn't sure who asked the question, but I tried to arrange my features to convey indignation and astonishment. But before

I had a chance to respond, Major Hunt asked venomously, 'Did you hack off Private Farrell's foot?'

'He was attached to my leg. I had no choice.'

'I wonder if Private Farrell appreciated your dilemma.'

'He was dead.'

The statement fell leadenly into the space between me and the three officers.

'He was killed by a piece of flying iron. It was a freak accident.'

It is truly extraordinary how a statement of irrefutable fact can sound more absurd and unlikely than the most elaborate and ridiculous lie.

'I was only inches from him. The wind was terrifying. Suddenly a sheet of iron flew off the hut and sliced off his head. It could have been me, but it wasn't. It was Farrell.'

My voice was beginning to sound desperate.

'Afterwards I couldn't bear the idea of being shackled to a corpse.'

There was no sympathy in their eyes. Major Purefoy drummed his fingers absently on the table.

'Sergeant Preston will never walk again, but he'll probably live.'

I must have looked puzzled.

'He was your driver.'

'Clarence?'

'You were on first-name terms?'

'It was written in his cigarette case.'

They conferred.

'There was no cigarette case amongst Sergeant Preston's effects.'

'It's in my pocket. I needed it to strike a match.'

'You stole Sergeant Preston's cigarette case?'

'I *borrowed* it.'

More notes were taken.

'I mention Sergeant Preston because we heard his version of events just a few minutes ago. He was dopey with morphine, and I grant you that his memory may be muddled. He told us that the jeep overturned, and that you and Private Farrell freed him and carried him to the hut. At least, he assumes that that is what happened. Is that correct?'

'Yes.'

'He was unconscious for a good deal of the time and, as I said, he may be confused, but he was anxious to tell us that he saw you chopping away at Farrell's body. He's convinced you were severing his head. Would that be right?'

'No, it wouldn't. I was severing his foot, and I'm perfectly aware how grotesque that sounds. Farrell was already dead. The only person to suffer any ill effects from the amputation was me. Do you think I enjoyed doing it? It's the most repulsive and abhorrent thing I've ever had to do, and I'll have nightmares about it for the rest of my life. Short of cutting my own foot off, how was I going to separate myself from Farrell's body? I wasn't keen on being shackled to him when he was alive, so you can imagine how I felt about being shackled to him when he was dead.'

I'd worked up quite a head of steam by the end of this speech, but it produced little in the way of a reaction.

'There's just one more question, Private Power,' said Major Purefoy, but it was Major Hunt who actually asked the question.

'Why was Private Farrell's penis outside his trousers?'

There was sufficient innuendo in his tone to satisfy the most demanding Tivoli audience.

'You think I interfered with him post-mortem?'

This was too much, and I leapt to my feet. All three officers did the same, and they were upon me before I could take a single step towards them. I was shoved back into the chair, but not before being thumped in the stomach. It was a perfectly judged and placed blow. It took the wind out of me. One of them grabbed at my shirt and removed the cigarette case. The three of them now stood before me in an arc. I was bent double and could only see their shoes, all of which could have done with a clean.

'We're fighting a war, Private Power. We don't have the facilities to deal with someone like you, or a case like this. It may well be that you're an innocent man, although nothing you've said convinces us of that. However, the law has to take its course and we're not authorised to pass any judgement, so we're sending you to Brocks Creek. You'll be held there until a decision is made about what to do with you and how to prosecute the case. I can tell you this, though. No one in the NAOU is going to be happy about diverting time and resources into investigating your killing spree.'

The three pairs of feet turned and left the tent. I remained hunched over, still catching my breath. The guard who'd been outside approached me, placed his hand roughly on my upper arm, and dragged me upright. This was an unnecessarily crude action. I would have been perfectly willing to stand up without his assistance. It was just one more gratuitous attack on my dignity.

The interrogation had left me feeling dazed and disconsolate, and with a crushing sense that I'd been tried and convicted for a series of crimes that I'd been sent to investigate, not perpetrate. What kept me safe from surrendering to complete despair was the knowledge that, at some point, Army Intelligence would be obliged to intervene. Ultimately, I'd be rescued. Brian would, I knew, be working towards my release. He'd be in a quandary, though. At what point would he need to go against our unambiguous instructions that we weren't to reveal the purpose of our visit? As I sat in the tent in Katherine, I turned this question over in my mind.

Now that the murderer was dead, did it matter that Intelligence had chosen to infiltrate the NAOU? Who would take offence at this? Surely, the over-riding response of the Nackeroos should have been gratitude and relief that the killer amongst them had been dealt with discreetly and efficiently. Or were they so touchy about their independence that any outside interference would generate resentment, whatever the outcome? I didn't know enough about military thinking to know how the various Commands viewed Intelligence. Did they despise that organisation, or mistrust it?

With nothing to do but sit and wait, I brooded over the interrogation. It had been most unsatisfactory, and I couldn't help but suspect that it breached every rule of law, even military law, which was no doubt less precious about the rights of an accused. Still, there must be processes that have to be followed, I thought, and that informal, nasty, and prejudiced little chat couldn't possibly conform to them.

When I reviewed the way in which I'd answered their questions, I was painfully aware that I'd done myself no favours. I was particularly aggrieved by the final insinuation of some kind of bizarre sexual impropriety, and all because I hadn't thought to re-house Rufus Farrell's private parts. My mind kept snagging on this mean query. It unsnagged itself when I began to consider the implications of the extraordinary fact that three Nackeroos in A Company had died prior to the deaths of Battell and Ashe. It wasn't feasible that anyone in A Company, let alone the officers in charge, could be ignorant of the fact. What was the reasoning behind their flat refusal to acknowledge my statement, and the absence of any curiosity about how I might have come by information that was closely guarded? I couldn't fathom it.

I have a tendency—and it gives me no pleasure to admit this—to allow imagination to triumph over ratiocination. In the past this has led me into errors of judgement that have had unfortunate consequences, and which I have sincerely regretted. With a tremendous act of self-discipline, I decided to suppress any further consideration of the three unacknowledged deaths. I firmly believed that as soon as Intelligence in Melbourne got wind of the successful identification of the murderer, their intervention would be swift, and of necessity there would be no fanfare. I'd be released and returned to Melbourne, and it would be as if nothing of any note had taken place up there.

For the first time in many weeks I thought of Nigella Fowler. Sitting there in that hot tent, handcuffed, unable to turn my head, accused of murder and sexual deviancy, I felt far removed from my naïve expectation that the solving of this case would bring us together. I closed my eyes and attempted to form a picture of her. To my surprise and disappointment, I couldn't bring her sharply into focus—a failure I put down to stress rather than any falling off in my feelings for her. I was, however, rather shaken by this small failure, and I saw with sudden clarity that her behaviour towards me all those weeks ago, at the beginning of this enterprise, had lacked the decisiveness of a woman in love.

At the time, I'd thought she was being careful. Now—and perhaps it was the situation in which I found myself—I re-interpreted her behaviour as indifference, perhaps even hostility. Allowing little flares of indignation against Nigella to leap inside me was a distraction. I might have wished that my feelings towards her were more positive at this time — that they would have been a comfort — but my circumstances precluded generosity of spirit towards anyone. I determined not to allow my mind to wander in the direction of Nigella Fowler until the worst of this was over and I could consider my position with the cool detachment of unhurried reason.

I'd been told that I was to be sent to Brocks Creek, and I was pondering where and what that might be when two Nackeroos entered the tent and manhandled me outside. I was once again the object of curious and disdainful stares as I was marched across an open patch of ground and bundled into the back of a car. Brocks Creek must be close by, I thought, if this ancient vehicle was being trusted to take me there.

The car pulled up at the railway station, and I was handed over without ceremony to two provosts who escorted me into a crowded carriage at the front of a train. Needless to say, we attracted a great deal of attention but, to their credit, the military policemen didn't respond to any of the raucous calls for information about who I was and what I'd done. They didn't speak to me, either. They sat stonily, one on each side, bored and radiating disapproval. Perhaps they'd been briefed on my alleged crimes; perhaps not. It probably made no difference to them what atrocity I had or hadn't committed. Like all MPs, there was no room in their steely hearts for sympathy. They exuded the complacent arrogance that marks the difference between the capturer and the captured.

I tried to shut down all my senses. I closed my eyes and recited Shakespeare in my head. The train lurched out of the station and headed north.

The first stop was at Pine Creek, and it was short. Some soldiers got off; some more got on. The next was Brocks Creek — officially called the 13th Australian Detention

Barracks—and the only people who disembarked there were me and my provosts. Brocks Creek wasn't really a place at all—not a place in the sense that you'd put it on your list of places to visit. It was a military prison that had been built in the middle of nowhere—nowhere being somewhere between Pine Creek and Adelaide River. The provosts escorted me through a gate and into a small hut. Three determinedly grim-looking soldiers took me off the provosts' hands. They returned to the train, which departed soon after.

The process of dismantling my putative rebellious spirit began with a shouted instruction to step forward. My handcuffs were removed, as was the length of chain that was still attached to my foot. In the time-honoured tradition of prison induction, I was ordered to strip. If this was intended to humiliate me, they would have had to work a lot harder. As an actor used to quick changes I wasn't prey to blushing modesty, and I was indifferent to their gaze.

I was issued with an unappealing set of clothes that smelled of the previous wearer's body odour, and pushed into an adjoining room. There, a red-faced, purple-cheeked, and wiry man in his fifties stood before a blackboard on which was printed, in an incongruously elegant hand, a list of rules and regulations. I faced him; he looked me up and down and snorted dismissively, as if what he saw was a particularly unimpressive specimen of the Australian soldier. My stiff neck created the impression that I was standing rigidly to attention, so I was spared any gratuitous instructions on that front. He didn't introduce himself, so all I knew about him was that he was a major. He made no inquiries as to my name. Indeed, thus far no one had addressed me by name. I presumed they had my details, but were pursuing a policy of dehumanisation. I was as nameless to them as a bug, and they wanted me to know it.

The major picked up a thin piece of dowel and began striking the blackboard with it. He shouted each rule at me to the sharp tattoo of the striking dowel. Somewhere around rule number eighteen the rule-makers had run out of ideas and inserted, 'You will not sing! You will not whistle!' When the major read this rule, his voice rose in pitch and he delivered it with particular ferocity, as if singing and whistling posed a greater threat to security at the 13th Australian Detention Barracks than the whole of the Empire of Japan. It occurred to me later that the major had probably been apprised of the fact that I was an actor, and that this rule was more likely than any of the others to be breached by me. At the end of each rule it was stressed that the punishment for breaking it was solitary confinement. This didn't seem too excessive to me, but at that point I didn't yet know what solitary confinement at Brocks Creek entailed.

By the time the major completed his fire-and-brimstone reading he was breathing heavily. His face was slicked with perspiration, and the whites of his eyes had become red as sweat crawled into them. It was, I admit, a fearful sight. This was no well-modulated, well-calculated performance. This was mania unmediated by sanity. The man was mad, and the terrible effect of his diatribe was to infantilise me. There was nothing I could do to prevent this regression. I'd been in Brocks Creek for no more than half an hour, and they'd already turned me from an independent private investigator into a compliant, frightened child.

After the reading of the rules, the major began a rapid, almost incomprehensible explanation of the workings of Brocks Creek. There were three compounds, numbered one, two, and three. Detainees were first confined in compound one, where there were few privileges and where one was entitled to write and receive one letter per week. All correspondence would, of course, be closely censored. If a prisoner behaved he might work his way into compound two, and thence into the luxury that was compound three. Here, apparently, a prisoner could write as many letters as he wanted, and receive his full complement of mail—parcels excepted. Parcels generally contained comforts, and Brocks Creek was dedicated to the eradication of comfort.

Just as the major's final words were battering my ears, a sergeant who was as tall as he was broad stormed into the room and bawled at me an observation that set a new benchmark in stating the obvious.

'You … are … now … in … detention!'

He took a breath after each word so that he could fill his lungs and bellow them individually.

'Now! On the double!'

He opened a door to the outside and indicated that I was to pass through it. I did so, took two steps down to the ground, and was shaken when he screamed, 'Run!' in my ear. The instruction confused me, and I hesitated. Had some danger appeared from which I needed to flee?

'In here, you run! Prisoners do not walk! Ever! Run!'

In the moment before I began running towards the barracks that housed inmates of compound one, I took in the spectacle of several men jogging in different directions—as well as the very strange sight of a group of men pulling what looked like an oversized concrete rolling pin. I learned later that this was Brocks Creek's equivalent of the treadmill. The men were required to drag this monstrously heavy object across a parched square of earth—laughably called a parade ground.

'On the double!!!'

I ran, and for the rest of that day I ran to and fro. When night fell, I entered the barracks for the first time.

The barracks in which the prisoners slept was a stiflingly hot, iron structure, built around a crude concrete slab. Not very much care had been taken with planing it smooth, and it was pitted and spiky. This mightn't have mattered if all we were required to do was walk on it. Unfortunately, we were expected to sleep on it as well, with no buffer between us and it apart from a thin, worn blanket. The blanket was made of wool, but an object further from the sheep's back I couldn't imagine.

There was only one good thing to be said for the barracks, and that was that they were dry—a state that made them unusually attractive to scorpions and other vermin. It was the smell of them, though, that stays with me still. At one end was a tin can that served as the lavatory for the twenty-five men who were confined there; the stench of the disinfectant splashed into it, combined with the stench of its contents, made for a nasty effluvium.

There was no light, and talking was forbidden, so we whispered like schoolboys, anxiously aware that one of the bloody-minded guards might burst in at any time and impose a petty penalty for 'creating a disturbance.' That penalty was decided by whim—it might be as vile as emptying the dunny can from each of the three barracks (carried on the shoulder and taken at a run so that the contents slopped over the carrier)—or as mean-spirited as a few days in solitary confinement. Thankfully, I didn't experience the former. I was propelled into the latter within twenty-four hours of entering Brocks Creek.

Conversation became less dangerous when rain began to pound the iron roof and walls. Voices had to be raised, but experience had taught the longest-serving inmates that the guards had an aversion to getting wet, so the possibility of being harassed by them was minimised. I can't say that my companions in compound one were salubrious, interesting, or even the victims of some miscarriage of justice. I was the only one there who could rightfully make that claim. Their crimes, which they weren't reticent in detailing (it was almost as if they believed that crimes committed within the world of the military weren't as shameful as they might otherwise have been), ranged from gross insubordination, to being AWL, to theft. I could have trumped them all by telling them what I was accused of, but my instincts insisted that the way to survive this was to be invisible, so I mumbled a bland confession of having been AWL, with a bit of drunk and disorderly thrown in to improve credibility. I felt no camaraderie with the men in compound one. Indeed, I found myself taking the high moral ground, and silently condemning each of them for reprehensively failing to do their duty. By morning, after a sleepless and wretched night, I'd decided that they were a species of traitor.

My spirits were low and they weren't improved by breakfast, which was a revolting sludge of army biscuit soaked in hot water — an unimaginative meal that was repeated at lunch and dinner, and was invariable, day after day.

Prisoners were kept occupied with so-called work parades, and it was in the execution of the duties imposed on me that I ran foul of a guard. I confess that I approached the task assigned to me in the wrong spirit. I would have had no objection to doing real work, even if it had been tedious. Instead I was told to run to a corner of the compound where a guard stood holding a bucket. When I reached him, I saluted, as required — an action that sucked self-respect out of me more efficiently than any other. I recognised the guard as the kind of brute who frequented rough pubs, and who would have lived in civilian life off the proceeds of petty crime or handouts. He upended the bucket, spilling hundreds of dead scorpions onto the ground. Each of them had been meticulously cut in half.

'I want,' he said impassively, 'all these little bastards lined up in neat rows, and I want them all put back together again. Humpty dumpty.'

He leaned down, chose a tail and a head, and pushed them together.

'Like that, see?'

'Why?'

The question made him start, and his face became contorted as if something very hot had been shoved up his arse.

'Because I fucking say so!'

His voice was loud enough to turn heads on the opposite side of the compound. By now I was experiencing my own little rush of blood, and was determined to win back some of the sense of worth that I'd squandered in saluting this Neanderthal.

'This isn't work. It's meaningless. It's demeaning.'

The punch to my solar plexus ended the discussion. I was dragged by the scruff of the prison shirt to one of the three solitary-confinement huts. They were small, solidly built boxes of corrugated iron that stood side by side, prominently placed so as to remind inmates where transgression might lead. One of them was occupied, as evidenced by the banging and obscenities that issued from it. It seemed that the silence rule didn't apply to solitary, although it was probably a measure of the success of a stint in one of these boxes when the prisoner fell silent through exhaustion and acquiescence.

That I could be condemned to this punishment without paperwork or recourse to appeal was devastating proof that Brocks Creek was a world unto itself, housing prisoners-of-war — prisoners who'd waged war on their own country. They were despised, and the niceties of laws and conventions were not to be lavished on them. However, the fact that I was temporarily and unjustly amongst them didn't arouse in me any sense of fraternity. I was 'me'; they remained resolutely 'them'. For a fleeting moment, the prospect of solitary confinement, while it had been perfidiously imposed, seemed almost desirable. At least it would separate me from the others.

I was ordered to strip, and was shoved into the box. In the brief moment before the door was closed, I saw that the only thing to sit on was the dunny can in the corner. When the door was shut it was almost as if I'd been struck blind — not the faintest glimmer of light seeped through from outside. The cells had looked flimsy, but they'd been built with care and clearly adhered to strict specifications for deprivation. I stood stock still: like Milton, light denied; but, unlike Milton, in no mood to fondly ask if God exacted day-labour, despite the inconvenience of blindness. I tried desperately to quell the rising flood of claustrophobia. It was the foul smell from the dunny can that rescued me. Somehow its putrid odours created enough of a sense of space to alleviate my fear. I can't explain why this was the case, but the nausea it induced became more physically urgent than the psychological compulsion of the phobia.

The box wasn't quite soundproof, and I could hear the muffled howling of the other prisoner. I wondered how long it would take for this experience to reduce a man to that state, and how long it would take beyond that to reduce him to silence.

I crouched onto my haunches and, having felt about on the ground for any impediment to doing so, I sat cross-legged. All right, I thought, if I keep very still, and breathe evenly, I might enter a trance-like state. But the smell made breathing evenly impossible. I became aware that I was sweating, that I was unbearably hot, and that I was thirsty. I became aware, too, of small, scuttling sounds nearby.

What was in here with me? Scorpions? Rats? Cockroaches? Centipedes? Achieving anything approaching a trance was now so remote as to be unattainable. In my fevered imagination, scorpions, cockroaches, and centipedes assumed the size of rodents. The thought of them moving about me — sentient, malicious, and patiently poised to exploit whatever it was my body offered that could satisfy their primitive needs — was unbearable. If there'd been arthropods in the Garden of Eden, that would explain why Adam and Eve got out of there.

I think I'd been confined for perhaps half an hour when the first urge to scream a demand for release hit me. I quashed it. My thirst was building, and to the panic about scorpion attack I added a panic about the effects of dehydration on the body and the mind. My breathing became rapid and, as if to further disrupt any potential for inward calm, I began to wonder how air could get in if light couldn't. This was when it occurred to me that I might suffocate in there, and it was also when the insanity of claustrophobia drove me to throw myself against the immovable and unforgiving wall. I didn't cry out, but threw myself again and again at the great, black solidity of the wall, uttering small, pathetic, whimpering sounds. For the first time in my life, a claustrophobic attack ran its full course uninterrupted by rescue. At some point I collapsed, my shoulders bleeding, my energy exhausted. I'd always thought that I'd die if I was ever in a situation where the phobia ran unchecked. But I hadn't died and, in a bizarre reversal of my emotional state, I felt a tiny surge of something like pleasure.

My thirst was raging, and now it was this more than any other discomfort that made solitary confinement intolerable. I tried not to focus on it by running through the poetry that was in my head, and this was quite effective until I inadvertently embarked upon 'The Rime of the Ancient Mariner', a poem I'd proudly committed to memory in school (a feat that had won me a copy of the complete plays of William Shakespeare, and changed the direction of my life). I stumbled at

> Water, water everywhere
> And all the boards did shrink;
> Water, water, everywhere
> Nor any drop to drink,

but ploughed on. Just three stanzas later, I truly regretted having begun:

> And every tongue, through utter drought,
> Was withered at the root;
> We could not speak, no more than if
> We had been choked with soot.'

Having entered fully into the world of the mariner, I felt my thirst more keenly than ever.

Looking back on it, it now seems odd that I should have found even the first few hours of solitary confinement so difficult to endure. I'd been thirsty, hot, and uncomfortable for most of my time in the Northern Territory. In solitary, however, the darkness exaggerated all sensation. Apart from the potent relief of having survived an attack of claustrophobia, all other sensations were horrible, horrible, most horrible.

My thirst was mercifully alleviated when the door was thrown open and a billy of water passed to me. I didn't see who'd delivered it, because the sudden light did such violence to my eyes that I had to turn away and protect them with the crook of my arm. The water tasted of tea and rust, but it was ambrosia to me. Although I ought to have sipped it and made it last, I drank it almost at a single gulp. There must have been a pint of it, so it successfully slaked my thirst. It gave me the luxury of being able to consider the stinging pain that was radiating from each of my shoulders, and I touched them gently. My fingers encountered sticky blood, and my thoughts immediately turned to infection. I knew that that way madness lay, so I attempted to gather the events of the last few weeks into a coherent shape.

It had been seven weeks since Brian and I had met with James and Nigella Fowler at Victoria Barracks in Melbourne. Intelligence would, no doubt, be pleased that the person who'd murdered five Nackeroos was now himself dead. Any hope of discovering his motive was lost, unless analysis of his relationship with each of the dead men turned up something. I suspected that Army Intelligence would have more pressing matters to worry about than the psychology of a lunatic. They'd be happy enough to consign the incident to history — a history that would never be written. It was an unsatisfactory conclusion, I thought. Knowing 'who' was all very well; knowing 'why' was the heart of the matter. Army Intelligence would most likely require that I stop digging about for motive, on the basis that settled dust was best left undisturbed.

Hours passed, rain fell, I was given bread (the open door revealing night) and another pint of water, and I managed a fitful sleep. Something crawled over my foot, and I let it, fearing that any sudden movement would excite it to strike. At some point, deep into the night, I wondered miserably how it was that I'd come to this. I was confident that I'd be exonerated and liberated — I had no expectation of an apology — but a bout of self-pity left me feeling most sorely hard-done by. I could draw the arc of events that had led me there, and I could see the awful logic at work, but at every point my trajectory had been fuelled by the incompetence and blindness of others. Even a man as clever as Archie Warmington had failed to comprehend facts that were self-evident. Fairly or not, I blamed him—and his determination that Rufus Farrell's accusations be given equal weight with my own—for placing me in the vulnerable position in which I now found myself.

When I thought of Archie and the last conversation I'd had with him, I thought, too, of the recent interrogation in Katherine. There'd been something very peculiar about it. The peculiarity might have been a consequence of their belief that they were dealing with a strange kind of sadist, but there was something else. It was their reaction to my mentioning the three deaths that had occurred before Battell's and Ashe's. They'd been perplexed and dismissive, and had thought the comment so unworthy of consideration that they'd moved on to another question, as if my remarks had been the product of a disordered mind rather than a statement of fact. Were they anxious to avoid discussion of the deaths? My memory of the look on each of their faces was strong, and I'd seen no anxiety there—only genuine, fleeting puzzlement. Their statement that Battell and Ashe were the first and only casualties in the whole NAOU, let alone in A Company, had been made with the unequivocal confidence that it was the truth.

And, of course, it *was* the truth.

There, in the bleak darkness of solitary confinement, it became brilliantly clear to me that it wouldn't be possible to hide three deaths from Command, and neither would it be possible to silence all the Nackeroos who must have had knowledge of them. I racked my brains, and couldn't dredge up even the vaguest hint from anyone that men had been dying in A Company. The claim had been made by James Fowler and

Army Intelligence, and by no one else. We'd been sent under false pretences. But why?

All the connections I thought I'd made began to unravel, and I was left with a series of incidents that made no sense at all. Ashe and Battell were dead, and Rufus Farrell had killed them. This fact now floated like wreckage in a sea of confusion. Why had he done it, and why had Intelligence put Brian and me at the scene of both crimes? Was Rufus Farrell working for Intelligence? As soon as I considered this, I knew I'd stumbled on a part of the puzzle. I couldn't put it anywhere, but at least I had it. It made me feel sick. I must have been turning these thoughts over in my head for hours, because when the door opened unexpectedly it was morning.

'Good morning, Will,' said a familiar voice. When I'd adjusted my eyes to the glare, I found I was standing in front of Archie Warmington. He was dapper, neat, and clean. I was naked, bloodied, and filthy, and I stank. I felt at a considerable disadvantage, and the thing I most wanted to do in the world was punch him.

'You look like shit,' he said.

Chapter Eleven

THE TRUTH ABOUT LIES

WHEN I'D SHAVED, SHOWERED, SALVED, AND POWDERED myself liberally with the luxury of Mennen Talc For Men, and after a halfway-decent meal, I felt slightly more well-disposed towards Archie, who was sitting opposite me in the office where, the day before yesterday, I'd been instructed in the rules. I'd been treated with considerable courtesy since my release from solitary confinement, although there'd been no suggestion that the punishment hadn't been richly deserved. I decided not to pursue the matter just yet. I'd wait until my release had been finalised, and then I'd lodge an official complaint about the inhuman conditions at Brocks Creek.

'Only you could get locked up in solitary within a few hours of entering this place,' Archie said, and an annoying chortle escaped him.

'I can't see the humour in it.'

He waved my objection aside.

'You'll laugh about it one day.'

This was one of those expressions that always got my back up, and I was disappointed to hear Archie use it.

'I've spoken to the three officers who questioned you in Katherine. I must say they painted a rather disturbing picture of you. They were of the opinion that you're a necrophiliac, and it took all my powers of persuasion to convince them otherwise—and I'm not sure I managed to fully convince them in the end. They were most reluctant to give up the idea. They really didn't take to you, Will.'

'Just add them to the long list of the like-minded.'

'Don't be so glum. It's just that things were rather stacked up against you.'

'Frankly, Archie, I think I've got you to blame for that.'

His raised his eyebrows.

'I didn't put you in solitary confinement, Will. You did that all by yourself, and I didn't decapitate poor, bloody Rufus Farrell.'

'*Neither* did I.'

Archie sighed, folded his arms, and shook his head.

'I know that, Will. Freak accidents happen. Admittedly, that kind of freakishness strains credibility, unless one knows the people involved. But that's its great strength as an explanation for what happened. Besides, the sheet of iron has been found and examined and, despite the rain, there was enough of Rufus's blood underneath it to support your story.'

'You needed evidence rather than my word?'

'I'm here to take you away from all this. Maybe you shouldn't be fighting me.'

'Over the past few days, Archie, I've been locked up, ritually humiliated, shackled to a dead man, subjected to impertinent and hostile questioning—not to mention vilification of the most odious kind—and you waltz in here and expect me to be pathetically grateful because you, and the powers that be, have finally accepted facts that were presented to you, by *me*, practically tied up with a ribbon and bow.'

'And what facts might they be?'

I was flabbergasted.

'The facts about Rufus Farrell.'

'Ah.'

Archie took the opportunity to light up a kretek.

'You know, Brian is terribly fond of you, Will. He really is, but he has pointed out that you have something of a record in backing the wrong horse.'

I was too tired to struggle, so I simply said, 'How fascinating. If you'd ever met his wife, Darlene, you'd know Brian has his own track record in that department—only he didn't just back the wrong horse, he rode it.'

Archie laughed.

'Are you saying,' I added, 'that you still don't believe that Battell and Ashe were murdered?'

'No, I'm not saying that. What I *am* saying is that Rufus Farrell didn't do it.'

'So you're accusing my brother Fulton.'

'No. Fulton isn't guilty of those crimes.'

'*Those* crimes? Who are you, Archie?'

'I'm your commanding officer, although in Intelligence we

don't insist on such distinctions, and you're not really a soldier anyway.'

I kept the expression on my face neutral, suspecting that this was some kind of trap. Was he trying to get me to admit that I was working for Intelligence? Was he trying to lull me into trusting him? Did people really just come right out and announce that they were Intelligence agents?

'You work for Intelligence? Is that what you've just admitted, Archie?'

'Why, yes, of course. There's no reason for you to be kept in the dark about that any longer.'

'Prove it.'

'You'll just have to trust me.'

This was where he lost me. He could have proved his connection with Intelligence in Melbourne simply by mentioning James Fowler's name. He didn't do it because he couldn't do it. Was he working for the Japanese? My mouth became dry, and I was careful not to let him see that my hands had begun to tremble slightly. Archie Warmington, it occurred to me, was the ideal fifth columnist—urbane, intelligent, above suspicion. I decided I wasn't going to play games.

'What's in it for you, Archie? What have they offered you? Money? Some kind of high rank in whatever mediaeval regime they impose?'

Even through my fear—and I was afraid—I managed a pretty decent sneer.

His eyebrows drew together in a heavy frown, and his hand stopped in midair on its way to deliver the kretek to his mouth.

'What?' he asked, and the frown deepened. 'What?'

His voice rose half an octave on that second 'What,' and I felt some satisfaction at having taken him by surprise.

'Wait here,' he said, and left the room. I knew before the door had closed that I'd been sent by Army Intelligence to unmask him. It made perfect sense. Rufus Farrell was an accomplice; but Archie, with access to high-level information about the NAOU and its positions across the north, was the traitor. Bali? Where else in Asia had he spent time before the war? James Fowler and his cohorts in Melbourne must have had their suspicions about Archie, and I could now deliver him to them.

I had no intention of waiting for him to return, and didn't believe that he *would* return. Without knowing how I would stop him, I opened the door. All I knew was that he mustn't get away. I knew all about him, and I wasn't going to let him simply vanish. He would be brought to justice for his treachery. Armed with the information he'd passed on to them, the Japanese might even now be preparing to invade at a vulnerable point identified by Archie Warmington as undefended. Doubtless, he'd helpfully supplied them with maps of the terrain; maps surveyed under appalling conditions by Nackeroos whose lives he held cheaply. It is always, always, always the person you least suspect.

When I emerged from the room I saw Archie walking almost casually towards a small, battered truck that was parked outside the gates of Brocks Creek. I hurried after him, silently. I had no clear idea what I was going to do. The imperative was to prevent him from getting into that truck and driving away. He'd passed through the gate when I began to run. Off to my left I saw the figure of an inmate, trotting from one side of the compound to the other, and on the road I saw a car approaching. Archie stopped to allow it to pass, and I saw my opportunity. I threw myself at him, putting my full weight behind the leap. When I hit him he lurched forward, and both of us stumbled into the path of the oncoming car. Its horn blew, and it struck us with the blind, impersonal force of the machine. I'd never been hit by a car before, and I was strangely aware only of a painless thud, the sensation of flying, the taste of dust, and a slide into unconsciousness that was achieved with the efficiency of an anaesthetic.

When I woke I was lying on my back in the dirt, and I was dimly conscious of someone at a great distance saying, 'They came out of nowhere. I didn't see them. I couldn't have stopped. It wasn't my fault. It's that bloke's fault.'

I knew the voice, but in my dazed state couldn't place it. Was he referring to Archie or to me? A moment later, I was left in no doubt. Glen Pyers leant over me and said, 'You're not badly injured, Will. What the fuck did you think you were doing?'

'Spy,' I managed to say. 'Spy. Archie Warmington. Spy.'

'Nong,' he said. 'Nong. Will Power. Complete, total, utter nong.'

Clarity returned when the generalised throbbing in my body narrowed itself down to the left hip and leg. I moved my toes and flexed my fingers, and assured myself that nothing was broken. Archie Warmington lay on the ground beside me, and his groans indicated that he'd suffered more serious injuries than I had. I propped myself up on my elbows and saw Glen kneeling beside Archie, who was only semi-conscious. Several guards from Brocks Creek had gathered around the scene, and a stretcher had been produced.

'His leg's broken,' Glen said, 'and maybe a couple of ribs. We need to get him back to Katherine.'

He nominated two men to take Archie to the Brocks Creek infirmary—a place I immediately imagined as solitary confinement with a bed.

'We'll stabilise him there and get him out of here as soon as possible.'

The medical authority in Glen's voice was surprising, given his squeamishness about blood and injury generally. I didn't feel sufficiently confident to stand up, so remained, like Gwendolyn in *The Importance of Being Earnest*, in a semi-recumbent posture while Archie was carried away.

'I'm not authorised to talk to you,' Glen said, 'except to point out that you're a very special breed of dickhead, and that people are going to be very, very angry when they find out that you threw Major Archibald Warmington under a car.'

'People? What people? Tojo?'

'I'm not authorised to talk to you.'

He helped me to my feet roughly, shaking his head all the while in exaggerated ruefulness.

'Are you authorised to shake your head in that incredibly irritating way?' I asked.

'I'm not authorised to tell you.'

A few minutes later, I found myself again sitting before the blackboard in the Brocks Creek induction office. This time I wasn't a prisoner, and it was Glen Pyers sitting opposite me rather than a maniac with a piece of dowel. He remained stubbornly uncommunicative, except to tell me that the Melbourne Cup was being run that afternoon, three weeks late, and on a Saturday owing to a string of government-enforced race-free days. I had no interest in horse racing, and asked him if he thought the information I had about Archie Warmington might be more pertinent to the prosecution of the war than the Melbourne Cup.

'You don't have information about Archie Warmington,' he said. 'You have misguided, silly, and bizarre misconceptions. They are not the same as information. The fact that you think they are is something of a nuisance. Now, I don't want to get into an argument with you, or antagonise you. Unfortunately, we need you and, believe me, that's not an easy thing for me to say.'

'We? You work in vaudeville. Who's we? The chorus line?'

A faint, roseate blush on his face indicated that he was fighting an urge to express anger.

'Archie should be sufficiently comfortable by now to speak to you. I hope so, because if I have to listen to you much longer, I'll kill you.'

I followed Glen, reluctantly, across the parade ground, past compounds one and two, and entered the barracks in compound three. These weren't salubrious by any means, and they smelled the same as the barracks in compound one, but at one end a section had been closed off. This was the infirmary. Archie was lying on a bunk, his leg immobilised in a rough splint, and his chest wrapped in bandages. He'd obviously been given a palliative shot of morphine—enough to take the edge off the pain, but insufficient to send him into a pleasant, dopey daze.

'Why?' he asked when he saw me. 'Why did you try to kill me?'

It was such a blunt question that the least I could do was give him a blunt reply.

'I wasn't trying to kill you. I was trying to stop you from escaping. I didn't see the car.'

The look on Archie's face was blank, as if I'd just spoken to him in Swahili.

'I'm sorry, did you say "escape"?'

I nodded.

'I know, Archie. I know who you are. I know you're a fifth columnist. I know you're spying for Japan.'

'Ah.' He drew the word out. 'And is Glen spying for the

emperor as well? He was driving the car I was attempting to escape in.'

I hadn't considered the peculiarity of Glen's presence, and I wasn't able to offer an explanation for it on the spur of the moment. With an attempt at insouciance, I said, 'I have absolutely no idea.'

'Nong,' I heard Glen say behind me. 'Nong, nong, nong.'

'That sounds almost Japanese, Glen,' Archie said. 'Has another piece of the puzzle fallen into place, Will?'

I wanted to face Glen, to see whether his expression was betraying anything, but I couldn't bring myself to turn around. I'd had enough of his special brand of ruefulness for one day.

'I'd laugh, Will, but I've been told it might lead to a punctured lung. Was it really only a few minutes ago that we were discussing your predilection for backing the wrong horse?'

'You sound like a trapped and desperate man, Archie.'

'Archie, please,' Glen said. 'Tell this fool of a man what's going on before I clock him.'

'All right. Now, Will, before I say anything else, I want to assure you that the only thing standing between me and fury about what your actions have done to me is morphine. I feel quite chirpy, but when it wears off and I appreciate fully how much damage you've inflicted, both to me and to this operation, I advise you to be several hundred miles from me.'

'It's probable that you'll be locked up here, Archie, so you don't need to worry about that.'

He closed his eyes in an ostentatious display of mastering his exasperation.

'I am not a Japanese spy, and Glen is not a Japanese spy. As I told you earlier, I work in Intelligence, and it should come as no surprise to you — although no doubt it will — that Glen also is in their employ.'

I opened my mouth to speak, and he held up his hand to silence me.

'Let me just say, Will, that despite every wrong supposition you've made, we do appreciate the fact that you have preserved your own Intelligence role, despite what must have been severe temptations to rescue yourself by announcing it. In all of my discussions with James Fowler I've been most complimentary about that aspect of your character. In an absolute sense, you can be trusted. You just can't be trusted to get anything right.'

I remained silent.

'On the fifth of October, you and Brian had a meeting at Victoria Barracks in Melbourne with James Fowler and his sister, Nigella. At that meeting you were told that someone up here was killing members of a secret unit, the NAOU. You were told that Intelligence needed you to go undercover and find out what was going on. It all had to be hush-hush because the NAOU was hush-hush—and it still is, I hasten to add. The civilian population doesn't know it exists, and neither do most other sections of the military. At any rate, they don't know exactly what it is or what it does. At some point, you were introduced to Corporal Glen Pyers here, and you were led to believe that he was a humble magician whose job was to entertain, and that was all. We were, I have to say, surprised that it didn't occur to you, or to Brian, that Glen might be in Intelligence, even though you were introduced to him in James Fowler's office. Again, the fact that you never made an attempt to quiz him on this, or to confide in him, remains, despite everything, an impressive demonstration of loyalty to Intelligence and to your idea of what was expected of you.'

'I need to sit down,' I said. 'My leg is hurting.'

My leg wasn't the problem. The fluid assurance of Archie's words, and his intimate knowledge of our mission, were slowly but surely altering my perspective, and I began to experience the sickening vertigo of having my world turned upside down. A chair was pushed into the back of my knees, and I folded into it.

'I'm afraid,' Archie continued, 'we lied to you and Brian on several fronts. But that's what Intelligence does—we're in the business of finding the truth, not telling it. You weren't sent to the West Alligator River to discover a murderer. You were sent as a smokescreen for an assassin.'

'I don't understand.'

'Decisions are made in a time of war which would be unthinkable in peacetime. Two men in A Company had been identified by your brother Fulton as Axis sympathisers—more in the line of fascists than Japanese imperialists; for them, Japan was an ally, not the enemy. We knew that they'd already passed some information to the Japs, because a few weeks back Tokyo Rose had sent a personal cheerio to an NAOU section and named their location. Now maybe a flyover had spotted them, but the blokes in that section swear they'd seen no aircraft. The information had to have come from within the NAOU. Fortunately, the unit is still finding its feet, and it's still deploying its members for maximum effect. The leak had to be plugged before seriously damaging stuff could be passed on.'

He paused.

'We made a tough decision to plug the leak, permanently. Corporal Pyers was assigned the task of assassinating both sympathisers.'

'No,' I said, not because I didn't believe it, but because these extraordinary words physically winded me, and the sound was simply pushed from my lungs.

'It was Glen you saw leaving Andrew Battell's bed, and it was Glen who shot Nicholas Ashe. Placing the gun in the wrong hand was a mistake—a bad one, and in a way it led to Rufus

Farrell's death. He'd noticed it, of course, and things began to go pear-shaped when you accused each other of murder.'

'Farrell had nothing to do with any of this?'

'Nothing. Absolutely nothing. I'm sorry to say, Will, that you scared the living daylights out of him. I don't know what you said to him, but he genuinely believed that you'd killed Battell and Ashe, and that he was next.'

I thought I might vomit.

'And who killed the three Nackeroos who died before we arrived.'

'That's one of the lies we told you. There were no deaths. It was Nigella Fowler's idea. It was important to the success of this mission that you and Brian agree to come to the West Alligator River.'

'Why?'

'I'll explain that in a minute. Nigella felt that you mightn't be able to be talked into doing this, but that you could certainly be flattered into it. I'm sorry if that sounds rather calculating. She felt that the twin drawcard of performing and being trusted to solve a nasty crime would be irresistible to you. Brian's personal circumstances made his decision an easy one. Nigella was right, as she usually is, and away we went. Having you believe that you were investigating crimes that had already been committed meant that you were always looking in the wrong direction — a talent that you have in spades, if you'll pardon me for saying so.'

My mind was now so crowded with revelations that I felt no compunction to defend myself.

'Why us? You could have chosen anyone.'

'There were all sorts of advantages from our point of view. James Fowler wanted you out of Melbourne, just in case there was any trouble after the Archbishop Mannix affair. That helped in persuading his superiors that you were a better choice that anyone else. There was, however, a more compelling reason for sending you. A favour was being called in. You're aware, of course, that your mother is about to marry a man named Peter Gilbert. I don't know how close you are to him, but I don't think he'll mind my telling you that he's one of our most respected men, or he was before he retired. Perhaps you knew that already?'

I shook my head.

'He's not completely out of the loop—our people never are—and he knew that Fulton was the one who'd done the work of identifying Battell and Ashe. He knew, too, that your mother was frantic about Fulton's safety. We don't know why she was so excessively worried, but we suspect that he let her know in one of his letters, in code that escaped the censor, that he'd discovered traitors in his section. What better way to reassure her that he was all right than to send his older brothers to be with him? Sentimental, but it suited everybody. I think Peter saw it as a gift to the woman he loved.'

'Fulton is his son,' I said flatly.

'Yes, we know that, which is why he exerted pressure to get you up here.'

'He wouldn't have believed that Brian and I could protect Fulton.'

'No. That was our job. You weren't meant to be anything more significant than a living comfort-package. We saw an opportunity for extra value.'

Archie was tiring, and this last, brutally honest assessment of our usefulness might have been symptomatic of a lapse in concentration. Here he was, declaring that Brian and I were no more than pawns in this monstrous war, to be moved here or there, in consequence of a favour being called in. My loathing for

Peter Gilbert was at that moment fierce, and Army Intelligence and all it represented began to seem poisonous to me. I suddenly felt the alarming force of the discovery that, to these people, to James Fowler, to Nigella, Archie, Glen, and Peter Gilbert, I was of use but not of value.

Archie had by now run out of energy, or interest, or both, and Glen indicated that we should leave him to the soothing buzz of morphine.

Outside, under a leaden sky, Glen told me that a train to Katherine would be arriving in half an hour, and that all three of us would be on it.

'The hospital in Darwin is too risky, and Archie refuses to be evacuated to Townsville. He wants to be relatively close to Roper Bar so that he can supervise the next part of this operation.'

'No. That's it. I'm not coming with you. I've had enough of it. I've been lied to, mistreated, used, slandered, humiliated, and battered. I don't want anything more to do with Army Intelligence. You disgust me, all of you.'

Glen closed his dextrous fingers around my wrist.

'You can't just pull out because you feel personally hard-done by. You're not in a bloody play.'

'I agreed to come to this hell hole because I thought I'd be doing something useful. It turns out that I'm here because of a cosy little arrangement between Peter Gilbert and Intelligence. Well, that just isn't good enough.'

'I've never met your step-father, but his reputation is impressive.'

'He is *not* my step-father.'

'He will be when he marries your mother.'

Was that a smirk on his face?

'I'm not going to discuss my family with you.'

'I'm not interested in your family. Believe it or not, the war with Japan isn't actually about your family. Which is why you can't pull out now. You don't have a choice. Well, you do have a choice, but spending the rest of the war in Brocks Creek isn't much of one.'

'Are you threatening me?'

'Yes, I'm threatening you, but what I really want to do is throttle you.'

The fact that Glen Pyers was experienced in the dispatching of enemies made me think that there might be more than conversational hyperbole to this remark. He did have a point, and I'm not deaf to the reasoned arguments of others, and not so stubborn as to maintain a position in the face of evidence that contradicts it. Glen was quite right to point out that the war was larger than its effect on me, and the mention of Brocks Creek underpinned his argument strongly. I put my hands up in a gesture of surrender.

'I give up, Glen. Whatever it is you want me to do, I'll do—we're on the same side, after all. But perhaps you can understand that I'm not feeling very proud of myself at the moment. I've put Archie in hospital, and I'm at least partly responsible for Rufus Farrell's death.'

'No self-pity, Will. It's a luxury none of us can afford.'

'It's not self-pity. It's self-awareness.'

'If it's any consolation, you did everything we thought you'd do. You and Brian weren't picked out of a hat. When James Fowler recruited you in Melbourne, he did a lot of background work on you and on Brian. Having Peter Gilbert on the inside was a stroke of luck. Intelligence work must be in the blood.'

'Gilbert is Fulton's father, not mine.'

'But Gilbert worked with your father, in Intelligence, in the First War.'

This was one piece of information too many, and I told

Glen that I didn't want to hear any more. When I got back to Melbourne I'd confront both Peter Gilbert and Mother with what I knew, and demand a full explanation. Standing here, inside the gates at Brocks Creek, all I could contend with was what lay immediately ahead for me. The past could wait, even if it had, in some inexplicable way, pushed me into this present.

'I presume when you say that I did everything that was expected of me, you're being offensive, and you mean that I did everything wrongly.'

'Well, that's a bit harsh. Let's just say that James Fowler's predictions, based on Peter Gilbert's predictions, were played out more or less as described.'

Rather than draw attention to his poor diplomacy skills, I pressed him to explain why this operation was not yet complete, given that the two traitors had been disposed of.

'We've lost Fulton.'

'Lost?'

'He's gone AWL, and we can only speculate on what his desertion means. The one thing we hope isn't true is that he's working for the Japs.'

I was taken aback by this, and was beginning to appreciate that the casual annihilation of other people's reputations was something of an Intelligence specialty.

'But he uncovered Battell and Ashe. Archie said so.'

'Spying is a messy, complicated business. Battell and Ashe might have been sacrificed to shield Fulton; they mightn't have even known about him. Don't underestimate the Japs, Will. Disguising Fulton as a hero would be well within their capabilities.'

'The more I know about Intelligence, the more repellent it becomes.'

'Intelligence will win this war.'

He said this with some passion but, when he realised he'd been caught in the act of expressing a real emotion, he coughed to disguise his embarrassment, and sought to reassure me about Fulton.

'You can relax about Fulton. We don't think for a minute that he's a Japanese agent. I'm just letting you know that no one gets special treatment, and that we consider all options. What is far more likely to have happened is that Fulton's had some sort of breakdown. He's very young, and he knows that if it hadn't been for him, Battell and Ashe would still be alive. Maybe he liked them. Maybe he didn't want to believe what he knew to be true. On top of everything else, his brothers arrive, and one of them, you, winds up being carted off in chains for murders he *knows* you didn't commit.'

'So he knew you were here to kill his mates?'

'Well, he knew they'd died because they were traitors. Whether he knew it was me or not isn't important. The thing is this: it all seems to have been too much for him, and he's taken off. We want him back, and you're our best chance of getting him back.'

'You want to court-martial him for desertion?'

'No. Intelligence wants to train him up. The NAOU might want to court-martial him, but they're not going to get their hands on him. We're going to find him—you're going to find him, and convince him to come back with us to Melbourne. He's a very valuable young man.'

'If Intelligence knows so much, you should know that he's unlikely to listen to me. Why haven't you organised for Brian to do this?'

'He was our first choice, obviously. Unfortunately, he's temporarily out of action. He was bitten by a scorpion, and he's had a serious allergic reaction to the venom. His whole leg looks like it'd burst if you pricked it with a pin. He can't walk. He's still at Roper Bar, so you can talk all this over with him when we get there.'

The startling and troubling fact that Brian had been incapacitated might have been considered by anyone other than someone in Intelligence as of sufficient moment to take precedence over all other matters. For Glen it was no more than a useful snippet to be produced at the point in a conversation where it would have maximum effect.

The train pulled in to the Brocks Creek siding, and I watched as Archie was carried towards it on a stretcher. His hand was covering his eyes.

'So,' Glen said, 'are you in?'

'You make it sound like there's a viable choice. Yes, I'm in. I can't bear the idea of Fulton being sent here. What kind of reward is that for doing his duty? And I certainly want to talk to Brian.'

'Good man. Archie said you'd do the right thing, the honourable thing.'

I didn't believe Glen Pyers had the faintest idea what honour meant, and I didn't believe that delivering Fulton to Army Intelligence, where he would, by degrees, be turned into Glen, or Archie, or even Nigella, had very much to do with honour. I got onto the train with a heavy, muddled heart, which lightened slightly as we pulled away from Brocks Creek.

Chapter Twelve

RESOLUTION

I DIDN'T SPEAK WITH ARCHIE ON THE TRAIN, and at
Katherine he was whisked away to have his leg set in plaster
before I could confer with him. The big news on the platform
was that Colonnus had won the Cup, on a wet track, by seven
lengths. I couldn't have cared less.

Glen and I were found bunks for the night, and he settled
back into taking money from the gullible. I was glad of the
distraction it offered, and no one bothered me. Fulton was out
there somewhere, hiding in the grim reaches of the Roper River,

distressed and maybe desperate, believing that as a deserter he would be punished and shamed.

We left for Roper Bar before daybreak, on a motorcycle, with Glen driving and me clinging to him like a limpet. My bruised leg suffered, but the motorcycle negotiated the bogs more successfully than a car or a truck could have done. Twice we found the road impassable, and had to carry the bike a small distance. We sped past two trucks that were firmly bogged, and caught the tail end of abuse for failing to stop. Even with this clear run, we didn't complete the four hundred and thirty miles to Roper Bar until just before midnight.

Brian had been moved under cover, and when I found him he was awake and feverish. Glen had made the consequence of the scorpion bite seem almost humorous, but Brian's bloated leg and his wild eyes alarmed me. He recognised me, but he was incapable of a sustained conversation. His water bottle was beside him, and I held his head while he drank from it.

'I'm going to bring Fulton back,' I whispered. 'He's not going to be charged with being AWL.'

Brian nodded, and the movement shook loose his grasp on the situation.

'The stronger we our houses build,' he said, 'the less chance we have of being killed,' and he laughed.

I stayed with him, half-sleeping, half-waking, until Glen came for me at dawn. He handed me a piece of warm bread, spread with an extravagance of jam—a gesture I appreciated, despite my distaste for that condiment.

'What do we do now?' I asked.

'We start looking.'

'We?'

'I'm coming with you. You won't find him on your own—and we're taking Isaiah.'

I followed Glen through the camp and down to the wharf, where Isaiah stood on the bank beside a long, flimsy-looking canoe.

'Why are we going by river?'

'Fulton took a canoe, and he was seen heading downstream.'

This made sense. Why would he paddle above the Bar, against the current?

I clambered into the canoe awkwardly and made my way to the back, very nearly tipping it over in the process. Isaiah followed, and sat in the middle. Glen took up his position at the front, and we pushed off into the wide expanse of the Roper River. We were carrying only one small pack of supplies, which seemed like madness to me.

'We don't need a lot of supplies,' Glen said. 'We've got Isaiah. Fulton's got a thirty-six hour head-start on us, so we have to move fast. Fortunately, we're better equipped. He's on his own to begin with and, like I say, we've got Isaiah.'

Isaiah turned to me when his name was mentioned.

'Ulcer gone, boss?'

'Yes, all gone.'

'Good medicine, you bet.'

We moved rapidly, with the three of us finding a good rhythm to our paddling. The canoe felt unsteady to me, so we were fortunate that the current was benign. The vegetation along the banks began to change as the waters of the Roper became more brackish. After several hours the mangroves began to dominate the fringes of the banks, their finger-like roots splayed and probing into the grey mud. It was Isaiah who spotted the canoe that Fulton had taken. It was lodged amongst mangroves in a section of the river that branched into a sluggishly flowing stream. Even when he pointed to the spot, it took my eyes a few moments to interpret the dark shape as a canoe.

'Why would he pull in here?'

Isaiah shrugged.

'Must be reason. Must be problem.'

The problem was apparent when we came close to the canoe. It had sprung a leak, and had taken in so much water that it was half submerged. We had no option now but to follow Fulton on land.

Isaiah quickly discovered which way Fulton had walked, and he showed me sections of mangrove root where heavy boots had scraped at the slime and bark. Our progress through the clutching, choking mangroves was slow, and a viciously protruding branch almost put my eye out. Hour followed hour, during which we were cooled, and our thirst slaked, by steady rain. Isaiah led us on, his energy so boundless that I had to beg for a rest.

By late afternoon I was weak with hunger, and muscles in various parts of my body began to twitch independently and rebelliously. Isaiah pulled a few berries from a fruiting tree, telling us that they were good to eat. By 'good' he meant 'not poisonous'. They were sour but edible. It was the rest we took while he picked them that was more reviving than the food.

We'd reached a point of high ground from which we could survey what lay ahead. It was a dispiriting vista of mudflats. Glen conferred with Isaiah, and they agreed that Fulton would try to stay as close to the river as he could, and that it must originally have been his intention to reach the coast — although what he'd do when he managed that was unclear. He'd taken a rifle, some ammunition, and a pack with rations that might last him two days at the most. As he was facing a journey of many days, he'd have to rely on his bush skills to furnish him with food. Isaiah was dubious. He didn't think much of any of the Nackeroos' food-gathering abilities, and he told us that in this country, unless Fulton encountered a water buffalo or a goat, and shot it, he'd find survival difficult.

There are surprising patches of extraordinary stillness and beauty secreted in the vast monotony of this landscape. We came upon one such place, and drank from a lagoon of clear, fresh water, its banks thick with reeds, ferns, and pandanus. Isaiah assured us that there were no crocodiles, but I was wary nonetheless. If a place looked like Paradise up there, a serpent was sure to be lurking in it somewhere.

Fulton had been there before us. Isaiah found the ashes of a fire—it was a remarkable feat that he'd managed to get one going in this damp world—and the remains of a few, blackened rhizomes.

'Bush tucker,' Isaiah said, and seemed impressed that Fulton had the nous and the knowledge to find and prepare it. There were also the shells of hermit crabs which he poked at, and declared, 'No good. Not sweet.'

The sun had almost set, and it was agreed that we'd spend the night there. Using the charcoal of Fulton's fire as a base, we lit our own, and Isaiah gathered the white rhizomes from ferns, just as Fulton had done. They were indigestible raw, but after a good bake in the coals they became starchy, if fibrous, and the taste wasn't objectionable. Isaiah failed to produce a cornucopia of bush food, so we ate the remaining rations—bully beef and more peaches. I swore that when this war was over, I'd never eat another peach.

We built the fire into a smoking pile, and curled up near it on the ground. I was so sore and tired that I endured the mosquitoes, and barely noticed the rain when it came.

There was no breakfast. We headed off while it was still dark, trusting that Isaiah had picked up Fulton's track. The rain had obliterated any footprints Fulton may have left, but Isaiah pointed to a discarded crab shell and said, 'Breakfast.'

Further on, another shell confirmed that Fulton had been eating while he walked. We were heading back towards the mangroves. When we reached them, Isaiah stopped and said, 'Good tucker here. Sweet.'

He found a rotting, sodden log and tore it open. From within its soft fibres he withdrew a long, glistening worm that hung from his fingers like a string of mucous. He gripped one end between his thumb and forefinger, and put the protruding tip into his mouth. Slowly he began sliding the body between his fingers until a line of mud oozed from its far end. He drew the purged upper body into his mouth as he did so. He was so practised at this that it was almost a single, fluid movement, and in a matter of seconds all that remained of the worm was a neat casting of extruded mud, coiled on the ground between his feet. He found another and handed it to me.

'That one tastes like oyster,' he said, so I overcame my revulsion and began feeding it into my mouth. I didn't get all the mud out, which made the initial experience more ghastly than it might otherwise have been. The worm had the slippery consistency of an oyster, but lacked its compactness. It tasted of brine and foul mud. I could see, though, that if properly purged it would offer sustenance to a desperate man—and I was a desperate man. I tried a second worm, after Isaiah had cleaned it out for me, and found that if the mind could see it as an oyster, it did indeed taste vaguely like an oyster, in that it was all texture and salt, with something, too, of rotting wood. These ship-worms, as I later learned they were called, would never grace the tables of restaurants, but they had a restorative effect on us all, and we moved on in pursuit of Fulton.

As we walked I began to rehearse what I would say to him. I knew he'd be disappointed that it was me who'd been sent to find him, and not Brian, but he'd also be relieved to see that I'd been released from custody. That was at least one thing he could stop feeling guilty about. I knew so little about him that I couldn't predict how he'd react to being discovered. I'd never thought of him as being unstable, or capable of rash, self-destructive behaviour. In truth, though, I'd never really thought of him as anything other than a child, and so far from me in age that familial ties seemed meaningless.

Remembered images of the small boy Fulton used to be began to crowd my mind. As I trudged wearily behind Glen, I experienced a kind of delirium of sentimentality, and fraternal feelings for Fulton welled up from a deep, unexamined part of my psyche. I was suddenly fiercely proud of what he'd done, of his measured, patient response to discovering two traitors in his section. No wonder Intelligence wanted him. His instincts were obviously superb, and unusually subtle in one so young. With careful training he'd become a formidable agent. With mixed feelings, I had to acknowledge that I lacked those qualities essential to a career in Intelligence. I could never do as Glen had done, and coolly and without remorse kill a man, even if that man was my enemy and threatened my country. I didn't have the stomach for it. Fulton, I thought, probably did, and once the hiccough of this absence without leave had been dealt with, he would please his father no end by following in his footsteps.

We stopped briefly, and Isaiah deftly collected a handful of small oysters. They were much enjoyed, even if they did create a strong thirst. This was easily quenched—we'd filled our canteens at the billabong. Eventually the mangroves became too dense to negotiate, and we were forced inland. I was glad of this, as having to constantly pull my limbs out of the mud was playing havoc with the leg that had been heavily bruised in the car accident.

Isaiah was quite confident that he was still on Fulton's trail, and just before midday he halted abruptly, crouched, and signalled that we were to do the same. Following his pointed finger, I peered through the ti-tree and wattle and saw a figure, seated, with his back to us. He was leaning forward, and his posture suggested that he was ill. He hadn't heard our approach — not because we'd been particularly stealthy, but because the green grass and soft, damp earth muffled our footfalls. Glen, who was in front of me, pulled his pistol from its holster. I tapped him on the shoulder and indicated that I thought the gun was unnecessary.

'We don't know his state of mind,' he whispered. 'It's just a precaution.'

'He's not a criminal.'

'If he panics and points his rifle at us, I want to be prepared.'

We approached cautiously. Fulton didn't move. When we were within a few feet of him he raised his head, but didn't turn around. His rifle was on the ground beside him, and he made no move to touch it. I was relieved, and was about to approach him when Glen placed his hand on my chest and held me back.

'You've found me,' Fulton said. 'Have you come to kill me?'

'Yes,' Glen said, and in a swift, precise movement he stepped forward, put his pistol to the back of Fulton's head, and pulled the trigger. I have no memory of the echo of the gunshot, just a sharp crack. Fulton's body slumped forward and fell sideways. Isaiah's face showed no shock, but his eyes were swimming with tears, and I realised he must have begun weeping before the shot was fired. My mind and my body refused to assimilate what had just happened and, for a brief period, I was in a catatonic state, unblinking, rigid, aware only of Isaiah's eyes.

'There were three of them, Will. Fulton was the third.'

I'd emerged from my state of shock sufficiently to hear Glen's words, if not to fully comprehend them. Fulton's body had been removed from view, and the patch of blood where his head had touched the ground had been covered over. It might never have happened.

'I did tell you.'

'You told me that you didn't think it was true.'

'Yes. I lied. We do that. I needed you to come with me.'

'Why me?'

'I wanted Brian. I ended up with you.'

I didn't hate Glen Pyers at that moment. He seemed so remote from whatever it was I understood as human that no emotion made sense in relation to him. I didn't feel in any danger, either. He'd done what he'd come there to do, and had no investment, for the moment, in harming any other living thing.

'Why did you need me here?'

'You're a witness.'

'Isaiah is a witness.'

'Isaiah can't tell Peter Gilbert what we want you to tell Peter Gilbert.'

'He doesn't know that his son was a traitor?'

'No.'

'You lie to each other in Intelligence?'

'Peter Gilbert has earned the right to believe that he has raised a son of whom he can be proud, and not a misguided little fascist whose sympathies were with the enemy.'

'I don't understand the moral universe you inhabit, and I still don't understand why you needed me, or preferably Brian, as a witness.'

In a chilling perversion of the word's meaning, Glen said, 'It's a courtesy. We wanted a member of Fulton's family to be able to report to his parents that he'd died quickly, painlessly, in the defence of his country, and that they should take comfort in the fact that he'd made an honourable death.'

'Do you seriously expect me to tell this monstrous lie to my mother and to Fulton's father?'

'Yes,' he said simply. 'We not only expect it; we insist on it. I think, when you reflect on this, you'll agree that injuring your mother with the truth about her son achieves nothing. If, however, you find yourself unable to offer her the protection of a generous lie, the gag of the Official Secrets Act can be applied.'

'Lies protect, and truth injures. My God, it's all smoke and mirrors with you, isn't it?'

'We want you to report something like this ...' He began pacing in front of me, constructing the scenario.

'We were out on patrol, just the four of us. Brian, of course, was laid up with a scorpion bite. It was a routine patrol, down along the Roper River ...'

Chapter Thirteen

INDEPENDENCE

'... AND WE WERE GLAD TO BE AWAY FROM ROPER BAR. Fulton liked patrols. He felt like he was doing something. He knew he was one of the best signallers in the NAOU, but he liked the bush.'

Mother had fallen against Peter Gilbert, whose face was grimly set against the threat of tears. We were seated in the front room of Mother's house in Garton Street in Princes Hill. Brian sat beside me, his head bowed.

The unspeakable news of Fulton's death had been told to

them before our arrival. It had taken us two full weeks to return to Melbourne, during every day of which we'd talked ourselves hoarse about Fulton and about what could have led him to despise his country so much that he would turn against it. I had no insights to offer, and Brian couldn't recall a single word or act that hinted at his discontent, let alone disaffection. He must, we thought, have been seduced by the politics of someone he met after joining up. Battell perhaps, or Ashe.

'I would never have thought he was so impressionable,' Brian said.

'Did he know that Peter Gilbert was his father?'

'I'm not sure. We never talked about it. He was the only father he ever knew, and he knew that Peter loved him. I never, ever saw him express any anger or lose his temper. He was happy, always happy.'

Mother's eyes were open and staring into space. Her hands clung to Peter Gilbert's arm, giving the impression that if she let go she would slip from her chair and collapse at his feet. I thought now that Glen had been right. If I'd told them the truth they might both have simply died of grief.

'There was no warning. We had no radio with us. We'd only intended being out overnight. It was the afternoon, and we were sitting, chatting, having a mug of tea. I saw the shadow of a plane move across the ground, but there was no sound of an engine. It was strange. No sound at all. Suddenly it was above us, gliding low, almost touching the tree tops. There was a burst of machine-gun fire, the plane's motors were switched on, and it banked away from us. I could see the pilot's face, they were so close. I didn't know that planes could do that. Fulton was hit, and he died instantly. He wouldn't have even known what had happened. He certainly didn't suffer in any way. The wound was just above his heart.'

'Who else saw this?' asked Peter Gilbert. His Intelligence training obviously made him sceptical about the clinical neatness of his son's death.

'There were two other men — Corporal Glen Pyers, who was with Brian and me in the Concert Party, and an Aboriginal man named Isaiah.'

He nodded. I could see that he knew I was lying, but I hoped he thought the lie had to do with the speed and ease of Fulton's death.

'There was nothing anybody could do,' Brian said quietly.

Mother raised herself upright.

'I'm sorry you had to see your brother die, Will. Truly I am. I'm glad, though, that Fulton didn't die amongst strangers, like so many soldiers do. I'm glad of that.'

She came across to me, leaned down, and kissed me on the top of my head.

'Thank you for telling us what happened. It can't have been easy.'

I caught Peter Gilbert's eye, and felt he knew I'd made it easier than it ought to have been.

'I'll make a pot of tea,' Mother said, and left the room. Her tone and movements were dull and muted, and I wondered whether Fulton's death had robbed her permanently of the capacity for joy.

Peter Gilbert cleared his throat. He and Mother had had a fortnight to accept Fulton's death, so he was calm when he spoke.

'I think Agnes and I both know that what you just told us isn't quite how it happened. I'm grateful that you spared your mother the whole truth. I, however, would appreciate knowing it.'

Glen Pyers had assured me that Army Intelligence would support the version of events we'd settled on, so I had to assume that Peter Gilbert had already heard that Fulton had died in machine-gun fire from a Japanese aircraft. Just because the stories matched wouldn't reassure him of their accuracy. Brian and I had also been instructed that we were not to tell Peter Gilbert that his former position in Intelligence was known to us, or that we had knowledge of his role in sending us to the West Alligator River. Perhaps they didn't have absolute confidence in Peter Gilbert. It was more likely, though, that this was a part of the wretched mechanics of allowing no one to see every piece of the puzzle.

'What I told you was essentially true,' I said, and made a show of finding what I was about to say awkward and difficult.

'Go on,' he said.

'Fulton *was* shot from a gliding Japanese plane.'

'What sort of plane?'

'I'm not an expert on planes. It was a twin-engine job. I was told it was a Mitsubishi something or other.'

That seemed to confirm something for him, and I was glad that Glen had insisted on this detail being a part of the story. It lent verisimilitude to the version Gilbert heard from me and the version he'd heard from someone in Intelligence.

'He was shot, but I'm afraid he didn't die immediately.'

'Ah,' Peter Gilbert said, and he visibly relaxed, as if now he could accept the reality of Fulton's death, because now he was hearing the truth.

'How long?'

It had been Glen's idea to offer an alternative fiction of a slow death if Peter Gilbert refused to accept the preferred fiction of a quick one.

'Not long.'

'How long?'

Again I hesitated, apparently reluctant to speak the words.

'He wasn't shot in the heart. He was shot in the stomach and in the throat, and he must have ...' I stumbled '... he must have lived for more than an hour. I'm sorry. I'm so sorry.'

'Thank you, Will. I'm glad you were with him. I'm sure it made a difference.'

'No, Peter. No. It made no difference, no difference at all.'

This was the only truthful thing I'd said, but Peter Gilbert heard in it only the lie of grief and impotence in the face of an innocent young man's death.

'I'm sure, Will. I'm sure it did make a difference.'

He offered a comforting smile, and I felt ill with self-loathing in the presence of his ability to find sympathy for me amongst all the violent emotions that must attend the death of a son. The truth injures, and lies protect, Glen had said. As I looked at Peter Gilbert I was obliged to accept and acknowledge his sympathy. Who, I thought, is protected? I felt naked, ashamed, and morally bankrupt, and that is why I began to cry. Even as I sobbed, I knew that Peter Gilbert thought I was crying for Fulton.

Brian and I arrived at Victoria Barracks at nine o'clock in the morning. It was Wednesday, 9 December—just over two months since we'd sat in James Fowler's office and accepted his assignment. We were sitting there once more, as instructed—and I was determined that this was to be the last instruction I would take from Fowler or from anyone else in Intelligence. He was late and, as I looked around me, I marvelled that decisions made in this mean, little space he'd been allocated could go out into the world and result in three men being killed, in secret—and that the deep, obliterating shadow of secrecy could close over these acts, so that no one would mention Andrew Battell, Nicholas Ashe, or Fulton Power (he never wore the name 'Gilbert') again, unless it was to lament their deaths as accidents of war. I knew that if there was to be any investigation into how it was that they came to betray us, neither Brian nor I would ever be privy to it or to its findings.

James Fowler entered the office, sat behind his desk, and looked solemn. I hated him.

'Well done,' he said.

I didn't trust myself to speak.

'Our brother is disgraced and dead,' Brian said. 'What exactly is it that you think we did well?'

'You stayed the distance. You did everything that was asked of you, and you may well have helped prevent a Japanese invasion of this country.'

'Do you know of a young soldier named Rufus Farrell?' I asked savagely.

'He was attached to your brother's section, wasn't he?'

'He was attached to *me*.'

'Oh, yes. That sounds like it was a most unfortunate accident.'

'It shouldn't have happened. It needn't have happened.'

'It was Major Warmington's judgement that he needed you and Private Farrell away from Roper Bar at that time. Whatever his reasons were, I have absolute confidence that they were justified and correct. Private Farrell's death was a tragedy, but it is only one amongst thousands.'

Brian jumped in.

'Archie wanted it to be me, and not Will, who saw Fulton's death. I didn't know that at the time. He thought Fulton's father would prefer me as a witness. I confided too much in Archie. I told him more than I should have about our family.'

'Where is Archie?' I asked.

'I'm afraid I'm not at liberty to tell you that. He's recuperating well, and he doesn't bear you a grudge, Will. You took him completely by surprise, and no one's done that for a long, long time. He did want you to know, though, that the surprise wasn't a good one. He hadn't expected you to be quite so spectacularly wrong-headed. They're his words, not mine.'

'I see. I'm glad in that case that he didn't get out of this unscathed. Please let him know that I'm proud of my contribution to his discomfort.'

'And Glen?' Brian asked hurriedly.

'Corporal Pyers has been redeployed. He's one of our best men. It's unlikely that you'll see him again. Intelligence is a bit like that, I'm afraid.'

'Don't be afraid,' I said. 'Intelligence seems to produce people I never want to see again. Believe me, I wasn't looking forward to catching up with Glen over a cup of tea and nostalgically discussing his kills.'

I hadn't heard the door behind us open, and when Nigella Fowler spoke I turned my head rather more quickly than was good for my almost-repaired neck. Consequently, the expression on my face was one of pain and not pleasant surprise.

'That's not a look that makes a girl feel very attractive,' she said.

When she spoke, I became immediately confused about the antipathy I'd been feeling towards her. Proximity to her disrupted all my powers of critical thinking. I'd once, in what now seemed a distant time and place, made a declaration of love to her, and I had hoped then that the success of this enterprise would encourage finer feelings in her for me. Through the static of the adolescent emotion I was feeling, I was only faintly sensitive to those qualities in Nigella Fowler that gave one pause. She could deceive without compunction—I knew that—and she was fearless. She'd also killed a man—a salutary achievement in a woman one might wish to marry. Through all this I felt, as I looked at her now, what I'd felt on our first meeting: beneath her plain, dressed-down exterior there were great reserves of kindness and sympathy—and kindness and sympathy were elements I would welcome into my life.

She held out her hand, and I rose and shook it. She shook Brian's hand as well, and asked if he'd fully recovered from the scorpion bite. Clearly, she'd been properly briefed.

'There's still some numbness in the foot. Apparently I should avoid scorpions,' he replied.

'You're not in uniform,' she said to both of us.

'They were rags,' Brian said. 'And the Tivoli isn't going to be happy about the state of the costumes. They're mostly mould with a bit of fabric in between.'

'So you'll need new ones,' she said lightly.

I was smiling, and my smile froze. Something passed between her and her brother, some flicker of unease that she'd made a misstep.

'Will,' she said quickly, 'can we walk for a bit? It's stuffy in here.'

Brian seemed oblivious to this rather obvious ploy to separate us, but I had no real objection to leaving James Fowler, who'd become the focus of all my disquiet about Army Intelligence.

I'd forgotten, in the humidity of the Northern Territory, that a Melbourne summer could produce days of enervating, blazing heat. This was such a day. It was barely nine-thirty in the morning, but it must already have been close to a hundred degrees in the shade. We stood on the curb of St Kilda Road, waiting for a break in the traffic so we could cross into the gardens opposite.

'I see your propaganda unit is still busy,' I said. On a lamp post there was a poster showing the mask of a smiling Japanese face being removed to reveal the sneering, leering creature beneath. 'Beware the mask of friendship,' it read. 'It hides Japanese greed and treachery.' Above it, a simpler poster reminded people what to do, 'If the air-raid siren wailed tonight … Don't rush. Don't panic. Don't telephone.' Having experienced a Japanese air raid, my own inclination would be to both rush and panic.

'The crypt in the Shrine is cool,' Nigella said.

'Maybe we could just sit in the shade of a tree and pretend that this bloody war isn't happening,' I replied.

We sat cross-legged, and I enjoyed the relative luxury of having only a few flies to swat away.

'How much do you know about what happened up there?' I asked her.

'I know what they want me to know.'

'Fulton?'

'Yes. I was sorry to hear about that.'

'How can you work for those people, Nigella?'

'I am one of those people, Will.'

Her expression was cool.

'Yes, I suppose you are. Are you meant to be talking me into another job? Is that what this is about?'

She looked back towards Victoria Barracks.

'No, Will. You're here with me so that James can talk with Brian.'

I thought about that, and was seized by a chest-gripping sadness.

'When Brian walks out of there,' I said, 'I'll never be able to trust a single thing he says.'

'He mightn't want to work for us. He might want to return to his normal life.'

'I'll never know though, will I? Not for sure.'

'No,' she conceded quietly. 'Not for sure.'

There was silence between us after that, and the distance that separated us became unbridgeable.

'What will you do?' she asked.

'I really don't know. I might have to learn to juggle.'

'You're too old to run away and join the circus.'

'I used to think the circus and the Tivoli were grubby professions. Now I know there are worse choices that people can make.'

Nigella stood up and dusted off her skirt, immune or indifferent to the insult.

'Goodbye, Will.' This time she didn't offer her hand.

On the opposite side of St Kilda Road, Brian appeared at the gates of Victoria Barracks. He saw us and waved. I waited while Nigella crossed the road. She spoke briefly to him and went through the gate. He stood with his hands on his hips, clearly deciding what to do. His mind made up, he began to dodge the traffic, and when he reached the footpath on my side he was smiling broadly. He walked up the grassy incline towards me, and I arranged my features carefully in readiness to hear his first lie.

ACKNOWLEDGEMENTS

For information about the North Australia Observer Unit, I am indebted to two books: *North Australia Observer Unit: the history of a surveillance regiment* by Dr Armoury Vane, Australian Military History Publications, New South Wales, 2000; and *Curtin's Cowboys* by Richard and Helen Walker, Allen & Unwin, New South Wales, 1986.

For information on the concert parties, I am indebted to *An Entertaining War* by Michael Pate, Dreamweaver Books, Sydney, 1986.

I would also like to acknowledge with gratitude my extraordinary editor, Margot Rosenbloom, whose tact and unerring judgement are peerless. Thank you, too, to Henry and to everyone at Scribe. It is a privilege to be published by such a house.